PRAISE FOR NATHALIE SARRAUTE

"There are few living writers I admire more than Nathalie Sarraute. Every sentence that she writes is priceless. The first to do so since Proust, she has introduced something new."

—Claude Mauriac

"Here is welcome relief from the passive entertainment that standard fiction provides."

—*Saturday Review*

"Technically the book is a remarkable feat."

—*Atlantic Monthly*

"Queen of the New Realists."

—*Time*

"*The Planetarium* is a wonderfully believable account of a short, sharp struggle between an exploitative young man with literary ambitions and his rich, domineering relatives."

—*New Yorker*

"The best thing about Nathalie Sarraute is her stumbling, groping style, with its honesty and numerous misgivings, a style that approaches the object with reverent precautions, withdraws from it suddenly out of a sort of modesty, or through timidity before its complexity, then, when all is said and done, suddenly presents us with the drooling monster, almost without having touched it, through the magic of an image."

—Jean-Paul Sartre

Other Books by Nathalie Sarraute in English Translation

Fiction

Between Life and Death
Do You Hear Them?
"Fools Say"
The Golden Fruits
Here
Martereau
Portrait of a Man Unknown
Tropisms
The Use of Speech
You Don't Love Yourself

Criticism

The Age of Suspicion

Drama

Collected Plays

Autobiography

Childhood

Nathalie Sarraute

THE PLANETARIUM

Translated by Maria Jolas

Introduction by Ann Jefferson

DALKEY ARCHIVE PRESS
Dallas / Dublin

First published in French as *Le Planétarium* by Editions Gallimard, 1959
Originally published in English by George Braziller, Inc., 1960
Copyright © 1959 by Nathalie Sarraute
English translation copyright © 1960 by Maria Jolas
Introduction copyright © 2022 by Ann Jefferson

First Dalkey Archive edition, 2005
First Dalkey Archive Essentials edition, 2022
All rights reserved

Library of Congress Cataloging-in-Publication Data available.
ISBN: 978-1-62897-389-1

Dalkey Archive Press
Dallas / Dublin

Printed on permanent/durable acid-free paper and bound in the United States of America.

Introduction

When *The Planetarium* came out in May 1959 its author was one year shy of France's official retirement age. However, for Nathalie Sarraute, the book's publication signaled the start of her belated recognition as one of the leading writers of the day, and consolidated a writing career in which she would remain active until her death in 1999. Begun in 1953, the novel's gestation had coincided with the rise of France's postwar boom, the so-called "Trente Glorieuses," and although little of that period is directly reflected in the book, its optimism is evident in Sarraute's bold embrace of novelty. Literary experiment was in the air, and in 1956, after her postwar association with Sartre and Simone de Beauvoir had come to an end, she published some of the essays previously written for *Les Temps Modernes*, under the title *The Age of Suspicion*. The volume was immediately read as a call to arms for a "new novel," and in association with a younger generation of writers such as Alain Robbe-Grillet, Michel Butor, and Claude Simon, the "Nouveau Roman" became the banner under which outdated convention could be challenged and innovation licensed.

Unlike Sarraute's two previous novels, *Portrait of a Man Unknown* (1948) and *Martereau* (1953), *The Planetarium* was widely reviewed in the French literary press. There were interviews with the author, including one in *Vogue*, and she was invited to give lectures in Italy, Switzerland, and Scandinavia.

An English translation by Sarraute's friend Maria Jolas, cofounder with her husband Eugene of the interwar avant-garde journal transitions, came out in 1960 in the US, where the book met with considerable interest from readers enthused by recent developments in contemporary French literature. It was reviewed in the anglophone literary press, the *New Yorker* ran a profile of its author, and her work was already being studied in university French departments. Sarraute always felt well received by her North American readership and, starting with a successful lecture tour in 1964, she was a regular visitor to the US well into her nineties.

As was the case for several other French writers of the twentieth century (Beckett, Irène Némirovsky, Elsa Triolet), France was an adoptive home for Nathalie Sarraute, and French an adoptive language in which she was both insider and outsider, an alternation that became an integral element of her writing. Born in 1900 to Jewish parents in the Russian industrial town of Ivanovo-Voznesensk, she had lived in France from the age of eight, acquired degrees in English and law at the Sorbonne, practiced desultorily as a lawyer for a few years, and, after marriage and three children, made a tentative start on writing in 1932 with a single short, generically nonspecific text. This was the first of what eventually became nineteen such texts, sometimes described by their author as prose poems, and they were eventually published in a slim volume under the title *Tropisms*. After the book's appearance in early 1939, a short sequel was set to follow under the title *The Planetarium*, but with the outbreak of World War II publication was canceled. Its contents were not, however, forgotten, and the texts were included in a second edition of *Tropisms* in 1957, while the title was revived for what became Sarraute's third novel.

There was more to the redeployment of the 1939 title than a word. The earlier text established a vision and an outlook that were carried over and scaled up in the novels published after the war. In the words of the first *Planetarium*, the "frightful clarity" and "blinding light" that entrap people in socially sanctioned views of the world are contrasted with the "shadows and asperities"[1] of the inner mind, or what Virginia Woolf—a writer much admired by Sarraute—had once called "the dark places of psychology." This opposition between a conventional surface reality and the murkier, semi-conscious underworld of permanently restless minds remains central to the novel written two decades later. And, in a final negative gloss on the title, the planetarium itself appears on the closing page of Sarraute's as a metaphor threatening fixity and artifice, a "motionless sky in which, as before, familiar stars would shine."

The familiar stars whose restoration Sarraute is most set on resisting are the forms of characterization inherited from the nineteenth-century novel and anachronistically maintained in a certain strand of twentieth-century fiction, where their "frightful clarity" obscures the shadows and asperities of a truer psychology which cultural and literary developments had helped to bring to light. (Sarraute cites both Freud and Proust as key figures in this phenomenon.) In an "age of suspicion," fictional characters can no longer provide the means of understanding the realities of human experience as they are lived in the modern world.

Instead, as *The Planetarium* repeatedly shows, "character," or character-type is activated primarily as a mask that people apply to others as a form of aggression, domination, or ingratiation. The surface action of the novel is relatively trivial: Berthe installs a new door in her dining room; her nephew, Alain Guimiez, has hopes of taking over her apartment; his mother-in-law wants to buy him and his wife, Gisèle, a pair of leather armchairs while they hanker after an antique

1. Nathalie Sarraute, *Tropisms, and The Age of Suspicion*, translated by Maria Jolas, London: Calder & Boyars, 1963, p. 47.

bergère; he begins to frequent the circle attached to the writer Germaine Lemaire. But there is no continuity of plot, and the novel is made up of a series of disconnected scenes, staging the characters in a variety of combinations and confrontations, each a minidrama of its own that provides them with an opportunity for their strategic projections.

Alain ingratiates himself with his mother-in-law's guests by describing his aunt Berthe as "a card," "cracked" like the rest of her family as she frets over the marks left by an ugly door-handle on her new oak door. He in turn is characterized by his mother-in-law as a "spoilt child, exacting and capricious, wasting his strength on trifles," while Alain conjures up a picture of her as "bossy" and "possessive," generous "only in order to dominate." Berthe appears in her brother's eyes as having compensated for her own childlessness though an overindulgent attitude toward her coddled nephew. And in the eyes of Alain's father, the famous novelist Germaine Lemaire appears as nothing so much as "a secondhand clothes dealer, or an out-of-date actress," whose attempt to express "regal simplicity" with the gesture of her hand merely looks ludicrous. And so it goes on, as these provisionally fixed points appear and fade in the artificial sky of the Planetarium, the London version of which is, by telling coincidence, next door to Madame Tussaud's waxwork museum, the repository of lifeless replicas that in Sarraute's estimation are the material equivalents of fictional platitude.

The novel conveys the violence behind the deployment of these platitudes through a series of images that have Gisèle's mother experience Alain's image of her as a "mask which he had plastered down on her face from the very first, that grotesque, outmoded mask of the vaudeville mother-in-law," while he in turn is left feeling like "an insect pinned to a cork plaque, [. . .] a corpse laid out on the dissecting table," and subjected to an "embalming process that will make a tiny mummy of him, a shrunken dried-up head which people will examine as a curiosity, exhibited in a glass case." The extreme effects of the clichés that the novel's characters inflict upon each other can be likened to what Sarraute once wrote about words, which she describes as "the daily, insidious and very effective weapon responsible for countless small crimes" because, as she explains, "there is nothing to equal the rapidity with which they affect the other person at the moment when they are least on their guard."[2]

Constantly caught off their guard, the inhabitants of Sarraute's universe live uncertainly between conflicting views of their fellows. With the exception of the writer Germaine Lemaire and her circle, the dramatis personae of the novel are linked in a network of family relations: husband and wife, mother- and son-in-law, father and son, mother and daughter, aunt and nephew, brother and sister. In Sarraute's hands, relationships in a family facilitate the easy characterizations that its members foist upon each other, while long familiarity makes these portraits more labile. Memory stores material for several—equally plausible, equally insidious—versions of the same person. They are also seen alternately from within, as they experience themselves, and from without, as others see them. Berthe and her brother Pierre meet twice in the course of the novel, and on each occasion the encounter is depicted from the point of view of both, the same moments and the same dialogue shown in two very different lights.

There is no ultimate truth to be had in these shifting permutations, and instead, Sarraute's aim as a novelist is to find a means of capturing human experience in terms that dispense altogether with the fixity of character. Convinced that this underlying experience is ultimately and most truly a universal that lies beyond individual difference, she allows Alain to

2. *Tropisms, and the Age of Suspicion*, p. 109, translation modified.

express her belief that "somewhere, farther down, everyone is alike, everyone resembles everyone else . . ." And so, he adds, "I don't dare judge . . . Right away I feel that I'm like them, as soon as I take off my carapace, this thin varnish . . ." It's in these terms that he backtracks after entertaining his audience with his portrait of Berthe as the crackpot devastated by the damage done to her new door by the wrong door handle. On the inside, we're all the same, and it's the outside—the carapace and the varnish—that divides us from each other with false differences.

Armed with this conviction and resisting the simplifications of "character," Sarraute goes in search of a "language that could express instantaneously what we perceive at a glance: an entire human being, with its myriads of little movements, which appear in a few words, a laugh, a gesture," an ambition that she also lends to Alain, although he is not himself (or not yet) a novelist. Her pursuit of this new literary idiom is evident from the first sentence of the novel, which, through a form of semi-reported inner speech, plunges the reader directly into the mind of an as yet unnamed character musing on the refurbishment of her apartment: "No, really, try as you might, you could find nothing to say against it, it's perfect . . . a real surprise, a stroke of luck . . . an exquisite combination, that velvet curtain." This opening in medias res is supported by Sarraute's trademark *points de suspension*, deployed repeatedly throughout the novel (in an average of more than eleven per page) to convey the tentative, shifting movements of the inner mind. The semiarticulate language that she dubbed "sub-conversation" alternates with the rarer instances of actual "conversation" or dialogue proper. And this alternates in turn with moments of narrative in the present ("The apartment is silent. There's nobody. They've left.") that capture the immediacy of felt experience and preclude the stability and distance that might be provided by retrospective narrative.

The reader shares the tentative perspective of the characters, whose experience is nonetheless strikingly illuminated by images that suggest analogies for the shadows and asperities of their semiconscious responses. These analogies go from the fleeting (Berthe's builders have "that imperturbable expression, the slow gestures and professional calm of a doctor, while the family waits") to more extended mininarratives, such as the one that conveys her sense of lurking threat in her nephew's designs on her apartment: a guard dog is found lying dead outside a ranch, unfamiliar tracks of bare feet are seen in the dust, a servant discovered scalped and riddled with arrows, while cruel eyes are glimpsed spying through the surrounding thicket. Sarraute is not afraid of hyperbole and the imagination that generates these analogies is often quite graphic, the most conventional forms of fiction (novels of the Wild West in this instance) being mobilized to provide legible equivalents of sensations for which ordinary language has no established currency.

The analogies also provide a way of tacitly linking characters to each other through echo and parallel. The image of an imperturbable doctor surfaces briefly for a second time as Germaine Lemaire is able to observe Alain's father's male appraisal of her with "no more repugnance than a doctor examining a wound." Berthe and Germaine Lemaire are linked again through similar scenarios of ruin and devastation in which each feels utterly deserted and alone, Berthe in the face of her spoiled door and Germaine Lemaire confronted with her own writing and finding it quite lifeless: "a woman abandoned among the ruins of her bombed-out house, stares dazedly, amidst the rubble, at just anything, the most commonplace object, an old twisted fork, the battered old lid of a pewter coffeepot, picks it up without knowing why, and with a mechanical gesture, starts to rub it, she stares blankly, in the middle of the unfinished page, at a sentence, a word, in which something . . . just what is it? the tense of the verb is not right." The writer's rubbing at the something that's "not right" echoes Berthe's rubbing at the marks left on her door by the unwanted door handle, while the repeated scene of devastation tacitly supports the claim that, however different the external circumstances, "On the inside, we're all the same."

This sameness of the inside and the rejection of preestablished categories are integral to Nathalie Sarraute's conception of the novelist. If she herself happened to be a woman, Jewish, and Russian-born, none of these, in her view, had any relevance to her novels. Although she lived in a society that denied women the vote until 1944, and although she had survived the German Occupation only by going into hiding and living with false papers to conceal her Jewish identity, these experiences were incidental to her writing, because for her literature provides a means for transcending such differences. And, as she once said in an interview, the self who writes is in any case "neither man nor woman, nor cat nor dog."[3]

The issue was an important one, and *The Planetarium* is as much a "novelist novel" as a psychological one, since for Sarraute the two are inextricably linked. This pits Alain Guimiez, the potential but untested writer, against the established and adulated Germaine Lemaire. His gift for entertaining an audience with "priceless" anecdotes is no index of potential literary talent, and his creative experience has gone no further than his interminable doctoral thesis, but Sarraute endows him both with moments of insight into the workings of the mind behind surface reality and with an awareness of the need for a new language to translate that insight. It is these

3. Sonia Rykiel, "Nathalie Sarraute : Quand j'écris, je ne suis ni homme ni femme ni chien," ["When I write I am neither man nor woman nor dog"] Les Nouvelles, February 9–15, 1984, p. 39–41 (p. 40).

that have the potential to make him a novelist in the future.

Germaine Lemaire, by contrast, embodies the fixity and divisions that are the antithesis of Sarraute's conception of writing. Ominously hailed by critics as the "Madame Tussaud" of fiction, she performs the role of successful writer for the benefit of her admiring acolytes, and treats each of those acolytes according to her sense of their allotted place in some hypothetical pecking order. Judged by Sarraute's own criteria, it's no wonder that Germaine Lemaire's work proves to be devoid of the slightest sign of life, as empty as the "hollowness inside a painted wax mold." But in her own resistance to fixity and once-for-all categorizations, it is to Germaine Lemaire that Sarraute gives the final insight of the novel, when in an echo of Alain's earlier claim about the underlying psychology that we all share, she suggests that "we're all of us really a bit like that." At the point when Sarraute herself was about to attain a certain celebrity as a novelist, *The Planetarium* is a reminder that the writer is an essentially protean being, the inner life the only one that matters, and writing always a work in progress with no ultimate point of arrival.

Ann Jefferson
2022

The Planetarium

No, really, try as you might, you could find nothing to say against it, it's perfect . . . a real surprise, a piece of luck . . . an exquisite combination, that velvet curtain, made of very heavy velvet, the best quality wool velvet, in a deep green, quiet and unobtrusive . . . And at the same time, a warm luminous shade . . . Marvelous against the gold glints of the beige wall . . . And the wall itself . . . How effective . . . You'd think it was skin . . . It's as soft as chamois . . . One should always insist on that extremely fine stenciling, the tiny dots give a texture like down . . . But how dangerous, how mad, really, to choose from samples, to think that she had been within a hair's breadth—and how delightful it is to think back on it now—of taking the almond green. Or worse than that, the other, the one that tended towards emerald . . . Wouldn't that be something, a blue green against this beige wall . . . It's funny how this one, looked at in a small piece, had seemed lifeless, faded . . . What misgivings, what hesitations . . . And now, quite obviously, it was just what was wanted . . . Not the least bit faded, it looks almost bright, shimmery, against this wall . . . exactly the way she had imagined it the first time . . . That was a brilliant idea of hers . . . after all the trouble, all the looking round—it became a real obsession, she thought of nothing else no matter what she was looking at—and there, at the sight of that green wheat gleaming and rippling under the cool little wind in the sunlight, at the sight of that straw-stack, it had come to her all of a sudden . . . it was that—in slightly different shades—but that, in fact, was the idea . .

. exactly what was wanted . . . the green velvet curtain and the wall a gold like that of the straw, only softer in tone, a little nearer to beige . . . now this brightness, this shimmer, this luminosity, this exquisite freshness, like a caress, they too come from there, from that straw and from that field, she has succeeded in robbing them of all that, in capturing it, standing rooted there on the road looking at them, and she has brought it back here, to her little nest, it's hers now, it belongs to her, she holds it fondly to her, she snuggles up to it . . . She's made in such a way, and she knows it, that she can only look attentively and lovingly at what she can appropriate to herself, at what she can possess . . . It's like the door . . . but one thing at a time . . . she's coming to that, there's no need to hurry, it's so delightful to go back over things, to relish them—now that everything has turned out so well, that all obstacles have been cleared—to go back over each thing, one by one, slowly . . . this door . . . while the others were admiring stained glass windows, columns, arches, tombs—nothing bores her so much as cathedrals, statues . . . ice-cold, impersonal, distant . . . nothing much to be got from them, not even from the stained-glass windows which are nearly always too bright in color, too gaudy . . . as for paintings, they're not so bad, although the color combinations are more than often strange, disconcerting, or just plain ugly, shocking . . . however, you can still occasionally get ideas from them, as for instance those flea-greens and purples in the dresses of the women kneeling beside the cross, they were really darned nice, although you had to look twice, and be very wary, you risk something in the way of disappointments . . . that day in that cathedral, she would never have believed it. . . but she had really been repaid for her discomfort—it was freezing cold—and her boredom . . . that little door in the thickness of the wall in the back of the cloister . . . made of dark wood, solid oak, in a delightful oval shape, and glossy with age . . . it was that oval shape especially that fascinated her, it was so intimate, so mysterious . . . she would have liked to take it, to carry it away with her . . . have it in her home . . . but where? . . . she had squatted down on a piece of broken column to think about it, when all at once, and why not? nothing was simpler, she had found the very place . . . they would only have to change the little door of the dining-room that leads into the pantry . . . cut an oval opening, order a door like this one in beautiful solid oak, in a slightly lighter shade, a lovely warm shade . . . she had seen it all at one glance, everything together . . . the green curtain opening and closing before the big square bay giving on to the vestibule, instead of double glass doors with awful little gathered curtains (it's really terrible, the things people used to do, and to think that we got accustomed to them, we didn't notice them, but one look was enough), the walls repainted a golden beige and, at the other end of the room, this door, exactly the same, with medallion-shaped bas-reliefs, in beautiful solid oak . . . It's a fact that things, the good as well as the bad, always come to you in series . . . This summer, they came one right after the other and it had all turned out beyond her fondest hopes . . . The whole effect will be enchanting and the door will be the best part of all . . . How impatient, how excited she was a little while ago, when they brought it, while they carefully took off the tarpaulin in which it was wrapped . . . their delicate, precise gestures, their calm . . . excellent workmen who know all the secrets of their trade, who love it, it's always best to deal with reputable firms . . . they unwrapped it gently and it appeared, more beautiful than she had imagined it, flawless, entirely new, unblemished . . . the beautifully rounded convex bas-reliefs, carved in the thickness of the oak, brought out its fine veining . . . you would have thought it was watered silk it was so glossy, so lustrous . . . it was stupid of her to have been so afraid, this door had nothing in common—what an idea even to have imagined it, but she had begun to see oval doors everywhere, she had never seen so many, it's enough to think about a thing for you to begin to see nothing but that—nothing in common, absolutely nothing, with the oval doors she had seen in suburban bungalows, in country houses, hotels, even at her hairdresser's . . . her fright when, seated under the dryer, she had noticed just in front of her, an oval door of veneered wood, it looked so fake . . . so vulgar, pretentious . . . she had had a shock: the oval opening was all ready, it was too late . . . she had run to telephone . . . why, of course not, one gets upset over nothing at all, her decorator was right, everything depends on the surroundings, so many things enter into play . . . this beautiful piece of oak, this wall, this curtain, this furniture, these little odd pieces, what has all this got to do with a hairdresser's parlor . . . one should rather think of the Romanesque doors in stately old mansions, or in châteaux . . . No, she has no need to worry, the whole thing is in perfect taste, quiet, distinguished . . . she feels like running . . . now is the moment, she can go home, they've had ample time to finish . . . everything must be ready . . .

The exquisite excitement, the confidence, the joy that she feels as she goes up the stairs, takes her key from her bag, opens her door, she has often noticed it, they're a good sign, an auspicious portent: it's as though a fluid emanated from you that acts upon things and persons from afar, an amenable universe, peopled with favorable genii, falls harmoniously into place about you.

The apartment is silent. There's nobody. They've left. Their jackets and caps are gone from the bench in the front hall. But they haven't finished, everything is in disorder, sawdust on the floor, the toolbox is open, there are tools scattered here and there . . . they didn't have time to finish . . . And yet the curtains are up, they are hanging on each side of the bay, and the little door is in its place at the end of the dining room, on its hinges . . . but it all has a strange, skimpy, lifeless look . . . It's that green curtain against the beige wall . . . it looks crude . . . a dull, facile combination, you've seen it everywhere, and the door, there's no doubt about it, that oval door in the midst of these square openings has a faked, added-on look, the whole thing is ugly, common, trashy, the stuff in the Faubourg Saint-Antoine would be no worse . . . But she must combat this impression of distress, of collapse . . . She must beware of herself, she knows herself, this is just nervous irritation, the reverse of the excitement she felt a while back, she often has these ups and downs, she goes so easily from one extreme to the other . . . she must concentrate her thoughts, examine it all calmly, perhaps it's nothing . . . But of course, that's it, it hits you right in the eyes: that handle, that awful nickle-plated door-handle, and that horrible aluminum fingerprint plaque . . . that's the cause of it all, that's what ruins everything, what gives it such a vulgar look—a real washroom door . . . But how could they? . . . of course it's her fault too, what madness to have gone away, to have left them, she has only got what she deserves, she'll never learn her lesson, and yet she knew perfectly well that they can't be left alone a moment, you have to be after them all the time, supervise each gesture they make, a single instant of inattention and it's a disaster. But that's the way it is, we are always too tactful, she's so afraid of upsetting them . . . we imagine that it keeps them from working well, our being there all the time right behind them . . . the absurd confidence, the faith she has in people . . . laziness, really, cowardice, she so loves to dawdle, to daydream and let things take care of themselves, let them fall like ripe fruit into her hands . . . Now the wood is marred, the big screws that hold the horrible aluminum plaque go deep into the flesh of the wood, they will leave marks . . . And it would have been so easy, this morning, when they came, to prevent it, this misfortune . . . she should have discussed each detail in advance, on the other hand, how could she tell, even the most vivid imagination would not permit you to foresee what they are capable of doing . . . fools, idiots, not an atom of initiative, or interest in what they're doing, not the slightest sign of taste . . . taste! for it's a matter of that, really, but that's the last thing you should ever mention to them, they're incapable of distinguishing beauty from ugliness . . . better still, they like ugliness . . . the more vulgar, the more hideous a thing is the better pleased they are . . . They did it on purpose . . . there's some hostile, cold-blooded will, some sly malevolence behind this disorder, this silence . . . If they would only come back, if only she knew where they are . . . they are probably taking a drink somewhere, laughing together, leaning on the bar-rail, swapping stories . . . she feels like running to fetch them, she would like to explain to them just the same, there's perhaps some way of convincing them, of appealing to them, it may yet be possible to repair it . . .

A bell rings . . . it's the kitchen door . . . a traveler lost in the desert, who perceives a light, the sound of footsteps, experiences the same joy mingled with apprehension that rises up in her as she runs, opens the door . . . "Oh! it's you at last, so there you are, I thought you would never come back . . . you know, it won't do at all . . ." She realizes that she had better be careful . . . a crank, an unbearably spoilt old child, she knows that this is what she is for them, but she hasn't the strength to control herself, and besides, she feels it is preferable, on the contrary, to give ludicrous emphasis to the features of this caricature of herself that she recognizes in them, to make fun of herself a bit with them, to coax them, to disarm them . . . She assumes a childish, whiny tone . . . "You know, it has made me positively sick . . . It's a catastrophe, a real disaster . . ." They start slowly unbuttoning their leather jackets, rub their hands together, numb from cold; they have that imperturbable expression, the slow gestures and professional calm of a doctor, while the anxious family waits . . . she would like to push them, take them by the hand . . . "Come and see . . . it's simply awful . . . it spoils everything . . . see how that looks on there, that handle and that plaque . . ." Their faces are unmoved, inscrutable . . . "Well, what's the matter with 'em That's what they gave us. We only carried out the boss's orders . . ."

Orders . . . that's all they understand . . . automatons, blind insensitive machines, pillaging, destroying everything . . . With orders they can be made to do almost anything, burn cathedrals, books, blow up the Parthenon . . . it's useless to attempt to appeal to them, to humanize them . . . but she doesn't feel that she has the strength not to try . . . "You could have seen for yourselves that they would not do, you might have waited . . ." She feels like crying, out of sheer rage and helplessness . . . "Everything is spoiled now, it was not worth the trouble to make the change, it was even better before, it's awful . . ." They stand there with their arms dangling, their eyes blank . . . "It's the very first time anybody ever complained, we put in those same handles everywhere, nobody ever said anything against 'em, it's the standard model, the customers never do object . . ." One of them turns to the other . . . "And yet they're the same ones, ain't they, as those we put in the other day at the Brazilian Embassy?" The other shrugs his shoulders . . . "Of course they are . . . That's what they use everywhere . . ." She perceives in her own voice a childish bitterness in which may be sensed nevertheless a touch of hesitation, almost of hope . . . "Handles like those in an Embassy . . . that I'm ready to believe . . . Perhaps on the kitchen or bathroom doors . . . —Not at all . . . everywhere . . . in the bedrooms . . . in the reception rooms . . . they decided to change everything . . . have it modern all over . . ."

They don't realize the force of the contrivance they are now handling, and this ignorance, this unawareness, lends to their gestures, as it does to those of lunatics, great skill, great assurance: they set it just in the right spot, and it explodes with an awful blast, everything flies into pieces, old oval doors and convents, old châteaux, woodwork, gilding, moldings, cupids, crowns, horns of plenty, chandeliers, paneling, velvet hangings, brocades, golden rotundities of straw-stacks shining in the sun, young wheat bending under the wind, the entire downy, warm world in which she had dwelt so snugly, and now, across these smoking ruins, which they are trampling under foot, the conquerors advance . . .

They are setting up a new order, a new civilization, while she wanders miserably amidst the rubble, in search of old debris.

In their immaculate palaces, built on pure, straight lines, with broad plateglass windows, a subdued light that comes, like daylight, from no one knows where, plays softly over the vast, smooth surfaces. Everything is quiet, calm, serious and pure, nothing dubious, faked, useless or pretentious disturbs the eye . . . There, the doors disappear, they blend with the walls, the metal furniture, the slender fins of the door-handles give forth the joyful, youthful reflections of airplane wings, the long white voile curtains have the light consistency of the smoke drawings that airplanes make in the sky . . . "That handle, after all, I don't know . . . it's not so ugly, really . . . but then, don't you think . . . there's a humble, begging note in her voice . . . then the door should be painted . . . so as to blend with the wall . . . natural wood like that, after all, personally, I don't know . . ." They look at her with surprise . . .

"Paint the door? A handsome, solid-oak door like that? . . . Why, certainly not, that would be too bad . . . in that case, it really wasn't worth while . . . But it don't look bad . . . that's just an idea of yours, come on, now, it's just a matter of habit, you'll get used to it, you'll see . . . it's very nice, it's real good . . . just leave everything the way it is . . ." That protective tone of theirs, that familiar manner . . . they are already settling in like conquerors, making themselves at home, their drunken soldiery, their hardened troopers are patting her cheek, pinching her chin . . . There now, that's better, getting a little easier to handle ain't you, my girl, she's beginning to come round, beginning to listen to reason . . . Come on, now, you'll get used to it. . . . Serves her right. It's her punishment for being so cowardly . . . How could she have fallen so low as to place herself at their mercy, accept their rule, ask them for aid and protection, offer to cooperate with these ignorant creatures who are ravaging, disfiguring the entire countryside, who destroy works of art, tear down charming old homes which they replace with those cement blocks, those hideous, lifeless cubes in which sinister objects out of dentists' offices and operating rooms float about in the icy, sepulchral despair that filtrates from indirect lighting and neon tubes . . . She draws herself up, gathers her strength together, the only survivor of a shattered world, alone in the midst of strangers, of enemies, she folds her arms, looks straight at them . . . "Well, no, it positively will not do . . . I don't want it, at any cost. It must be removed. Tell your boss that he should have realized that. You don't put such awful things as that on an oak door . . . It should be some sort of antique . . . out of old brass . . . But I'll call him up . . ." Have it your way, girlie, nobody's forcing you, what we said about it, that was for you, as for us, eh? . . . it's nothing to us . . . They pick up their tools in silence, they don't give her another look, but start talking among themselves as though she weren't there . . . "So, what do we do about the handle? Take that one back? Better leave it for the time being." She is seized with the kind of rage a child feels when it is about to be left alone in its room, she feels like shouting and stamping her feet . . . "Why of course, you must leave that handle, first you put in just any old thing, and then you want to leave me with a door that won't close. I prefer even that for the time being . . . Only I hope I'm not going to wait six months the way I did to get those wall-brackets up in the parlor . . ." They pick up their toolboxes, put the straps over their shoulders, give a hunch to get the straps in position . . . "Oh, that depends, first you gotta find the kind of handle you want. . . But you talk to the boss about it. That don't concern us, that's not our department . . ."

The sharp click of the latch, the quick slam of the kitchen door, the diminishing sound of their heavy soles on the cement steps of the service stairway, reverberate like a stealthy threat; they are the premonitory signs of the deep silence of loneliness, of abandonment . . . Now she is left entirely to herself. Forgotten amidst devastation and ruins . . . There is sawdust everywhere . . . The floor is strewn with bits of wood and rusty screws, the furniture, which has been pushed in every direction, assumes absurd positions, even the door has a strange look, a look of being out of place . . . patched up, added on . . . a look of pretentious trash in the midst of the thin walls of this mass-produced apartment . . . But above all, she must not get panicky, she must pull herself together, to calm that feeling of emptiness, of chill, she must examine everything carefully . . . there's no doubt about it, it's obvious, it's that hideous handle, a handle suitable for a washroom, or a bar, that gives to the door, and to everything about it, such a faked, tawdry look . . . She makes a great effort, she's got it, she pulls . . . and in the place of the thin aluminum tube, with its weak imitation of a sort of fin, there alights a heavy old brass handle, with a delightful patina, the kind of old handle to be found in châteaux: slightly curved, and the end, which turns up a bit, swelling into a little globe with soft highlights that reflect the veining of the wood and the gold of a brass plaque with finely etched arabesques . . . No, nothing, no plaque at all, just the wood . . . but they've bored holes, their gimlets have bored into the tender flesh of the oak . . . they've spoiled everything, destroyed everything, on purpose. Why pretend? It's no use. All her efforts for nothing . . . Her hopes . . . her struggles . . . To attain what? In anticipation of what? For whom, after all? Nobody comes to see her for weeks on end, for months . . .

All at once she finds herself in a big, dark room with a smoke-blackened ceiling—she recognizes it: it is this same big room in a dilapidated old house, that she has already seen like this, in similar moments of distress, of doubt—her old uncle's study. Newspapers heaped in piles on the floor, books everywhere, on the furniture, on the beds, the hangings are faded and worn, the upholstery on the chairs is frayed, the leather of the old sofa is covered with cat scratches, the corners of the soiled carpets are chewed by young dogs' teeth, and she, in the midst of all that, has a strange sensation, one of well-being, that's what it is: among these battered, submissive objects, which are kept at a distance, and which no one has deigned to look at for years, except to glance at them absent-mindedly, people seem to move about with lighter gestures, she herself feels relieved, released, it seems to her that she is floating delightfully, wafted with every breeze, borne aloft on every wind . . . she is being carried, but where to? . . . she's slightly frightened . . . She can't . . . she won't have the heart

. . . no, for her, it's impossible . . . She can't stand disorder, dirt, it exhausts her, it gives her the staggers . . . that sawdust there, at least she should take that up, sweep it . . . Then, all at once, the ground becomes firm, it stops moving, the dizziness has disappeared, she regains her foothold . . . there . . . on the baseboard, that spot, a mark left by their hands, and beside it, but they're all over the wall, they've left spots everywhere, and underneath there, all along the floor, those black streaks are marks left by the knocks they gave to the still fresh paint with the toes of their heavy shoes . . . that won't come off, it's become incrusted in the very fine grain of the wood . . . they will have to do some retouching . . . but how will they get the same shade? the walls will have to be repainted . . . Better try right away, only, watch out, all the grain, all the velvetiness will disappear at the slightest rubbing, it will leave big light-colored spots, the way it did that time when she had been so stupidly impatient . . . above all, not lose her head . . . not be in a hurry . . . a very clean basin, that one there, in the sideboard . . . some hot water, a very fine rag, this batiste handkerchief, couldn't be better, there's not a moment to lose, if it's spoiled it can be thrown away, no sacrifice is too great, succeed, at all costs . . . there . . . don't rub . . . press gently . . . the soapy water is being slowly absorbed . . . She waits . . . lifts up the wet handkerchief . . . a miracle . . . it's gone, the spot has disappeared . . . the difference in shade, that's nothing, it must be allowed to dry . . . Now, to finish, go gently, pat it lightly, let it dry . . . we get panicky about nothing at all . . . it's like the door, too, just a question of nerves, the door will look very nice, the tiny holes can quite well be stopped up with a little putty, then, after a coat of stained furniture polish, even with a magnifying glass, nobody will see a thing.

Oh, he must tell you that one, it's too funny . . . they're priceless, the stories about his aunt . . . the last one is worth its weight in gold . . . Do tell it to them, it's the best of all, the one about the door-handle, when she made her decorator cry . . . You're such a good storyteller . . . You made me laugh so hard, the other day . . . Go on . . . tell it . . ."

That abrupt way she has of taking you by the scruff of the neck and throwing you right in the middle of the ring, for people to gape at . . . that lack of tact she has, of sensitivity . . . But it's his fault as well, he knows it. With him it's always that desire of his to have people approve of him, make a fuss over him . . . What would he not give them to make them have a little fun, to make them feel contented, make them grateful towards him . . . His own mother and father he would turn over to them . . . But he, himself, how often he has made an exhibition of himself, has described himself in ridiculous positions, or in ludicrous situations . . . piling up disgraceful details to make them laugh a bit, to laugh with them a bit, delighted to feel that he's among them, near them, to one side of himself and quite stuck to them, clinging to them so closely, so dissolved in them that he even saw himself through their eyes . . . It was he, again this time, who came, of his own accord, to offer . . . he can't resist . . . "Oh, listen, I must tell you, you'll die laughing . . . my aunt, what a card, ah! what a family, and no denying . . . We are really all a bit cracked . . ." So it's rather late now, to bridle up in protest, to pretend to be fed up, as we make our bed, so must we lie in it . . . they're there, all in a circle, waiting, they're counting on his act. He sees already in their eyes that little gleam of excitement, he feels that they're making scarcely perceptible movements inside themselves to clear the boards, to settle themselves more comfortably.

But how glum he looks suddenly, what a wry face he's making . . . What has come over him? . . . The dry little tone with which, all at once, he refuses, and that derisive glance . . . Usually, he's more accommodating, less timorous . . . But you never know with him . . . It's enough for him to feel that she is very keen . . . Or else it's a lack of confidence in himself all of a sudden, unsociability, laziness . . . How complicated, how difficult to get along with people, she can't understand it . . . he needs a good shaking up . . . "Come on now, don't be ridiculous, don't make us beg you . . . you're keeping us on tenterhooks . . . come on, be nice . . . tell it . . ."

Why can't she let the poor boy alone? He's quite right . . . It's incredible, such a lack of sensitivity, such crassness . . . despite the thirty-five years they've been married, she can still make him blush the way he did the first day, when she goes blindly on, head down, pestering people, walking roughshod over everything, putting her foot in it, committing every possible blunder . . . Now there's nothing to be done about it, she'll never leave the poor fellow in peace. She can see that he's reluctant, that she has either hurt his feelings, or that he is in a bad humor, but she doesn't give a rap . . . That's her way of making people ridiculous, of getting her revenge on them for God knows what. . . She's more aware than she appears to be, she knows perfectly well what she's doing . . . Or else, she doesn't know anything, but it amuses her, and that's all; I do what I want, it suits me like that, what are all these niceties and complications about? Little does it matter to her . . . Now she has decided that this is the moment to serve up that idiotic tale . . . gossip . . . of no interest, not a word of truth in any of it, as usual. . . Generally he gives in only too easily . . . It's sickening to see him strutting there before a lot of morons, making a bid for their admiration, getting all worked up over a lot of old women's talk . . . For once he has reacted as he should, and is holding his own . . . "Why don't you let him alone, you can see perfectly well that it annoys him. And what is there so interesting about those stories? She's an old crank, and that's all there is to it."

Now he feels it, that's what is paralyzing him, keeping him from launching out, it's that heavy mass beside him, an enormous swollen pocket, stretched to the cracking point, which is weighing upon him, pressing. If he makes a move, it will burst open . . . idiotic gossip, idle talk, lies . . . vulgar chatter . . . a lot of females . . . and he, the worst of all, parading, wanting to shine, a regular little whore . . . it's demeaning to associate with them, so much straw in your hair . . . it's going to roll over him, stifle him, fill his mouth and nose with an acrid, burning, nauseous liquid . . .

But she's not afraid. No, indeed! she's not afraid of his explosions of fury, of scorn, he'll never succeed in browbeating her . . . after trying for thirty-five years . . . As soon as she opens her mouth, she feels him trembling . . . what will they think? is it stupid? isn't it a bit vulgar? immoral? crass? did anyone take offense? . . . he jumps down her throat right away, crushes her. At first, when she was young, it used to make her timid, it gave her complexes . . . Fortunately, she has plenty of pluck, she stood up under it, he had to deal with a powerful opponent . . . He can tremble as much as he wants, he won't keep her from doing what she pleases, from leading the conversation as she sees fit. She doesn't care what people think, she doesn't need for people to like her, she's not afraid of hurting their feelings. If they are cut to the quick, so much the worse for them . . . Moreover, that's just an idea of his, all that, one of his manias, she never gives offense to anybody . . . It's walking on eggs like that with people that makes them oversensitive, suspicious . . . You have to take them simply, they are grateful if you do . . . they like her very much, she knows it, they forgive her everything . . . an occasional outburst . . . they know she means no harm, that she has a heart of gold, is filled with the milk of human kindness . . . With him . . . if she let him have his way, they would die of boredom. Never anything exciting, always heavy subjects of conversation, finance, politics . . . And, above all, he must occupy the center of the stage, he must be the one to talk, to spread his tail-feathers, otherwise he doesn't listen, everything bores him, people are stupid, tiresome . . . Now she's not going to let him browbeat that poor boy . . . Nobody ever has a right to say a word. Everything is for him . . . "Oh! I beg of you, let us laugh a bit, we can't always be serious . . . when you are present, nobody dares to speak, everything bores you, it must all be for you . . ."

The enormous pocket, that was pressing so hard and keeping him from moving, has burst, she has pierced it through with one of those quick, telling stabs, such as they all know how to give, that is, the innocent, unaware, instinctive people, who don't stop to think, or who never hesitate; and what the pocket contained was not so terrifying, not so repugnant as all that . . . a little of the exasperation felt by a selfish, conceited old man, by a jealous old baby, ravaged doubtless God knows when, by God knows what rebuffs . . . He suddenly appears crestfallen, deflated, he utters a resigned sigh, looks elsewhere, like a frightened dog, withdraws into himself, scowling . . . But above all, no pity, as soon as you give in, you become his prey . . . She's right, he keeps you from breathing, he stifles you—a real damper . . . the boorish way he puts you in your place . . . just to think about it makes you piping mad . . . every time people get a little excited in his presence—that impatient shrug of his . . . "Well, what's so remarkable about it? Quite a discovery, isn't it? . . . People have known that forever. They went into raptures over that twenty years ago . . ." Not the tiniest puddle of fresh water in which to splash in the sun, strut a bit, preen one's feathers . . . She's right, one shouldn't let oneself be intimidated, he will not give in, he's not afraid . . . the friends surrounding him encourage him, smile at him, go ahead, make a start . . . he tries his voice, gives a little cough . . . It's not good when you're plagued like that to begin with, pestered from every side, announced in glowing terms . . . Things should happen, quite naturally, without thinking about them, worming their way in gently at first, then expanding little by little, but in this case, the boards have been cleared in readiness for them, the space set aside is too great, they will float about in there, ridiculously puny, barely visible . . . but it's too late, the open space in front of him attracts him, sucks him up, he feels himself being pushed from behind, he leaps forward, gets off on the wrong foot, he senses how false, how unnatural his voice is . . . "Well, all right, but there's nothing so very funny . . . I don't know why you think it's so amusing . . . As usual, it's about my aunt and her manias . . . the things that happen when she does over her apartment. . . lately, it's been something unbelievable . . . She woke me up in the middle of the night . . . I was reading, on the point of going to bed, when I heard the telephone ring . . . I looked at my watch: eleven o'clock . . . Gisèle was asleep

. . . I thought something awful had happened . . . It was my aunt. . . She was speaking in a wee little voice . . . Hello . . . did I wake you? Excuse me, I'm extremely sorry . . . You can imagine how little she cares, I know her . . . it's not the first time . . . she would move heaven and earth when she feels like it . . . She would walk roughshod over anybody . . . Listen, it's this . . . there's something that is upsetting me . . . I can talk to you? you're not too sleepy? You remember I told you I wanted to put an oval door between the pantry and the dining room? You disapproved of it . . . Well, I should have listened to your advice, I should never have changed it . . . however, what's done is done, I'm not going to turn everything topsy-turvy again, I'm going to keep it . . . But you can't guess what they've gone and done; imagine, they've put a nickel-plated fingerprint plaque and door-handle on that solid oak door . . . It's your friend Renouvier (a very nice fellow whom I had had the misfortune to recommend to her) . . . he's a nitwit, a good-for-nothing, who doesn't know his job . . . I took it all off . . . but do come, please, I can't explain it to you like that . . . no, not tomorrow morning . . . jump in a taxi, come on . . . I was crazy to listen to you, to have engaged that Renouvier fellow, everything is spoiled now. So, believe it or not, I went . . . at eleven o'clock at night . . . I know her. In any case, I was done for, she would have waked me at six in the morning . . . she would have spent the entire night walking up and down in front of her door like a caged animal . . . I saw right away, as soon as I got there, that she was in a bad way. She looked fairly haggard. And the entire place was in what, for her, was terrible disorder; a can of furniture polish on the table, bottles and rags of every description on the floor . . . She let me in, a rag in her hand: Come and see, it's incredible what they've gone and done, your friend Renouvier is no good . . . Look at the door . . . I saw an awful new door such as you see everywhere, a pretentious, interior decorator's sort of door, which was there nobody knew why . . . A mad idea she had had all of a sudden . . . But I didn't say anything, it was too late, there was no longer any question of that . . . the fingerprint plaque had been removed and it had left holes in the wood, tiny marks that had been stopped up with putty and which she was rubbing, painting with all her might . . . Almost weeping, she begged me . . . Look . . . tell me the truth, I can't judge any more, I can't see anything but that . . . The nail marks were undoubtedly visible . . . If she had said nothing, I shouldn't have noticed anything, but now that she had told me . . . It was, indeed, too bad, but there was no doubt about it, I did see them. Some devil must have prompted me, I couldn't help saying to her: Oh, if you don't think about it, you can hardly see anything, but now that you've told me, I do see the filled-in spots . . . But so tiny . . . you'd have to know they're there . . . But that was just it, that little defect, that minute flaw, that little wart on the face of perfection . . . it must be dominated, annihilated, she must rub . . . She stepped back . . . And at moments, in certain lights, if you stood in certain places, you couldn't see anything, but then it would reappear, she couldn't see anything else . . . the door, the room itself, were gone, but the little round spots were there, her eye guessed them, made them appear at regular intervals, counted them . . . it was torture . . ." he hears their laughter, gentle chuckling, dove-cooing, a caress, an encouragement, a vote of thanks . . . They allow themselves to be led, they let themselves go in brotherly fashion, and he feels that he is gaining in confidence, he would like to splash about and shake his feathers . . . "But do you know that, two years ago, she got like that for even less . . . She noticed that a bit of wood had been scraped off her bedpost, the one against the wall . . . well, it had to be matched, filled in . . . and you could see it . . . or you couldn't. . . she was continually pulling the bed out. Finally she decided to replace the entire bedpost."

But this is too much; there's too much freedom, too much lightheartedness . . . the pocket beside him starts swelling again . . . he sees a shoulder being shrugged, an eye staring straight ahead; the thumbs of both hands folded over a protruding belly are turning wildly round each other; quite near him he perceives that little hissing sound that a snake gives when it is about to empty its poison duct . . . enough of this nonsense . . . it's all pure invention, anyway . . . straws in your hair . . . of no interest . . . And the pocket keeps emptying, it's empty, the stream of acrid liquid is spreading . . . "Well, what of it? Why get excited? She's a crank, and that's all there is to it . . ." A crank. That's all there is to it . . . The luxuriant forest into which he was leading them, the virgin forest into which they were advancing, astounded, towards he knew not what strange regions, what unknown fauna, what secret rites, is about to change instantaneously into a cross-country boulevard black with cars and bordered with filling stations, signposts, billboards . . . Don't listen to him, let's continue to press onward . . . Have faith in me, follow me . . . my white plume . . . don't hesitate, you will be rewarded, forward, ho! . . . All of a sudden, he looks quite serious, he has stopped laughing, the moment is a solemn one . . . "It may seem stupid, all that, true enough . . . absurd, even . . . but just the same it's curious, when you come to think about it . . . Here's a woman who has known real suffering . . . the loss of those she loved, that of her husband . . . She knows that her own death is not far distant, she told me that she feels her strength is failing, that she's aging, and then, what happens? All the anguish that has gathered in her becomes fixed there on that bit of wood, those holes in the wood, everything is there, concentrated on one point—in reality, it's a lightning conductor . . . I myself, I must admit, after a while, was rubbing and painting and planing with all my might, I too was struggling against something threatening, to restore a sort of harmony . . . It was an entire universe, in miniature, there before us . . . And there we were, trying to gain mastery over something that is very forceful, indestructible, intolerable . . ."

That laugh, there, at his rear, he recognizes it: nothing in common with the gentle cooing, the tender chuckles . . . ponderous, wallowing laughter, thick, oily laughter that rolls over everything, then all at once plunges into the throat, almost disappears, reduced to a sort of hoot, proceeds for a long while somewhere down below—and no one makes a move, they're waiting—then reappears, throaty, grating, long-drawn . . . excoriating.

The person who's laughing, he doesn't even have to look at her, he knows her . . . He should have foreseen it—but he had foreseen it, he knew it—the moment was badly chosen, the atmosphere was not favorable, the company was made up of ill-assorted persons, some hostile to one another, the kind that can never be charmed, never won over . . . At present, he is in their hands, he has surrendered to them . . . he has spared himself nothing to try to inveigle them to come with him . . . out yonder, unknown wonders were perhaps awaiting them . . . he can call forth mirages: towering cities, skies perhaps about to cast their reflection in a little puddle of muddy water . . . he has that power . . . He has given of his talents unabashed, without haggling, he thought that he could risk relying on them like that. . . But with that female, there, there's nothing you can do . . . You can surrender to her, you can put yourself entirely in her hands, counting on her generosity (it's not possible that she would avail herself of this fact—that would be too easy—to do you harm, or to take unfair advantage of the situation) . . . You can commit hara-kiri before her very eyes, all your entrails exposed, and you won't arouse her compassion . . . How many times in the face of that manner of hers, when she is observing people, seated comfortably to one side, with a self-assured, contented, narrow-minded expression, he has felt impelled to throw down his arms and go up to her . . . "Look, this is how I am made, I am stupid, I react in a ridiculous way, but I can't make myself believe in a fundamental difference between people . . . I always believe—it's perhaps idiotic—that somewhere, farther down, everyone is alike, everyone resembles everyone else . . . Then I don't dare judge . . . Right away I feel that I'm like them, as soon as I take off my carapace, this thin varnish . . . Don't you? Don't you think so? . . ." She can't refuse, simple human respect, decency, honesty will force her to join in, to nod her head with an air of vague comprehension: all sincerity deserves some attention, some slight gratuity, you have to, when a person surrenders to you like that . . . Well, no, right away, at the sight of this stripped body, blushing and trembling under the garish light, the thick, oily laughter bursts forth, she leans back, in order to see better, she throws her head back, the laughter strangles in her throat in an endless hoot, a long whistle, before the enormous, final explosion . . . "Ha, ha, ha, what a comical creature you are . . . What a queer card . . . Oh, no, I can assure you, I'm not like you, I don't put everybody in the same basket . . ." They're comical . . . What cards . . . She almost dies laughing when she sees their poor bent backs while they rub, stand off, stoop, the better to see the marks of the holes . . . Crackpots, ridiculous puppets . . .

But in the name of heaven, don't allow yourself to be impressed, don't listen to her. The goal is near, you will be rewarded, you must exert yourself a bit, come on . . . that's what the entire game consists of . . . "I assure you, no, don't laugh, because it's true, I didn't resist either, I rubbed, I polished . . ." come on, rub with us, the holes are disappearing . . . there now, however, if you stand a little to the left, then they all reappear . . . "That handsome piece of oak, with its polish and veining, was pitted with awful little circles, no matter how much you camouflaged them, how much furniture polish you put on them, how much you rubbed them, it was impossible to make them shine . . ." We should try staining them, they're too dark, let's scrape off the polish, let's start all over again, let's cut out little wooden circles to stop up the holes . . . but the little surrounding circles are visible to the naked eye, no matter how hard we rub . . .

There's nothing we can do, we'll have to give up, we'll have to resign ourselves, tear ourselves away from it, but we can't . . . We're all shut in here with her, aren't we? We are being herded down a narrow, dark corridor with no exit, we are going to keep endlessly tramping along, locked up with her in this dark, closed labyrinth, going round and round . . .

But never fear . . . It's a game, you know that perfectly . . . There's no risk for any of us. Our hearts are exquisitely wrung, we feel like crying aloud, the way we do on the scenic railway, when the little train dips down, we laugh . . . We are so strong. A single movement on our part and the dungeon will open, the marks of the holes will disappear forever, the walls will move apart . . . Outside, an entire universe, our own universe, diversified, luminous, open to every wind, awaits us . . . We are so free, so supple . . . We can disport ourselves and play about as we please. We can plunge very deep, down to the bottom: our healthy lungs contain an ample provision of pure air . . . One good push off and we'll be back up again . . . That is what I offer you, this brief incursion, this amusing excursion, this exciting impression of adventure, of danger, but you can turn back when you want . . . In an instant, if you feel like it, you can be back home again, whereas she will remain there forever, in that hole she has dug for herself, too weak to escape, tramping endlessly along, endlessly going round and round . . .

"Oh! listen, I can understand you, I would have helped her rub too, if I had had the time. Why not? If I had leisure and money, I would spend my time the way she does, polishing doors and matching handles. If the woman enjoys that, whom does it harm? It's as good a way as any other to keep busy and give other people work . . . That, or something else, really, after all. . ."

Good shot. She's a very good shot, this one too, with that idiotic look of hers. A half-wit, he says that to himself right away, in order to reassure himself: that's what they are alluding to, the others—to such statements as the one she just made—when they say she is stupid: "Madeleine is silly." He himself has never understood very well exactly what they meant by that. But they must be right: that's what is meant by half-wittedness. She can see no farther than the end of her nose. There she is now, her nose glued to these objects . . . why not change door-handles and stop up holes? When she herself does nothing else her livelong life, supervising everything about her with the shining, glassy eye of a magpie, scouring, mending, calculating . . . No lightning conductor in her—why rack one's brains, no anguish, no foreshortened death which must be vanquished at all cost, death itself, she can look at it from close range, she's not afraid . . . "The poor man, my poor husband, it was the thought of what he had become there, under the earth, that made me feel the greatest pity . . . Already, when they laid him out, I didn't recognize him any more. He so loved to be comfortable, any old jacket, an old pair of trousers, that was what he really liked, old clothes . . . and would you believe it, they put his frock coat on, which he hadn't worn for twenty years . . . It was twice too big for him . . . the poor dear had simply melted away during his illness, he looked like a poor plucked chicken . . ." Idiot: that's quickly said. That way she has, that pitiless way she has, like a Lord Chief Justice, when she says before people her own age, who shrivel up right away from fear: "Whatever you may say, age counts, doesn't it? My strength is failing . . . After all, I'm no longer so young as I once was, we mustn't forget that . . ." She resigned herself to the inevitable a long time ago . . . dark clothes, white hair, a black velvet ribbon round her neck. Her hard little eyes took stock of it all, made the inventory a long time ago . . . She has a detailed list, a complete description of the premises, she's known for a long time what it's all about. And it's not so brilliant, I can assure you. But you have to take things as they are. There's nothing you can do, that's sure. It's disgraceful, really, the childish games people play, the way they act like frightened ostriches. Let them rub spots and fill up holes—fine. That or something else, what's the difference? It's better, in any case, than disorder, or dirt. But incursions into dark, underground regions, exquisite contrasts with the iridescent world to which one accedes with a push-off, just so much literature, all that . . . Come on now, a little courage. And expect nothing. It's all alike, outside, inside. You get along as best you can, with what you have at hand. And you look things straight in the eye, gamely.

They have all understood quite well. Very quickly, without needing any long explanations. Nobody has yet discovered the language that could express instantaneously what we perceive at a glance: an entire human being, with its myriad little movements, which appear in a few words, a laugh, a gesture. Everybody feels a bit uncomfortable now, the downgrade on the scenic railway turned out badly, they got a bump. They feel a bit ridiculous, a bit ill at ease.

But not this one, fortunately, not he. Never. You have only to see the dim, reassuring, peaceable little light in the depths of his pale gray eyes—and his smile. He didn't hurt himself, that's obvious. He never takes part in these excursions, he doesn't like the scenic railway, and he remains quietly on the solid earth upon which he is accustomed to walk, where he feels perfectly secure . . . Come, come, they make him smile, they should pick themselves up now, they should brush off their clothes and put their hats on, come, come, a little dignity . . . "Where does she live, anyway, your aunt? in Passy? It's a big apartment? How many rooms has she got there?" And right away they feel better. In no time, they find themselves in a place they should never have left. A place that is well known, comfortable, protected and fenced in, but still sufficiently spacious to allow people to move about at ease. Soft lights, air-conditioning, an exactly appropriate, even temperature. Everybody feels at home.

The hostess immediately resumes her role: "How many rooms? Why, five, imagine, for her alone." The little show would have amused her, the sleight-of-hand trick could have been funny, she thought it would entertain her guests, but since it misfired, that's that . . . He can come on off now, it's finished, get the hook. Therein lies her strength—and he admires her, in spite of everything, the poor magician, standing there on the stage, still holding in his hands the hat from which no doves have flown—therein lies her strength, in these immediate relinquishments, these prompt recoveries. She makes a gesture with her hand: "Yes, indeed, five rooms for a woman alone, when so many young couples are living in attics, or with their parents-in-law."

But she should not desert him, not yet, she should let him try his luck . . . If they would turn his way, if they would look again, just one second: "Five rooms and she entirely alone. But that's just it, that's where her madness lies. I was about to tell you . . . That's the funny part. She never has any company. But she must have her two parlors, a big dining room, a guest room . . . That's why she's always getting things ready, so as to invite people. Everything must be perfect, spotless: it probably seems to her that their eye is there, always, ready to seize upon the slightest mistake, every imperfection, every error in taste . . . People's opinions frighten her so . . . It's never perfect enough. Never entirely ready . . . she doesn't want it to be. In reality, she doesn't care to see anybody: what she needs, in fact, is this getting ready. For her, that suffices . . ."

But there's nothing to be done about it. It's too late, the moment has passed. They are hardly listening to what he says, leaning towards one another; they turn slightly to cast an irritated glance in his direction . . . what are all these "deep" considerations about, anyway, they're bored, what is he driving at with all that? As a good hostess, she feels obliged, this time, to stop him, firmly. Besides, he is beginning to irritate her, too: a poor sport, maladjusted, come on, now, this has lasted long enough, that's enough, he must come off . . . She laughs, wags her finger . . . "Now, tell the truth, it's an obsession with you too, you adore it . . . she fascinates you, your aunt does. You understand her only too well. In reality, you take after her . . . I always thought so . . ."

It was to be expected, of course. That's his just reward. It had to happen. Distant. Smug. Amused, the guests turn toward him. They adjust their monocles. They take out their lorgnettes; a queer card, that chap. All those crackpot stories.

He feels that he can no longer control his voice. In him, too, an enormous swollen pocket is emptying with a whistle, he himself is surprised by his own tone, which is filled with repressed violence, with hatred, by his sneer: "Indeed! you've just discovered that? Really? Why, of course I am like her. We are as alike as two peas, did you never notice that? Otherwise, I should not be so much interested by her. And you, I shouldn't make you laugh so much, at certain moments . . . I can be so funny, you are continually forcing me to tell you stories. Nor would you be so interested, you either, if you yourself and all of us here, didn't have a little something, somewhere, well hidden, in some well-closed, remote recess . . ."

They stand up, this time for good. Scandalous. The fellow is impossible. Fairly indecent. He overrides people's rights . . . "Good heavens, it's awful, we enjoy ourselves so much at your house that we forget how late it is . . ." Noise of chairs . . . and he, scowling in his corner, ignored, almost forgotten already . . . "It was delightful. So when shall I see you? Oh, very soon. Don't forget to let me hear from you. One of us will telephone at the beginning of next week. I'll count on you, then, surely?"

THAT'S GOING TOO far, she feels herself blushing again. That's really a bit strong. What a dressing-down he should have got! But she didn't turn a hair, of course . . . not a word. She had even smiled, flushing a bit, no doubt: she had felt, as she does now, a slight warmth in her cheeks. It's always the same thing, she accepts all the knocks with a smile. Everything rolls off her, doesn't it, they probably say that, "she has the skin of an elephant" . . . Never a word when, without warning, like that, people begin to attack . . . In reality, she's afraid, it's very simple. He always frightens her a bit. Since the very first moment, with him, she has always felt this same uneasiness. You never know where you stand, you never know what might happen, he's capable of all kinds of outbursts in front of people . . . Livid, all at once, filled with hatred, sarcastic . . . and right away, she draws in her horns. A coward. It's nothing but cowardice on her part, and he feels it . . . cowards scent one another out . . . He knows he can go safely ahead, he makes no bones about it. Cowardice? Why, that's out of the question. She a coward! Nobody is more liable than she to suddenly come out with a violent retort, to smash everything, at those moments she's not afraid, and each time people draw back, amazed. That highly disdainful saleswoman, that time, in the fur shop on that little street behind the Madeleine, who had thrown the coat at her . . . what an insolent gesture . . . what a tone . . . She had drawn herself up abruptly . . . The poor woman couldn't get over it, started backing out, wide-mouthed, stammering excuses . . . And right away, inside her, a sensation of overflowing force, of excitement . . . a feeling of intoxication . . . And that other one, the big fat trained nurse with the enormous hips, revolting . . . who, as a result of too much spoiling, had really taken leave of her senses, had permitted herself all sorts of liberties . . . People take advantage of her kindness, of her considerateness, of her attitude of equality, of the regard she has for everybody, no matter who it is. Kind. Too kind. That's what it is. But that's not all. There's something else about her when she remains spread out there before them, motionless, acquiescent, taking all the snubs without answering back. There's a sort of slowness, a torpor, a lack of flexibility, of vivacity in her reflexes . . . She's like that: heavy, slow. She has difficulty getting under way . . . The sky's blue, the weather's fine, peace reigns, we're among friends, among decent people, there are conventions which everyone respects, we say little insignificant things, people throw very light little darts at one another to put themselves in a cheerful mood, to tease one another a little, they laugh . . . It was to set him off to advantage before her friends that she had brought up the subject of his aunt's little manias . . . he can be screamingly funny when he's in one of his good days. But it didn't go very well, what of it, you go on to something else, and that's that, he made a mistake to insist . . . she wanted to stop him, to tease him a bit, it was so harmless, anybody else would have laughed it off . . . but he . . . right away that look of hatred he had, that pallor, that hissing tone, those insinuations . . . So what of it? What did he say that makes her blush now again, out of embarrassment, out of rage? (this is the ransom she must pay, she realizes it, these belated blushes, these eternal harpings on the same thing, they are her punishment for not having retorted at once, for having swallowed it all down) what was it he said exactly that makes her feel so like . . . if she could get hold of him one day, here, just the two of them alone, he would get what's coming to him . . . but what was it that was so corrosive, so scalding, she had withdrawn blushing, they had all looked embarrassed . . . "Ha! so you've just discovered that, have you . . ." Yes, that's what it was: you with your paltry female brain, no, really, that's too funny . . . will wonders never cease . . . the little mole, nosing about, dug that one up and dares to show it to him, she pretends to know him, to tell him something he didn't know, she thinks she can catch him napping, get at him, pique him, make him blush . . . oh, indeed. When it's he, he alone, who sees, knows, judges. He, the eagle, pounced upon her, and right away she was in her hole. With wings spread wide, he soared . . .

She who had imagined that she was urging him on with encouraging little protective pats: come on, don't be so shy, for goodness sake, do your act to entertain our guests, don't force us to beg you . . . when in reality it was he who was leading them about, he was escorting them with a firm hand—a pack of dogs on leash—toward a goal known only to him . . . "It wouldn't interest me so much if I weren't like that myself . . ." he didn't care a rap about the effect he had on people, what they might think or not think, there was something there, inside him, which he wanted to see; he was like these people who start out to do their errands and take you along with them so you can enjoy their company while they attend to their business, and you follow them docilely, like so much refuse tossed about at the mercy of the current.

But that's nothing. All that is nothing. What makes you thirst for vengeance, what makes you feel like running and taking him by the shoulders to tell him some home truths, the kind of truths that are not pleasant to hear, very unpleasant for him to hear if you dared, if you weren't ashamed to humiliate him, it was his having had the nerve to put her in the same basket, to insinuate that she too, like that family of lunatics . . . "And you yourself, if you didn't have that in some well-guarded secret recess . . ." He had had the nerve to insinuate that . . . But it's because she's too kind, too generous, too considerate of him, spoiling him as though he were her own child, doing everything he wants . . . you can give him anything on earth, everything is due him, but if you refuse him anything whatsoever, or fail to give in to his slightest whim . . . One single time was enough, just one . . .

It's extraordinary how she feels these things in advance. It's a source of wonder each time, to find that everything that was going to happen was already there in the bud, she had felt it at the moment, she knew that it was there, all ready, foreshadowed, she had sensed it quite clearly, she never makes a mistake, everything was going to come out of that and unroll, as astonishingly for the innocent onlooker as those long rolls of paper, the ribbon that keeps coming out of the magician's hat: everything that had already happened, everything that's coming now, came from the following brief question: she had hesitated to ask it, she had turned away . . . watch out, we mustn't allow ourselves to be tempted, let's forget it, Lord knows what that might stir up . . . But her friends—how could they have guessed it? how could sane, normal people think it?—her friends, in their simplicity, in their guilelessness, had encouraged her: "You're looking at our new easy chairs. They're nice, aren't they? We've got a little upholsterer who does perfect work . . . He furnishes only the best quality of leather . . . He used to work for Maple and has now gone into business for himself . . . It's as well finished as at Maple's . . . Extremely sturdy . . . And much less expensive . . . You ought to tell your children about him, since they're fixing up their apartment. This will last them all their lives . . ." And that was true: it was exactly what they needed, what she would have liked to give them—robust, long-wearing, magnificent leather. She had run her hand along the arm, she had felt the cushion, springy, silky, the back comfortably and simply shaped, in the best English taste . . . But there was no use asking the address. That's not for us, all that kind of thing, not for such as us out there. Here everything is as reliable as these chairs, everything is simple, clean-cut. But out there, at her daughter's . . . shadows, dark holes, disquieting swarmings, soft uncoilings, dangerous layers of ooze that open up, engulf her . . . it's enough for her to set her foot there, it's enough for her to say a word, to give her advice, for her merely to pronounce the name of her friends, and right away it never fails: silent withdrawals, contained shrugs, hardly perceptible ironic smiles, exchange of looks . . . no . . . she's too frightened . . . she prefers to remain apart, avoid all temptation, not stick her finger in the machinery, turn aside . . . But her friends keep after her: "Now do look at them. They're really the very best quality. And if we told you the price . . . Guess, how much would you say? . . ." She shakes her head with an air of appraisal, amazed: "Ah! that really is dirt cheap."

But they're ridiculous, after all, those ideas of hers . . . Nervousness—she'll dismiss all that. It's she, her excessive tact, her fits of diffidence with them, the desire that seizes her all of a sudden to curry favor with them, to get them to like her, which makes them that way . . . Her friends would certainly say that if she spoke to them about it: they're just a pair of kids . . . kids with no experience, excessively spoilt, rotten, rich kids who've never done anything except what they wanted . . . what's all this about, what are all these flickering shadows, these troubled waters, these disquieting reactions . . . She should be with them as she is with other people: be someone who is quite simple, straightforward, frank, not be afraid: they'll pretty well accept what's given them, that would be the last straw . . . and delighted at that . . . life will teach them . . . they are very comfortable, these chairs are, and there's no use smiling on the side of your faces and looking at each other like that, you'll be glad enough one of these days, when you're a little older, when you'll be working harder, when you'll be more tired than you are now, to sit down in these easy chairs . . . they'll last forever, they certainly will, and that's important, believe it or not, ask your father, he was the one who earned the money to buy them with . . . Yes, we're going to be like everybody else, we too, they're completely ridiculous, when all's said and done, all these complications, these finicky tastes, we're going to be like my friends here who look at me with their good, innocent eyes: "Why don't you have a pair made like that for your daughter and her husband? They are really a bargain. —Why not, true enough, you're right. What's the name of your upholsterer? Let me have his address for my daughter. They're exactly what she needs . . ."

What could be simpler, more natural? A mother filled with solicitude—and what had she not done for this child, what wouldn't she do?—gives her daughter and son-in-law the address of a good upholsterer, makes them a present of two handsome easy chairs . . . "Exactly what you need, you won't find anything better. I got the address through the Perrins, you can tell him they sent you. He used to work for Maple. He will give you a special price. They are comfortable, sturdy and very pretty . . . made of splendid leather." But it's doubtless her voice, something in the tone, in the sound of her voice, a note of hesitation, of uneasiness, a lack of self-confidence, which must have set everything going. They are like dogs that grow excited from fear, even when it's hidden, they feel it . . . it was that barely perceptible waver in her voice, which started everything, which upset everything . . . they hesitated a moment, they looked at each other . . . "Oh, thank you Maman—we want, Alain and I . . . We had thought we should like to have an authentic *bergère*, we saw one in an antique shop . . . It will be a little more expensive perhaps than the leather chairs, but I assure you, it, too, is a bargain, and it's so much prettier . . ." These words, apparently harmless—but only the uninitiated could make this mistake—these words, like those that once revealed heresy and led directly to the stake, showed that the evil was still there, as alive and strong as ever . . . her heart started to beat, she blushed, anybody else, except them, would have been surprised by the violence of her reaction, the hatred, the rage in her tone all of a sudden, in her false, icy laughter, she herself felt sick when she heard it: "Oh, how stupid of me . . . I keep forgetting . . . that's true . . . it's enough for it to come from me, poor fool that I am . . . or for it to come from friends of mine . . . I knew it, I didn't even want to ask them for the address . . . But I couldn't resist, it was such a bargain . . . I should have bought them for us, if I could have done so just now . . ." The look they gave each other . . . They always have awful looks . . . their eyes seek each other out, find each other right away, become motionless, stare, stretched wide, as though they were full to splitting. She knows what composes this silent transfusion that takes place up above her while she lies prone between them, powerless, inert, floored: it's there, eh? We were right. Did you see that? I did. Congratulations, that was certainly the reaction that had been foreseen. We are very clever. It's exactly as we thought, it's what we always say . . . she has to call the tune . . . as soon as you take a step off the path chosen by her, she sets herself up as a flouted victim . . . She's bossy . . . possessive . . . She gives in order to dominate . . . to keep us forever under her tutelage . . . And that little pique at the end . . . Did you notice that? —I did . . . To hear her tell it, she takes the bread out of her own mouth to give to us . . . her eternal sacrifices . . . What playacting . . . She feels a faintness, a dull pain . . . She shouldn't have . . . But they are the ones who drive her to do those things, to say things like that to them, now she's ashamed, she was already ashamed at the moment, but they are the ones who cause her to slip, who make her step in that dirt, that mire . . . what he calls "those little marshes" . . . He detects them right away. He sees everything . . . always on the watch . . . and he shows them to her, to her own daughter, to her little girl, who hadn't seen a thing: that clear gaze of hers, so pure, formerly, so confiding, there was nothing lovelier than her mama, but he, he spies, he hunts, he finds and he shows everybody: "Right this way . . . is there anybody who hasn't got his little recesses . . ." And she, pitiful, crazy old woman, ridiculous . . . smiling away . . . wriggling . . . oh no, you mustn't believe . . . you're mistaken, I assure you . . . there's none of all that about me, you must believe me, nothing except a real doting mama, continual little treats, presents, better than a mother—a friend. But he won't be taken in. No use to kick. With a firm hand, he holds the mask which he had plastered down on her face from the very first, that grotesque, outmoded mask of the vaudeville mother-in-law, of the old woman who sticks her nose into everything, the tyrant who keeps her daughter and son-in-law well in hand.

Very well, that's fine. She feels within herself a delightful welling up of strength that increases as her calm increases, a sensation of power, of freedom. No, not that mask; not that face, she'll have none of it, but this one, which she's going to wear now, which is so becoming to her, which is to her taste too—a face with the same features as the other, but harder still, more accentuated . . . No use exchanging looks . . . there'll be nothing left to show up, everything will be so clear, so obvious. That's what she should have done from the beginning. Only strong actions inspire respect. People accept you the way you are, people give in, they become docile, if you assert yourself with them, if you stand there, right in front of them, unshaken on your two feet: look at me. I don't need you to like me, I don't care a rap whether people like me or not—her father always said that when he spoke of his employees, and they all respected him . . . She should have taken a page out of his book . . . But, in reality, she's like him, she can be like him when she wants to be . . . Too delighted, all blushes with pleasure when he pinched her cheek, or laid his hand on her hair—it was rare for him to make her the tiniest of presents . . . the little perfume bottle, she still has it, with shepherdesses, outdoor scenes painted on it, an old-rose color, and its gently curved old-fashioned shape . . . it's still there in her drawer . . . it brings her good luck . . . Merely the idea of being cranky with her father, of questioning his good taste, exchanging looks! Everything he did had seemed perfect to her . . . But those two, if he had known them . . . spoilt, rotten, taking all sorts of liberties, never satisfied . . . You could give them the moon, they'd want more . . . Antique chairs, museum pieces . . . and to go where? . . . They'd do better to work a little harder instead of loafing about in front of antique shops, trying to impress their little playmates . . . but it's finished, all that. . . Quite finished. Look at me hard. I'm not afraid. Either the leather chairs or nothing. I'm the one who pays. It's hard to swallow, humiliating? It's sordid, cowardly on my part? Tyrannical old woman . . . Unsatisfied (another of those idiotic theories!) . . . I don't care a rap. They can take it or leave it. That will cure him, cure this unusually bright boy of making discoveries at my expense, of giving lessons in psychology. He'll lose his taste for getting me riled before people. A little common sense, at last. Some sense of the realities of life. These mere striplings who are so sophisticated, so complicated, must be made to come down to earth, they must learn about life. Simpler and coarser than they think, very simple and very coarse, in fact, I'll be the one to teach them that. This time they can count on me, they'll understand.

She doesn't have to wait long, no need to go and "get" them. They are never able to hold out, they themselves make the first move. They walk briskly along on the mined terrain: "You know Maman, we meant to tell you, about those leather chairs . . . We've thought it over, Alain and I . . . we don't really need them just now . . . We wouldn't even have room for them . . . It's such close quarters: you'd have to have a real office, those are office chairs. The Louis XV *bergère*, on the other hand . . . no doubt about it, it is very nice. We went back to see it. It's really marvelous. I thought that it was all the same to you, really, so I said that we would take it. We had to decide. It really was a unique opportunity." A fine opportunity for her, too. A unique opportunity. Chin up . . . This is the moment or never to turn over a new leaf at last, to stand there in front of them, steady, heavy, well-ballasted, an enormous mass, impossible to move. Perfectly poised voice. Indifferent look: In that case, children, you'll take care of it yourselves. I'll do nothing more about it. I'm no longer at all interested. I wanted to give you something useful, really sturdy, but museum pieces, especially just now, that, no. An immense rock spread out before them in the sun. They can go all over it, examine it at their leisure: avaricious; mean; prejudiced; boorish; a coward who takes brutal advantage of her strength; unnatural mother; "castratress"—one of their expressions; a real vaudeville mother-in-law. The furious little waves of their looks, of their thoughts, will come and break against her feet. Go ahead, make an effort. Everything will be so simple afterwards. So smooth, so clean-cut. No more ingrown rages that ooze with little scalding drops, no more torturing need for revenge, memories of shameful weaknesses, of exhausting regrets, nothing more to fear: there will be no more of those looks that pass between them, during which she fairly shriveled—little dried Indian head fit to put into their glass cabinet, in among their collection of unusual objects . . . They'll have to turn their looks elsewhere, tense, piercing adult looks, directed at real obstacles, real difficulties: You know, my mother refused point-blank. Well, it's not so bad as all that, you can't change her at her age. The question now is to see how we can get hold of the money.

All by themselves. What are they going to do? Babes in the woods, all alone in the big forest. They wander away, go deeper and deeper. She is going to lose track of them. She can run as fast as she likes, she'll not catch up with them now. When she holds out her arms to them: Don't you recognize me? I'm your maman, see here, I was just joking, you're really unreasonable, you must admit . . . It was just to frighten you a bit . . . Go ahead, buy what you want. . . they will look at her coldly, their faces will be hard, the rather sad, serious faces of adults at grips with the difficulties of life, that little wrinkle, barely outlined, will furrow the corners of their eyelids, of their mouths . . . they will answer politely, in the same remote, indifferent tone that she is going to use now: No, no, everything is going very well, don't worry. We don't need anything, it's all been taken care of . . . Impossible. She won't be able to stand it. It's too abrupt, too cowardly to use such means as these, to maltreat these young people, to leave them without help . . . God alone knows what the future holds for them . . . they will have plenty of time later . . . still such delicate, such innocent children . . . tender petal-like softness on her rounded cheeks, real down, her little girl's lips still smell of milk, pouting now, as before, as always, when she has her worried look . . . "Listen, darling, you know it's not my habit, I've never done that, to go back on something I've promised . . . And since I wanted to buy you a pair of easy chairs . . . You know that . . ." Her reaction, which she feels right away, of rapprochement, of nearness, her tenderness, her caressing look, her grateful smile . . . "Why yes, Maman, I know it . . ."

Tender, sweet child. So easy. So delightful to handle, to model. What would she not have done to please her maman? So careful . . . it was touching . . . conscientiously wiping her little white kid shoes on the doormat, so as not to soil anything . . . always spotless, with her big bows of ribbon. Passing through all the stages quietly, docilely, with no jolts—nothing that really counts—then this last stage, which she had so dreaded for her little girl. Together they had prepared it, waited for it, imagined it, never tired of listening, of telling, seated evenings huddled up close to each other on the little low sofa in the dining room . . . it had been her favorite story ever since she was eleven or twelve years old: Oh, tell me again, Maman, what the great day will be like . . . the wedding dress, the bridesmaids, the guests arriving at Auville as in the old days—that amused her no end—in old-fashioned carriages, in enormous charabancs . . . the bells of the old church ringing out, and she, coming slowly up the steps on her father's arm, her heavy train carried by little pages in lavender? in gray? she, Gisèle, it wouldn't be Gigi now, certainly not, but Gisèle what . . . let's think of a nice name . . . but a grownup lady, in any case, who would come out on her husband's arm and stand for a moment, smiling and rosy, on the church steps . . . And everything had gone perfectly, it had all taken place as if by a miracle, enough to make all the mothers, all their friends, turn pale with envy . . . the real Prince Charming, appearing at a given point . . . She herself had been beguiled, she herself, she's well aware of it, had encouraged them. There were a few drawbacks, of course . . . but he was charming, he was handsome, he was intelligent, very gifted . . . whom else should she look for? and where to find him? True, she had noticed from the beginning a few little knots in the beautiful tapestry they had embroidered: a few defects of workmanship, undoubtedly, in the so prettily woven wool . . . But it sufficed—or so she had hoped—not to pay any attention to them, not to look, no one else saw them, they were nothing really, tiny things . . . eccentricities . . . that furious expression of ingrowing violence all of a sudden when the photographer had tried to get them to pose, when she had insisted—they're always slightly ridiculous, that's well known, the poses they make you assume in those cases, looking deep into each other's eyes, holding hands, you have to make certain allowances, but between that and being filled with hatred, with fury: the traces of it are still to be seen in that cold, contracted expression, preserved for all time, in the photograph she has kept—she has no other—on her mantelpiece. And those smiles about nothing, when she would say the most innocuous things . . . those looks . . . It's not for herself, does she matter? It's ridiculous, they have neither rhyme nor reason, those moments of rage, like a little while ago, that desire for vengeance, against whom? In such cases, one only punishes oneself. It's not because she feels out of things, humiliated, that those smiles, those looks, make her suffer. No, she's afraid: they are disquieting signs, crevices in the walls of the fine structure that they had so patiently erected. It will bear looking into more closely, perhaps it's nothing serious, there's surely some way, if you take your courage in both hands, to fill in the chinks, to repair them . . . Let's look well, both of us . . . "You know, darling, I desire nothing but your happiness . . . I was just going to tell you, since we happened to speak of it . . ." Come close to me, quite close, snuggled up to your Maman, the way we used to sit, on the sofa . . . Let's examine it together, is it what we expected, is that how we had imagined it would be . . . "Your husband is adorable. You know how fond I am of him: like a son. And, in reality, he's fond of me, I know it, he's so sweet; he's so young, so charming, but it must be admitted that he is perhaps not exactly the husband your father and I should have wished for. He's not quite mature enough . . . I'm not speaking of his age . . . It's a question of temperament. Your father was mature when he was twenty-five . . ." Only look out. Her little girl withdraws slightly, she's about to take cover in one of her stubborn silences which it takes any amount of trouble to get her out of . . . "It isn't the question of his position, you know that. Other parents than ourselves would perhaps have taken it with bad grace, but you know very well that, for us, that hasn't mattered . . . You're both young, you're in love, you have the entire future before you. Only that future must be prepared for. And Alain—that's the dark side of the picture . . . His charm—I understand it perfectly, I succumb very easily to it, believe me—also comes from that, from his lightheartedness, from his frivolity. He doesn't think much about your future . . . Not enough, if you want to know what I really think." The girl listens attentively, as though fascinated; she won't try to get out of it; this is serious, she knows it: this is their serious, ceaseless work done together, occasionally painfully hard, but she knows that they are performing it for her, for her happiness, that it's only for her good . . . "You know, don't you, darling, that it's a question of you, of your entire life . . . You are both so young, so carefree, it's natural, there are things you never think about. . . But you, yourself, you can do a lot. You can change a lot of things, believe me . . . Alain is still very young . . . he listens to you . . . It's your role as his wife, my darling, to tell him . . . It's not always a good thing to close our eyes. I made up my mind to speak to you about it, and I am taking advantage of this opportunity . . . as for the *bergère*, you know perfectly well, that I don't give a rap about it. . . That's not the question . . . But I assure you, and it's not because I'm prejudiced, he is queer about certain things, he's not like other young men of his age." Slight withdrawal, haughty, satisfied little smile: "But I know that, Maman . . . It's for that very reason that I love him . . . —No, no, I know what you mean, but that's not the question . . . It's not a mark of superiority, but something which worries me a bit . . . you know what they're like in that family . . . His old Aunt Berthe . . . He spoke of her the other day with a sort of excitement that struck me. He feels very close to her, he's like her in certain ways, I couldn't help saying it to him, he was furious . . . But he acknowledged it . . . He certainly did . . . he admitted it himself, he said to me: Otherwise, I shouldn't talk about her like that . . . I wish you had seen his manner when he said that to me . . . He had a sort of sneer that made me wince . . . I thought about this *bergère* affair. I realize that it's natural to like nice things, up to a certain point, but in his case . . ." The poor little girl has grown pale, it's as though the ground had slipped out from under her, she's afraid, you feel pity for her . . . it's distressing, it's heartrending to see her in that state, but it must be done, this is not the moment to stop, one must have the courage to incise the wound, sooner or later it will have to come to that. . . "With Alain, it's a passion, it's a sort of frenzy . . . once he gets started, it becomes an obsession . . . I mentioned it one day to his father, he didn't deny it, I'm sure that he agreed with me . . . that's why his work is not getting on as he would like, why his thesis isn't finished . . . It's a way of escaping from himself, of compensating himself with trifles . . . A man has other fish to fry, he doesn't care a rap for such things, Louis XV *bergères*, easy chairs . . . what they are like, one way or the other . . . provided there's something comfortable to sit on, a place to rest . . . I know what you're going to say, that he likes nice things . . . I understand that very well . . . He can visit museums, look at beautiful old pieces of furniture, pictures, works of art, there's nothing to be said against that . . . but these excursions to antique shops, this need to buy . . . it must absolutely belong to him . . . all that effort . . . like Aunt Berthe, who passes her time fiddling over little details as though she were expecting the Pope, when she has never been able to give so much as a cup of tea to a friend . . . All that, you understand, no . . . that's not it . . ."

That's not the man who was supposed to give his arm to the pretty bride, a calm, strong, pure, unworldly man, absorbed in serious, complicated things that escape weak women like themselves, staring into the distance, his sturdy arm escorting her by degrees, making her go forward at his side with long strides, towards wealth? fame? . . . "You have to look things squarely in the face." They look. How little it resembles the picture they had envisaged, this spoilt child, exacting and capricious, wasting his strength on trifles when, meanwhile, time is passing . . . the best years of all . . . his work is not going ahead as it should, they're living in a tiny little flat . . . "I might understand if you had a handsome apartment, he could amuse himself furnishing it with authentic, *bergères* . . . But, in your place, you must see that yourself, darling, it's a real mania . . ." She's advancing now without encountering any resistance into conquered, subject territory . . . She can have plenty of elbowroom, take her time . . . Her enemy—it's his turn now—lies inert and prone at her feet, she can do with him what she likes . . . she takes her turn subjecting him to the embalming process that will make a tiny mummy of him, a shrunken dried-up head which people will examine as a curiosity, exhibited in a glass case . . . an excitement that she recognizes takes hold of her, it's the same that she always feels when she is able to engage like this, upon a prostrate foe, in these delicate, thrilling operations of drying and shrinking . . . how far would she not go, if she were to give herself free rein . . . But she feels, trembling up against her, as in the old days, when she was afraid of burglars, when she waked from a nightmare and came to snuggle up in her maman's bed, her most cherished treasure, her little girl . . . all aquiver, gentle and warm like a frightened young bird . . . the branch it is poised on is untrustworthy, it's going to fall, it's afraid, it must be taught, helped . . . "But, my darling, don't have that desperate look . . . It's extraordinary how life has spoiled you—you're absolute children . . . I wanted to put you on your guard, that's all. Alain is at the age when he can still change. You can do a great deal towards that. What I feel sorry about, you see, is that he should make you lose your own sense of judgment, that instead of trying to bring him to reason, you urge him, on the contrary, to satisfy his whims and his manias . . . This *bergère*—it's nothing, you know that quite well, but it's like that about everything. As soon as I take the liberty of saying a word, you look at each other, oh yes you do, don't say you don't, I see everything . . . you know I may appear like an old fool, but I see a lot more than people think, I can read you like that . . . like an open book . . . They amuse me, those glances you exchange as though I were your worst enemy . . . Come along, now, cheer up, it's time to approach life the way grown people do . . . Push him to work a bit, to have a little more ambition . . . And as for all of that, what nonsense! it's quite unimportant, come, come, give me a little kiss, and hurry, I'm sure he's waiting for you . . . with regard to the *bergère*, buy it if you want, that's not the question . . . But I know you have understood me, I feel sure that you will think about all that and that everything will be all right . . . And that's what matters most for me, darling, you know that very well."

Something inside her comes loose and falls . . . in the emptiness inside her something is quivering . . . Dizziness . . . Her head reels slightly, her legs weaken . . . But she must brace herself, she must hold on, just one second more, present a calm face for the light kisses on her cheek, offer a kiss in return, smile, talk . . . "Well, goodbye, Maman, we'll see you soon . . . Why no, I'm not depressed, no, I'm not annoyed, what an idea . . . Why, of course, Maman, I understand, I know . . . And you, don't you worry, either . . . They're nothing serious, you know, in reality, those fads of Alain's . . . You'll see, we're not as bad as you think. Yes, yes, I'll speak to him. You're right, it will straighten out . . ."

As soon as the door is closed, as soon as she is alone on the silent staircase, the dikes break . . . Something boils up in her, runs over . . . She knows what it is, it's the old sensation she used to have, her own peculiar fear, still the same, the terror that had never left her, she recognizes it . . .

She is skipping along the walk in the Petit Luxembourg gardens, holding her mother's hand. The big pink blossoms on the horse-chestnut trees stand erect amidst the soft foliage, the damp grass sparkles in the sun, the air trembles slightly, but it's happiness, it's Spring that trembles above the lawns, between the trees . . . she inhales delightedly on her bare arm her own odor, the odor that will always recall that Spring, that happiness, the cool, bland odor of her child's skin, of the sleeve of her new cotton dress . . . And suddenly a shriek, an inhuman, strident shriek . . . Her mother shrieked, her mother is pulling her back savagely, her head turned away, holding her nose . . .

The light has grown dim, the sun is shining with a dull luster, everything is wavering with terror, and a strange vehicle, a high, slender, nightmarish cart, filled with a livid powder that exhales a frightful smell, comes bumping along towards them on the walk . . .

She feels now, as she did then, like hiding her head so as not to see, like holding her nose, she's going to be sick, she would like to sit down just anywhere, there, on one of the steps . . . or preferably, over there, out of doors, on a bench . . . Everything is wavering . . . Everything is going to collapse.

Smiles, knowing looks, murmurs . . . later, later, you'll see . . . Images proposed on every side, songs, films, novels . . . Promised, heralded, awaited, finally manifested, handsomer than she could possibly have imagined . . . a little shy, perhaps, but highbred, smart, subtle smile of his gray eyes, everyone had agreed: a real Prince Charming. A little too young? Her father had patted her cheek as he gazed at her in his tender way . . . "Don't complain, my daughter . . . You'll see, youth is a very brief illness, one gets quickly over it, believe me . . ." And his studies not completed? his doctor's thesis not yet finished? But it's so hard, the Doctor of Letters thesis especially, it's the hardest of all . . . the blotchy-cheeked woman looked at her with shining, slightly bulging eyes . . . "Ah, my dear child, my husband was studying for his internship when we were married, and now, you see . . ."

No, nobody had had anything to say against it. If there had been something . . . the slightest crack . . . her mother, who saw everything, her mother who looked out for everything—nothing escaped her . . . No, there was nothing. It really was what you call happiness that people had looked at with tender smiles, moist eyes. You couldn't mistake it. It certainly was that. Everybody had been delighted with the very amusing fancies, the innocent teasing that happiness indulges in when its strength is overflowing, when it feels lighthearted, at ease, and sure of itself: the bridal train that an awkward little page had caught on a bench, as they started up the aisle . . . The "yes" that she had answered a little too soon during the civil ceremony . . . the right hand she had stretched out instead of the left to receive the ring . . . It was all so funny, so charming . . . and they had all been delighted, laughing there under the refreshing caress of this joyful outburst, of this overflow of happiness . . .

And yet, even that day—now that she looks with all her might at the beautiful structure, which is wavering, which is listing—even that day, there had already been something, a crack, a defect . . . What was it? She feels, as she hunts about, a sort of excitement, almost a satisfaction, which mingles with her suffering . . . yes, already at that time, the edifice had not been so handsome, so perfect. . . There had been that tiny cranny through which an evil-smelling vapor, exhalations, had leaked . . . That half-laughter, as she went from one to the other in the drawing-room, all excitement, people calling her from every side, congratulating her, that whisper, like a wheeze, of the two baleful old women, the wicked fairies, leaning towards each other . . . "How much did you say? How much? Eighty thousand francs a month? Really? no more than that?"

She turned away, she fled, she ran to take refuge with her husband, she laid her hand on his arm, they looked into each other's eyes, then and there, in front of everybody . . . And she felt very strongly, for the first time, she knew that the two of them . . . the pain comes back all of a sudden, throbbing harder than before . . . that they formed together something indestructible, unassailable . . . Not a flaw in the hard, smooth wall. No way for others to see what was on the other side.

On the other side, only they two knew it, everything was fluid, vast, without outlines. Everything was in a state of constant movement, changing. Impossible to find your way about, to give a name to things, to classify them. Impossible to judge.

Who would dare? Indeed, nobody dared. Silence. The baleful fairies themselves stopped talking, while they stood there like that, facing the others, leaning towards each other, looking into each other's eyes. Everybody kept a respectful distance and looked, with emotion, at the handsome, congenial young couple, joined together, the very image of happiness.

They two alone, he and she—they alone were able to enter at will into the intimacy of others, to penetrate without effort on the other side of the thin wall that others tried to oppose to them, behind which others sought to hide . . . It was so amusing, so thrilling, it sufficed to make a slight effort, everything was so well circumscribed with other people, each thing in its place, immediately recognizable, they pointed it out to each other . . . "Uncle Albert, don't you think he has a very hypocritical side? And Auntie, really she's stinginess itself. Frank, though, that she is, her heart on her sleeve." In the evening, after their friends were gone, taking one last drink, just between themselves—it was fun, this diversion, after all the effort, all the edginess, it was delightful, this little surplus excitement mingled with a sensation of relaxation—they amused themselves trying to find a set formula for each guest, pigeonholing . . . At times, the tiniest thing suffices to guide you . . . A word, a gesture, a mannerism, a silence . . . "Did you see that? Did you hear that? What do you think of it?" It's very curious, occasionally astonishing, these discoveries, these glimpses, these demolitions, they proceeded hand in hand, she let herself be guided by him . . . He was so witty when he took hold of people, held them in the palm of his hand, showed them to her, when he drew them with such accurate, vivid strokes, he knew how to get such a good likeness, he imitated them so well, she laughed till she cried . . .

No one escaped. Not even their parents. She had been afraid—it was this same fear, the same sensation, as now, of wrenching, of falling into space—when, huddled up to him, she had seen her mother, who, thus far, like herself, had been unsurroundable, boundless, abruptly projected in the distance, suddenly grow petrified in an unfamiliar form with very precise contours . . . she would have liked to close her eyes, she had drawn close to him . . . "Oh, no, Alain, this time it's not that, this time, I'm not so sure . . ." But he had forced her to look, he had laughed: "What a child you are . . . why, it's obvious, see here, think it over . . . It's so simple, I don't understand what you are so surprised about, for it's clear. Your mother is, above all else, bossy. She loves you, that goes without saying, I don't say she doesn't, she always has your welfare in mind. But you must walk the straight and narrow path that she has laid down for you. She has probably been frustrated herself, not had in her own life what she would have liked. She wants to make up for it through you. I, as her son-in-law, actually suit her very well. She would have her hands full with anybody else but me, somebody older, more independent . . . I put up no resistance; at least, so she thinks. Just a few snubs here and there, to frighten her, to amuse myself . . . But I'm what she needs, with me, she can imagine that she can do as she does with you, that is, that she can continue to teach me how to behave . . ." She had drawn back. Sacrilege . . . Yet no, they had the right: thou shalt leave thy father and thy mother. What strength that had given her; what relief she had felt at finally seeing things clearly, at being able to look calmly at what, for so long, she had felt moving in the darkness, confused, disturbing, what she had tried in vain to flee, what she had struggled against with the awkwardness, the angry weakness, of a child . . .

In front of her, all about her, he was clearing the ground, cleaning out the underbrush, laying out roads, she had only to let herself be led, to remain supple, flexible, as one does with a good dancer. It was curious, this sensation she often had, that, without him, before, the world had been a bit inert, gray, formless, indifferent, that she herself had been nothing but expectation, suspense . . .

As soon as he was there, everything fell back into place. Things assumed form, molded by him, reflected in his glance . . . "Come and look . . ." He took her by the hand, lifted her up from the bench on to which she had dropped to rest her swollen feet, looking, without seeing them, at the tedious rows of frozen-faced Madonnas, of large, nude women. "Do look at that. Not bad, eh? What do you think of it? He certainly knew how to draw, the old rip. Take a look at that draftsmanship, those masses, that balance . . . Not to mention the color . . ." From out of uniformity, chaos, ugliness, something unique emerged, something strong, alive (the rest now, all about her, the people, the view out the windows overlooking gardens, seemed dead) something vibrant, traversed by a mysterious current, organized everything round about, lifted, sustained the world . . .

It was delightful to delegate him to do the sorting, to remain confident, in abeyance, acquiescent, to wait for him to give her her beakful, to watch him looking for their feed in old churches, in the bookstalls along the Seine, in old engraving shops. It was good, it was cheering.

Little by little, a sense of relaxation, of recovered security, overspread her suffering, her fear. He is so eager, so alive, he throws himself into things with such enthusiasm . . . That is what permits him to make discoveries, to invent, it's that fervor, the intensity of his sensations, his unbridled desires. She feels quite well now. The tottering, unstable edifice has little by little found its poise . . . It's what she lacks, this enthusiasm, this freedom, this boldness, she's always afraid, she doesn't know . . . "You think so? In our place? Somehow I don't see it . . ." He laughed, held her arm tightly . . . "Over there, silly, no, not that one, that's a Voltaire armchair, no, there, upholstered in pale pink silk, that *bergère* . . ." She had suddenly felt excited, she had joined in right away, it had touched one of her sensitive spots, hers too, the building of their nest; she was a little frightened . . . "It must cost a fortune . . . Not that in our flat, Alain! That *bergère*?" Like her mother, she would have been more inclined to put comfort, economy before everything else, but he had reassured her: "Do look at it anyway, it's a beauty, a magnificent piece of furniture . . . You know, it would change everything in our place . . ." Only marriage permits such moments as these, of fusion, of happiness, during which, leaning on him, she had gazed at the old silk with its ash-rose, its delicate gray tones, the large, nobly spreading seat, the broad back, the free, firm curve of the elbow-rests . . . A caress, a consolation emanated from its calm, ample lines . . . at their fireside . . . just what was needed . . . "There would be room, you're sure?—Of course, between the window and the fireplace . . ." Tutelary, diffusing serenity, security about it—this was beauty, harmony itself, captured, subjugated, familiar, become part and parcel of their life, a joy constantly within their reach.

A passion had seized upon them, avidity . . . The door of the shop was closed, it was the lunch hour . . . they had to know right away, no obstacle could stop them . . . in those moments, he is seized with a sort of frenzy, and she too had felt within herself a kind of emptiness that must immediately be filled, a sort of hunger, almost suffering, that must be appeased at all costs . . . they had turned the door-handle, the shop door was closed but the handle had not been removed, this augured well, the dealer could not be far . . . they had pressed their noses against the pane, they had knocked, they had gone into the courtyard to see if there was not a back room, behind the shop, where he might be having lunch . . . but he was not there . . . they had questioned the concierge . . . doubtless he wouldn't be long . . . "We'll have to wait a bit, it's worth it, it's perhaps a unique bargain, you know, come on, let's go and look at it again . . ."

That's where it comes from, this sensation of weakness in the legs, this fear which she feels again now—our bodies are never wrong: before consciousness, they record, enlarge, assemble, and reveal with relentless brutality to the outside world, tiny, intangible, scattered impressions—that sensation of flabbiness in her entire body, the shiver running up her spine . . . Hadn't she already experienced them at the moment when they went back to look, while they waited, leaning against each other, soaking up what emanated from the sheen of the faded silk, from the soft luster of the mellowed wood, from the free, powerful curve of the armrests . . . Already at that moment, she had suddenly felt a sort of weakness, a pang in her heart, anguish . . . something like what the characters in a play she had once seen must have experienced. The scene was the bar of an ocean liner. The passengers gathered there were drinking and chatting, at first everything seemed commonplace, harmless enough. And then, little by little, something disquieting, slightly sinister, began to make itself felt, it was hard to say from where it came, perhaps from the strange manner of the pallid bartender standing behind his counter . . . Suddenly the hand of one of the passengers began to tremble, the glass it was holding fell and rolled along the floor . . . He had just realized that this liner on which they were drinking and chatting was the boat that transported the dead, they thought they were alive and they were dead . . . somewhere out there living persons had looked at them, touched them, examined them, turned them over, carried them . . . and they themselves didn't know they were dead . . . she too had suddenly understood at the moment when they were standing there waiting in front of the shop window . . . she had seen herself, she had seen themselves, the two of them, as others, her mother, the living, saw them . . . They were dead. They are both dead, embarked they don't know how, swept along, carried away without their knowing it towards God knows what country of the dead . . . a dream, all that, Louis XVth *bergères*, antique-shop windows, visions that cross the minds of persons in a swoon, of drowning, frozen persons . . . She must ask for help, call out, she must pull herself together, break away from all that, from these drowsy shops filled with things that are long since dead, she had drawn aside abruptly, she had felt like running away . . . "Oh, listen Alain, it doesn't matter, why insist, let's drop it, let's go home, shall we, don't you think we'd better go home?"

Complete fusion exists with no one, those are tales we read in novels—we all know that the greatest intimacy is constantly being traversed by silent flashes of cold clear-sightedness, of loneliness . . . what her mother had seen, she too had seen, during the brief second when she had come to herself again, when she had come to her senses, the two figures coincide, no mistake is possible . . . it suffices to step away from ourselves and see ourselves as others see us, and immediately it knocks your eyes out . . . her mother has just tried to resuscitate them both, come to your senses, I beg of you, pats on the cheek . . . Life is flowing by all round them while they are numb with sleep, clinging weakly in their dreams . . . to what? I ask you . . . what is all this morbid excitement, this sudden necessity? why?

Quick, she must go home, throw herself on her bed, examine it all closely . . . she almost runs . . . the little empty street is sad, dreary, like this whole neighborhood, she hates it. The entrance to the house, the neat, overheated stairway, remind one of a nursing home, a mental hospital . . . and the little nest, well, it's even smaller than she had remembered it . . . that enormous *bergère* in here would look absurd, ludicrous, it was ridiculous to think it could change the meager, cramped look, it would even bring out all the more the diminutive size of the room: a real little tenement. She runs to her room and drops face down on her bed . . . Lets herself sink, farther, still farther down . . . voluptuousness of going down . . . down to the very bottom . . . It's all a fraud . . . she sits up in bed: she and Alain are a fraud. Imitation, sham, pictures supposed to represent happiness, and there's something on the back . . . the old witches' laughter . . . And her father's shrug, the way he hissed the day they showed him that they didn't much like the glass-doored book case he had bought himself . . . "Oh, that aestheticism of yours . . ." It was like the overflow of an acrid vapor that had filtered between his clenched teeth . . . Frivolous, weak, spoilt child . . . His contempt for all serious ambition, his amateurishness . . . already disenchanted, bored, at twenty-seven . . . and she clinging to him, she being swept along towards death . . .

That contemptuous smile of his, that sneer when she had said to him as they passed in front of the *Collège de France* . . .

"Who knows? perhaps one day you will go in through that door to give your lectures . . ." He had drawn away from her, the better to see her, his lip had curled in that contemptuous expression he can have . . . "What do little girls dream of? So that's what you have in mind . . . What a joyful prospect to see me one day, bald and rotund, go and mumble a lecture before a lot of idiotic society women, tramps . . . No, really, you disappoint me . . . that makes me think of that poem of Rimbaud's, you remember? She, replying to all his invitations to go voyaging: and my office?" And she had felt herself blushing . . . How mature he was already, how clear-sighted, pure, strong . . . he sat enthroned, solitary, disillusioned, bitter, on the heights . . . all the others, dashing about somewhere down below, running stupidly hither and thither, with a busy air, comically lifting enormous burdens . . . She had snuggled up against him, they were alone, the two of them, very high up, she was a bit dizzy, she was a bit afraid, the air was hard to breathe, raw, rarefied. An icy wind blew against the bare peaks. She would have preferred—but she hardly dared to admit it—she would have loved to go down in the valley with the others, in that tiny miniature world that she saw in the distance, where everything was made for her, to her measure . . . peaceful villages, calm evenings, dreams of the future . . . He would have energy, ambition: you'll see, I'll be somebody . . . They would talk about their children's education, choose names for them . . . Everybody longed for that happiness, it was normal, it was wholesome . . . that was what she had expected, what had always been promised her . . . But her mother knew, her mother had understood a long time ago. It's unbearable, she can't face it . . .

What's done cannot be undone. Her mother finally decided to open her eyes, to show her things the way they are. They had been mistaken, it was not that, that was not happiness. She's not happy. Every one has noticed it. People remark about it, she has changed, grown thin, her eyes, her hair have lost their luster . . .

She hears the little click of a key in the lock . . .

The wrench, the frightful separation will soon be finished. Like the dead passengers on the boat, he knows nothing as yet. As in their movements, there is in each of his gestures, when he quietly hangs his overcoat on the hall rack, when he smoothes his hair in front of the mirror and moves towards the bedroom . . . "Is that you, Gisèle? You're back . . ." there is something in his voice, in his natural, carefree tone, which is off-key, strange. The gestures, the sayings of lunatics give normal persons observing them this impression of being disconnected, emptied of their substance. She hides her head in the pillows. It's impossible, she can't remain so far from him, watch him from a distance and then try coldly, prudently, with skill, the way a psychiatrist would do it, to slip the words into him that, without his being aware of it, are going to mold him, transform him, cure him . . . No, she hasn't the courage . . .

She feels the caress of his hand on her hair, he has that anxious, tender, protective tone, that he takes when she has one of her moments of depression, one of her crying spells . . . And she lets him do what he wants with her. She lets him fondle her, pet her like a child . . . "Gisèle, darling, what's the matter? What's wrong, Gisèle, tell me . . ." She feels her eyes fill with tears right away, she lifts her head, puckers her lips like a little girl: "I don't know, I feel blue. It's idiotic. About nothing at all . . ." That nice look he can have, a very attentive, intelligent look, which penetrates her, searches . . . Impossible . . . she can't . . . let him see for himself, she can hide nothing from him, there's nothing that doesn't concern them both . . .

it's there inside her, sunk down deep, buried, it hurts her, he must help her remove it, he alone can do it . . . "You know, it's a sudden feeling of anguish . . . it's idiotic, we've often said so . . ." She's a little afraid . . . she hesitates . . . "It starts from almost nothing . . . The slightest pretext will do . . . It's about that *bergère* . . ." She has the impression that he draws back a little, is on his guard: "The *bergère*? —Yes, you know, the one we want to buy . . ." Something inside him closes; a glaze, a hard varnish veils his eyes: "Well, what about it?" It can't be helped, she must risk everything . . . He must be made to see. It can't be helped if she appears hideous, second-rate, narrow-minded, she wants him to see her as she is . . . conceal nothing, she couldn't stand it . . . It's there inside her, let him look, it must be extracted right away, that must not be allowed to grow inside her, to embitter everything, he should not force her to withdraw within herself, to turn away from him and scrutinize herself all alone, he must not allow her to suffer far from him . . . "Listen, Alain, I'm going to tell you. I have the impression, at certain moments, but you're not going to be angry? You know I can't hide anything from you . . . I am talking to you as I should to myself . . . It seems to me that we care a little too much for all that, for those *bergères*, those handsome things . . . we attach too much importance to them . . . You would think it was a matter of life and death, whether to take that or something else . . . Sometimes it seems to me . . . how shall I say it to you? . . . that we are a bit on the edge of life, that we are wasting our strength . . ." If only he would wake up, if only he would come to his senses . . . His face is inscrutable, frozen, he'll have to be given a shaking . . . Other people are there, all round us, other healthy, calm, clear-sighted, normal people, they see us . . . They pass judgment on us . . . They are right. . . "Alain, listen to me, my mother spoke to me about it . . . I felt that it really hurt her when I refused her leather chairs . . . Not for herself . . . I assure you . . . for us . . . She is anxious . . ." He laughs with a laughter that rings false . . . "Ha, ha, and if we accepted the leather chairs, would that reassure her? —No, but what would reassure her would be for us to attach less importance to all that . . . The leather chairs are sturdier, more comfortable, less expensive, and that's that. And for her, it would give her such pleasure . . ." He should come, he should join them, they're all there about him, they are calling him, they are stretching out their arms to him, he should understand, he should finally see things as they are, he should see himself as he is: weak, childish, a rebellious child; she will take him in her arms, she will press him close to her . . . He can let himself go, there, in her arms, she'll protect him, she'll help him to grow up, to change . . . he can change, if he wants to . . . "Alain, I assure you, at our age we should have other fish to fry . . ." he laughs derisively, gives her a quick glance which skims lightly over everything with disdain, with loathing, a glance that judges things coldly, that classifies them rapidly: "What fish?" No matter, it's too late to turn back, the only thing left to do is to seize him round the waist, bind him hand and foot, throw cold water on his head, to get the best of him: "What fish? Well, work, imagine that. Some real work. Not just little amateur jobs that you do to earn a little money, but your thesis, for instance, you don't seem to care a rap about it . . . Something that really leads somewhere . . . there's our future, just the same, you should think about that, our children's future . . ." He draws back a little to examine her more closely and bursts into hate-filled laughter: "Ha! that's a good one, a fine one . . . That's what *bergères* lead to . . . they lead a far way . . . That's what comes of so-called good upbringing. You never depart for long from the right principles. The slightest call to order suffices to make you walk straight again. But if you think you can get me that easily . . . A man is supposed to maim himself to fit into your picture, which is the dream of every little stenographer, the nursemaid's ideal . . . a good, reliable husband, a family, a career . . . And all of that represented by sturdy leather armchairs. What a magnificent symbol! From Maple's. Long-lasting. Economical. In the evening, to satisfy you both, you and your mother, I'll put on my embroidered house-slippers and sit in the chair opposite you to rest from my labors. We'll talk of my future, of my promotion. But how scared you look, you are indignant, aren't you, at what I just said . . . It wasn't exactly that . . . Whom did I take you for? . . . No . . . I forgot . . . Leather chairs, that's something else: it's the lightheartedness, the negligence of the artist, of the scholar, which should make me accept them . . . I should not even notice them, absorbed as I am by my research, by my work . . . An over-rich inner universe keeps me from being interested in these trivial details . . . It's all right for my mother-in-law, for my wife, to think about such things, it's their task to build me a comfortable little nest in which I can blossom forth . . . That's their role . . . Oh, you know, my husband . . . he simpers . . . he's a demon for work, a real seeker, the only thing that matters is his work . . . But the *bergère*, horrors . . . what a frightful revelation. Your mother was ashamed, the other day, in front of her friends, of those dubious tendencies of mine . . . Imagine, I seemed to understand only too well . . . what am I saying? I seemed to approve of my old lunatic of an aunt . . . Your mother was ashamed of me before her guests, she disavowed me . . . Fie upon me! Think of it . . . But my word, young man, if you don't speak as though you were a connoisseur . . . You come by it honestly . . . I answered her pretty sharply . . . It took her breath away . . . I know them, I know all of you only too well, do you understand, it's too easy, it's not even funny any longer. But she'll regret not having urged me to take it, that *bergère* . . . She'll be the one who will have to insist to get me to accept it, you'll see . . . It's the only means she has to keep her hold on us, these little treats, these little presents . . . In that way, she can own us . . . She would fall ill if the umbilical cord were cut . . . But I've had enough. I've had enough for a long time, if you want to know . . . I didn't want any of that, you know that quite well. I don't give a hang about the apartment, the furniture and all the rest . . . I can live on a park bench, I prefer to live just anywhere to putting up with all your preaching, your teaching, your martyred looks . . . Oh, I beg of you, you make me laugh with your tearful airs . . . There's only one victim here, and that's myself. My life is ruined . . . All I want . . . a little calm, freedom . . . And I have to listen to all these stupid things . . . these insinuations . . . 'Your tastes . . . You came by them honestly . . . Your career, my darling, you make Maman anxious . . . ' I've had enough. She'll see . . . I've had enough . . . he's hammering each word: Enough, you understand . . . I'm fed up with all that . . . Well, I'm leaving . . . I'm going out. . . I don't know when I'll be back. Goodnight, don't wait up for me."

THEY'RE UPON HIM. They've encircled him. No way out. He's caught, locked in; at the slightest movement, at the faintest stray impulse on his part they spring up. Always on the watch, spying. They know where to find him now. He himself has submitted to their law, given himself up to them . . . so weak, confident . . . he's theirs, always within their reach . . . And she, supple, malleable—a tool fashioned by them, which they use to bring him to heel. Stupid faces, eyes shining with curiosity. Moist glances . . . It's such a touching sight . . . these turtledoves . . . so young . . . their little nest . . . Brief incursions, furtive leaps, prudent withdrawals, shy touchings, little surprises, presents . . . the old lady wiggling the mobile end of her nose, her skittish eyes under their worn lids . . . coy smile . . . holding out a lump of sugar . . . And right away he too, wretched dog, trained by them, wriggling, begging on his hind legs, eyes shining covetously, stretching out an avid neck . . . "Really, auntie, you would do that for us? . . . You mean it, you're not joking?" They grow bolder every day. They're going beyond all limits, they're not afraid of anything anymore. No shame in them, no reserve. They stick their noses into everything, attack openly. No more precautions, even before other people. No need to mind him, is there? With him, you can do as you like. Guileless fool, so sensitive . . . Pearls before swine . . . But they'll see. Of what stuff . . . he is skipping . . . Who laughs last . . . he almost runs, knocking into the passersby.

Indignation and rage have aroused him, all his strength comes surging, he must take advantage of it, maintain his momentum, it will be right away or never . . . But he must not lose his head, above all, not act too hastily, he would have to start everything over again, prolong this apprehension, this suspense . . . Go easy . . . with the forefinger thrust well in the little metal circle, push the dial frame entirely to the right, let it come back to its starting point . . . one letter, then the next . . . now the figures . . . It's the first move he has made towards deliverance; it's a challenge which he's hurling at them, at all of them out there, from this narrow booth in the basement of the little bistro, by dialing this number: a simple telephone number like any other in appearance, and this commonplace appearance has something thrilling about it, it heightens its magic character: it is the talisman that he carries with him always—his safeguard when he feels that he is threatened. It's the password divulged to the privileged few: permission to make use of it is conferred as the highest of distinctions. And he has been given it, he has been deemed worthy, he, quite so . . . But don't rejoice, don't boast too soon, all can yet be lost, in an instant he can be ignominiously hurled back to them, humiliated, vanquished, immediately taken possession of by them—this time, their prey for ever . . . He feels like a hunted man on foreign soil, who is ringing the bell of the embassy of a civilized country, his own, to ask for asylum . . . The bell echoes in empty space. Each regular, prolonged buzz holds his life in suspense . . . A click . . . Someone has taken down the receiver . . .

It's astonishing to hear his own voice, as though detached from him, who is nothing now but disorder, confusion, palpitating shreds, answer of its own accord, very calmly: "Is Mme. Germaine Lemaire in? This is Alain Guimiez speaking . . ." That name, Germaine Lemaire, which he has just spoken so calmly, constitutes a scandal. It's an explosion. That name alone would make them retreat. It would make those very perspicacious glances they're continually turning on him, those knowing smiles, disappear from their faces, the mobile end of his aunt's nose would stop wiggling, it would become set, tense, puzzled . . . But a few words can still make them rush upon him, hem him in . . . Those dreaded words, he might as well prepare himself, make a hollow to receive them, to deaden the shock . . . there they are, he feels them forming somewhere out there, he braces himself . . . Mme. Germaine Lemaire is out . . . when a deep, drawling voice, the voice he knows, replies: "Why of course. It's me. No, I shall be in for some time yet. You won't disturb me, do come. I'll expect you." The universe, calmed, subdued, charmed, stretches itself voluptuously and lies down at his feet. And he, standing there, very erect, strong, master of all his movements, deploying all his faculties, clear-sightedness, cunning, dignity, replies with perfect ease, in a voice that is so warm, so pleasant, so engaging, that he himself is charmed by it: "Very well, that's splendid. I'll come, then . . . In about half an hour, if I may . . ."

Thank God, he held his own, he didn't spoil things . . . What progress . . . In the old days, he would have lost his head, through some stupid weakness sacrificed these moments—one half-hour of happiness. Twenty-five minutes, to be exact. Seated on the banquette in the back of the little café, he can now relish this moment, when nothing has yet started, when nothing can yet be jeopardized, spoiled, when he still holds hugged to him his unimpaired treasure, absolutely intact.

Time stands almost still. The instants, closed in on themselves, smooth, heavy, full to the cracking point, advance very slowly, almost imperceptibly, move with precaution, as though to preserve their charge of dream, of hope.

In a little while, all will be haste, excitement, blinding

light, scalding heat, the instants, like a fine gray dust blown by a burning hot wind, will bear him along towards the harsh separation, towards the dreadful wrench, towards that lonely fall into darkness, into the void. The threat will be there at the first glance, the first words they exchange, it will continue to grow until finally, to cut short his torture, and take his own fate in hand, like a man condemned to die who commits suicide, he will rise all of a sudden before it is time, take leave too abruptly . . . or else, out of cowardice, feeling her embarrassed, impatient eyes upon him, he will do his utmost to put off the reckoning, the fatal moment.

But now he is free, he is the master. He can dispose of his time. He must prepare himself. It's the period of meditation, of purification, that precedes corridas, coronations. No alcohol. Beware of stimulants. One should not force one's luck, cheat, coerce an already propitious fate, that only brings bad luck . . . He must remain in full possession of his faculties . . . Weak tea, at the most . . . or rather, no, just a cup of coffee . . .

As he sits there motionless, he feels it forming inside him: something compact, hard . . . a kernel . . . But he has become all over like a stone, a silex: things from the outside that knock against him strike brief sparks, little light words which crackle for an instant . . . "How that stove of yours does heat, tell me . . . What make is it? A Godin? They heat like a house afire, those things do . . ." The waiter nods approval, looks interestedly at the stove. No hard kernel in him, that's obvious. Inside him everything is soft, everything is hollow, anything at all, just any insignificant object from the outside fills it entirely. They're at the mercy of everything. He had been like that himself a few moments ago, how had he lived? how on earth do all these people live with that enormous emptiness in them in which, at any moment, just anything at all surges in, spreads out, takes up all the room . . . The waiter stoops down and turns the knob that regulates the draft, stands up again, looks at the stove affectionately: "Oh, you can say what you want, Godins, there's nothing like 'em, they're as good as a furnace. They never go out. You fill them full at night, in the morning all you have to do is to empty the ashes . . . They'll never make anything better than those things. And today the weather is mild, but if you had come when it was really cold . . . it's so warm in here I can never stand a sweater . . . —Oh, you're lucky, I'm always frozen, I could wear two sweaters in midsummer. —Well, that depends on what work you do. But in our job, we are on the move, running back and forth all day long . . . Oh, I can guarantee you, there's no risk of our getting stiff. It's good for your circulation . . ." Rubbing, merry crackle: "Oh, with me, it's the same thing whether I move about or not. I've always been like that. Already, when I was a tiny child—no blood in my veins. My grandmother used to tell me even then: Why, you're more sensitive to cold than I am . . . What I need, to feel really well, is the good old dog days, the Sahara itself . . ."

But time, all at once . . . what time is it, anyway? Time—that couldn't fail, that had to happen to him while he was there amusing himself, watching the crackling sprays of words surge up and fall—time forgotten, released, has taken a leap . . . Only four more minutes, damn it. . . and he's not ready, he would have needed a few seconds more of reflection to prepare himself, he would have needed to pass first through a zone of silence . . . something has been put out of gear in the mechanism he had adjusted so well, he has jeopardized everything through sinful insouciance, unpardonable absentmindedness, he's being driven, jostled, he's going to take off badly . . .

Above all, he must not lose his head, better to be a few minutes late than to arrive all overheated, out of breath . . .

He steps as unhurriedly as he can through the old doorway, walks slowly across the vestibule, opens the door giving on to the courtyard . . .

Tall liveried footmen standing frozen on the steps of the grand stairway, a gold-braided majordomo preceding you slowly over vast expanses of slippery floors, all the display and outer signs of power and glory, all the ceremonial, flaunted hierarchy, etiquette, the conventional, required gestures, had something to recommend them. All that maintained you, guided you, it was less upsetting than this slip-shod concierge sweeping out her courtyard, who looks at you furtively, who sees everything, who knows, and answers quite casually: Mme. Germaine Lemaire? Across the courtyard, to the right, first floor; it was less disturbing than the cleaning woman with the tucked up apron who opens the door for you, lets you in with an absentminded, hurried air, then deserts you, left to your own devices, in the midst of sly threats, of invisible, unforeseeable dangers.

She has real beauty, "Germaine Lemaire has real beauty," they're right, obviously. There . . . in the line of the cheek, the eyelid, the forehead . . . something which recalls what he had discovered in the faces of certain pre-Columbian . . . Aztec . . . statues, what he had taken away from them . . . it's hard to discern, sometimes long initiation and great effort are required to catch it; a certain austere strength, a crude grace . . . And that rather weak, rather displeasing curve . . . meager . . . vulgar . . . of the nostrils, of the chin, it's nothing, one need only make a little effort, and the grace, the strength that he had caught in the faces of the Aztec statues, or were they Etruscan? he no longer knows, and which inflect the line of the forehead, of the cheek, must also be made to pass, to flow—the way a part of the water in a river is turned aside to irrigate the land—there, into the chin, the nose . . . they overrun everything . . . and the entire face . . . how could one mistake it? who would dare deny it?—radiates a secret, exceptional beauty.

From the effort he has just made to perform this sleight-of-hand with such ease, such speed, from the certainty he now has of finally being worthy to belong to the little cohort of the initiated, something has begun to ooze, it is that same note of annoyance he had heard in their voices when, in reply to the good people who, like himself at one time—he's ashamed of it now—expressed naïve surprise, didn't understand . . . "Not at all, Germaine Lemaire is a real beauty, how can you say that?" It's even, in his case, a bitterer, sharper feeling, it's exasperation, hatred almost, he can't bear, he is ready to exterminate, the ignorant, the faithless—those repugnant creatures who prefer to let their idle gaze wallow basely among the insipid curves, the facile and misleading sweetness of the noses, chins, and cheeks of cover-girls, of stars.

But something remains, nevertheless, of his very first impression—this uneasiness, this painful sensation, he retracts a little, exactly the way he did the first time he saw her . . . In the corners of the lip which cuts a little too deeply into the cheeks, which curls up a little too high, in the movement of that thin mouth, something is creeping, fleeing . . . he doesn't know what it is exactly, he has never tried to name it, he doesn't want to, one must not, it's nothing, no one but he sees it, it's a mirage, an illusion, bred of his uneasiness, it's his own fear which he projects, his own apprehension which he sees cowering there, hiding . . . he must not let his glance pause, settle there . . . it should barely graze . . . not see, not think about it any more, it will disappear . . . There now . . . There is nothing more. It has vanished.

But how could he not have foreseen it—in fact, he had expected it—it's the lesson his stupid vanity has cost him, it's the lie given once more to his romancing: she's not alone, of course, that would be asking too much, someone is seated beside her, at her feet, that tall, gawky lad with the long, anemic face, who is encircling his crossed ankles with his hands while he swings delightedly back and forth like a big monkey . . . His deeply set, bright little eyes are watching him as he advances awkwardly . . . And she too is watching him. Her big, limpid eyes are staring at him. A current emanating from her repulses, crushes his thoughts, his words . . . He looks about him . . . help will come perhaps from the outside, from just anywhere, from that big fire blazing in the fireplace in this mild weather, from that lap robe she has on her knees, he clings to that, something is springing up from it, the words are already forming . . . but watch out, they are driven back, dangerous corner, the crime of lese majesty, he's lost if he dares ask her a question as he would just anybody, put himself on the same level . . . she's going to draw herself up with that manner that he has seen her assume, the manner of an outraged empress . . . But again this time, while he is pulling them back to hold them in, the words break away, lurch a bit, then grow steady: "I hope . . . you are not ill?"

The tall fellow leans still farther backwards and laughs derisively, showing his big teeth, he's in seventh heaven . . . "Ill? The very idea! The lady has ironclad health, you didn't know that? Reinforced concrete, I shan't say more. But she loves her comfort, as is well known, and there's nothing she likes so much as to coddle herself . . ." She leans towards him: "Hold your tongue," and, with the back of her hand, gives him a little slap on the cheek, while he lifts his elbow in fun, ducks his head . . . The queen's jester, the buffoon jingling his little bells, turning somersaults on the steps of the throne, serving a learnedly dosed mixture of impertinence and provocation, has dared to say, to do, what should have been done . . . She laughs . . . They had both seen, that's certain, his paralyzed, over respectful manner, his fright. The buffoon had sought to bring them into greater relief, in order for her to enjoy them all the more; he had made an insolent display before the poor greenhorn, fresh from the backwoods, ignorant of court customs—of his own complete ease, his offhandedness, his privileges acquired long since, the liberties he may take. He spreads himself. His hands drop his ankles, he deploys his long, lanky body, stands up on his two feet . . . "Well, with that, I shall be off . . . it's high time . . ." He leans towards her, seated erectly, royally, on her high-backed chair . . . something flits from him to her, something barely perceptible . . . an invisible movement, more rapid, clearer, than words, and which she immediately records: There now, I'll be leaving you to do what you can with this clod, but try to have a little fun, just the same . . . you'll tell us all about it later . . . we'll have a good laugh . . . Ah, what's to be done about it, *noblesse oblige* that's the price of fame, all these avid little fellows who try to come and rub elbows, who want to glean what they can . . . The favorite, the fortunate sycophant bends, smiling, over the hand she holds out to him, straightens up again . . . "Very well, then, I'll call you tomorrow about that paper" . . . turns round . . .

Not a trace of the buffoon remains in the slightly gawky young man with the sensitive face and serious, direct expression, who walks towards him to say good-bye, his hand outstretched . . . no more jesting, you're allowed to laugh a little, but here we know what courtesy means, respect for others, the most complete equality, fraternity, reign, as is well known, in this house. Consideration is shown to all the foreigners who come here from distant lands, to all poor pilgrims: "I'm delighted to have met you. Good-bye, I hope we'll meet again soon . . . —Oh, yes, I too, certainly, I should be delighted . . ." He too, shakes hard this firm, helpful, friendly hand, which clasps his fingers, he holds on to it a second . . . But resolutely, pitilessly, the hand breaks away.

A moment ago, that malicious joy of the buffoon squatting on the floor, swinging, showing his big teeth, those secret signs between them, that current which had passed between them above his head, had been, nevertheless, security, it had been happiness, compared to this forlornness—alone here with her. In what moment of madness, of insane audacity had he let himself be roused by the impulse that had made him climb to these heights . . . he feels dizzy now, perched up there on the highest peak . . . one false move and he'll fall, he'll crash to earth . . . She's watching him, clinging there, not daring to budge, quite petrified, she must feel like smiling . . . how comical he is, really . . . she's not accustomed . . . usually the people about her have stouter hearts, their lungs are more used to breathing this tangy air. He's so weak, so awkward, he must make her feel sorry for him . . . how ridiculous he is, how tiresome . . . But there's nothing to be done about it, she rouses herself, pulls herself together. She must bear up, set to work. These are weighty obligations. She smiles at him, makes him a sign with her hand: "Now then, why don't you come and sit here, near me . . ." don't be frightened, it's nothing . . . you'll see, you won't fall . . . "There now, you'll be more comfortable near the fire, in this easy chair . . . It's been an age since I saw you . . ." do stop looking under your feet, think about something else . . . "What have you been doing that's interesting? Tell me . . ." now then, things are better already, aren't they? feeling calm again? make one more try . . . "What have you been up to? Has your work been going well? —Well, no, I haven't done very much lately . . ." At the sound of his own voice—the way it used to be when the examining professor had just asked a question and, his head empty and not knowing what to say, he heard himself reply—at the sound of his own voice, like sleeping soldiers who, at the sound of the bugle, jump up, shoulder arms, run, fall in, all the scattered strength in him that had become sluggish, surges up . . . all of a sudden, he feels sure of himself, full of confidence, assurance, free of movement, relaxed . . . "I must confess to you that I've been very lazy . . ." No cheating with her. No mock triumphs. No constantly threatened victories . . . "I let myself be led astray by all kinds of idiotic things. I've been stupidly wasting my time . . ." He has nothing to fear, he can allow himself that: she will know how to find what's hidden under the matrix . . . She had been the first to discover him . . . The proof is there, always worn next to his heart: the letter he received from her the first time . . . he hadn't believed his eyes . . . to him . . . it wasn't possible . . . at the bottom of the page, he had not been mistaken, in big letters, it was certainly that: Germaine Lemaire . . . Miracle . . . He knows every word of it by heart . . . Bits of phrases rise up to the surface at any moment, while he's walking along, lost in the crowd, while he listens to people's chatter when, seated in the bus, their empty gaze upon him, he hands his ticket to the conductor. They murmur inside him. He hears their call . . . for him alone . . . they are the secret sign of his preferment, of his predestination . . . "Well, yes, I've let myself be swallowed up. Upset by just anything. The entire family . . . Fixing up our apartment . . . But I don't know how to defend myself against that . . ." Verlaine and his "wretched fairy Carrot." Rimbaud. Baudelaire and his mother, and General Aupick . . . Lazy, childish, wasting their time, ruining their lives . . . the words he has just spoken make them rise up in her right away, she gazes at them . . . they are the models he wants her to draw upon. And she obeys him. He looks, enchanted, at the picture resembling them which he sees in her, his portrait which, he knows, he is sure of it, she is engaged in sketching . . . He leans towards her and looks deep into her gray-green eyes . . . "What joy, if you knew, what pleasure it is for me to be here with you, in your house." Now he can do anything he wants. He can strip naked. No more ridiculous fears, no more shame, no thought of his dignity. He can tell her what he wants. They understand each other over and beyond mere words . . . "It's a long time now since I've told myself stories, you know, those 'continued stories' such as adolescents and persons suffering from depression tell themselves, but I did like to imagine myself coming to see you, seated like this near you, talking, very brilliantly, of course . . . they both laugh . . . holding you spellbound. But I didn't very well see what your place was like . . . At that point, I always hesitated. At times . . ." all at once he has the impression—it's very fleeting—that inside her a long, avid arm with grasping fingers is reaching out, he doesn't know very well, he hasn't time to know, how he detected this movement in her . . . and right away, within himself, with the return of a sense of danger, that rapidity of adaptation—he himself is surprised by it . . .

In one second he has given up the idea, all dreams of intimacy are forgotten. Squatting at her feet, he shows her, he spreads out before her, his gifts, his offerings, all he possesses . . . of no great importance, but he's ready to give her everything, she should choose what she wants . . . but what does she want? "At times—it was the sparseness in your writing, that dry warmth . . . which trembles . . . which made me think of that—I saw you in a big Southern farmhouse with whitewashed walls, a large, bare room . . ." It seems to him that the long arm drops, there is something a bit misty in the big eyes . . . right away, he's going to show her, she should be patient, this is going to be better: "But I was foolish, it's reality, of course, that's in the right. As usual, reality upsets all preconceived ideas, all expectations. Now I see that it's all this—he looks about him—which gives greatest evidence of that molten lava . . . an incandescent stream . . . At times, in certain of your books, there is a flamboyantly baroque note, when you are stirred with enthusiasm, when the thirst for conquest carries you along. There is here, in this clutter of curious, very fine things . . . this sorcerer's mask . . . these fabrics . . . all your Spanish, conquistador side . . . They make one think of the fabulous spoils amassed by a pirate . . . set there at random, neglected . . . I adore that casualness . . . Beside it, all my fiddle-faddling seems so ridiculous, so petty . . ."

She is wearing a pleased little smile . . . "Oh, you're exaggerating . . . It's simply that things collect little by little . . . souvenirs, a few presents . . . True, I do like to pick up things wherever I can . . . That wicker cage there, for instance, I brought it back from the Canary Islands. This leather bottle was given me by an old peasant in Tibet . . . it's nice, isn't it? We accumulate a lot of things in a lifetime when we continue to live in the same place. And at heart, you know, I'm very much of a stay-at-home. But I'm sure your place too must be charming. I should love to see what it is like. You'll have to invite me one day to come and see you . . ."

It's moving to see her descend the steps of the throne with such simplicity, such modesty, mingle with the crowd, take an interest in each one, ask each one a question or two; bend over graciously to cross the threshold of the most sordid little hovel, the humblest cottage; sit down among the family, gathered round; allow the children's sticky fingers—oh, no, it's nothing, don't scold him—to rumple her silk gown; give a calm glance at the walls covered with vulgar flower patterns, at the color-prints, at the artificial flowers emerging from Japanese vases won at a street fair . . . at the pottery brought back from Plougastel . . . at the unspeakable leather chairs . . . "Oh, no, my place is very ugly. You'd be terribly disappointed . . . there are all sorts of presents, each one more frightful than the other . . . But there's no way of getting rid of them. We'd need a fire, an earthquake. And even then . . . the family would see to it that they were all replaced. Because they must have all that, my family must: platters from Plougastel, awful easy chairs . . . that's the flag they plant on newly conquered territory. Their banner, which marks the extent of their empire. As for me, I escaped them, but I have been brought into subjection. And this time, for good and all. I'm occupied, they're building roads, setting up boundary marks, measuring, administering, and vaccinating for the welfare of the population . . . But I'm boring you . . ." Useless precaution. Pure coquetry. He has a foot hold, he feels it, he's on his own ground, he's no longer afraid. He rises and starts walking up and down, and she watches him . . . At last . . . he knows that that is what she expected of him, that's the cream of the milk, for her alone, the hidden treasure that she alone has been able to discover, to bring out to advantage, and which, one day, she will reveal to the world . . . Never has he felt freer, more skillful . . . his gestures are sure, elegant: now, look at this. "Here, as you see, are two leather chairs, quite ordinary in appearance, the English 'club' type that exists in certain movie-houses. Well, bloody battles are being fought over them. I'm fighting not to have them in my house as though I were defending my very life. And I'm right. I am, indeed. Because these chairs, we all know what they are. But never a word on the subject. Absolute secrecy. There exists a tacit agreement, we don't speak of them . . . We use all the weapons in our possession, but never an allusion to what they really are: the badge of the order they want to force upon me, of their power, of my submission . . ."

This time, he has found his audience. An audience worthy of him. From his hat come cascading billows of ribbons, objects of every sort, they flow, get out of hand, form enormous piles all round him . . . world is confronting world . . . the angel is combating the beast . . . he brandishes his blade at their common enemy, hers and his . . . now he can amuse himself, take all kinds of liberties . . . he seizes hold of something in the air . . . "Look . . . take, for instance, my aunt, an old crank . . . she would amuse you no end if you knew her . . . she's a character for you . . . I'll introduce her to you one day . . . You should have seen her when she came to see us. Sweetness itself. Deeply moved. But her eyes were taking it all in . . ." He imitates her walk: "The end of her nose moves the way a dog's does, she keeps wiggling it: Why, children, it's as cute as anything, your place is. That towel rack, it's marvelous . . . A quick look at the view out the windows. Just here there's a smell of heresy. Here, rebellion smolders. I tease her, I provoke her: Come and look, auntie, isn't it lovely, that view, and those old roofs, in the distance, over there . . . Right away she gets her back up: I think that's what you paid for especially, that view . . . Because the rest, it's very cute, but when all's said and done . . . in a few years, ho, ho, let's hope so, anyway, you're going to be cramped for space. With that she gets a hold over us, my wife and myself. We're caught. We're disarmed. Bound hand and foot in no time. And then she begins to amuse herself a bit, it's too tempting: But you know, children, what you should have? My apartment, why, of course . . . It's exactly what you need . . . We don't dare believe our ears, we tremble, we crane our necks, we stare at her with eyes filled with the most despicable cupidity, we ask her: But auntie, how is that possible? Do you mean it?"

She settles upon him a gaze in which he sees a gleam of recognition, of approval. He comes to a halt in front of her. She can look closely now. He feels this is the moment. Luck is with him. All his gestures are sure, bold, free, he is free, he does what he wants, he is skipping along, brandishing his sword, he's going to dismay the dislocated ranks of the enemy, he charges, nothing can stop him . . . "But that's finished, you understand. I've had enough. I'm going to break with all that for good. Escape. And you will be the one to have helped me. That's what I came to ask you today. Now I know it, I can't come to terms with all that . . . It's all or nothing . . . Why tell ourselves lies? I'll have to resort to surgery, there's no other way . . . And that means . . ." The telephone rings. She rises, without ceasing to look at him: "No other way, really? You think so? . . ." She said that a bit mechanically. He has the impression that she has caught hold of just anything, the words he has just spoken, and which were still inside her, and that she is repeating them without knowing very well what she is saying, in order not to interrupt too abruptly his roulades, his serenading . . . She shakes her head, sighs; she is walking slowly, as though the tie by which he is holding her impeded her movements; finally, still gazing at him, nodding impatiently . . . Oh, what a bore, I'm so sorry, how tiresome they are, all those people . . . she slowly stretches out her arm, takes down the receiver: "Hello . . . Hello . . . Yes . . . When? I'm surprised at that. Why yes, I was in, I haven't moved out of the house. She laughs. Oh, nothing in particular. Same old sixes and sevens. What? her voice grows lower, softer, assumes an intimate, warm tone . . . In a little while? Yes . . . When? In an hour? Very well. Fine. No, nothing as yet. Oh, we'll talk about that another time. I'll tell you all about it. Don't be late."

She comes back towards him. But he knows that the play is over. A little belated applause. People are already thinking about getting their coats from the checkroom, they must hurry, they will miss the last *métro* . . . "Yes, well, all that is very thrilling, what you were telling me . . ." It seems to him that she is collecting all her strength to make a final effort . . . "But personally, I believe, on the contrary that, if I were in your place, I should accept. Only too delighted. I mean it. They ought to be of some use at least, all those people. So take what you want. It's darned pleasant not to live in cramped quarters. And it will take more than that to make a slave of you. We're swallowed up only when we are willing for it to happen. You have to be more cynical than that, since you say you like . . . she looks about her, smiles . . . pirates and conquistadors . . . —Yes . . . after all . . ." he has difficulty in recognizing his own voice. As always, in moments of breakdown, of collapse, someone speaks the words for him, saves his face . . . "After all, you're probably right. But here I am talking away . . . When I'm with you I can't stop, I'm making you waste your time . . . —Oh, I like to listen to your stories . . . you must come again, often . . ." He feels that it would be dangerous to linger, to beg for a few moments more, there's something threatening in her slightly remote, society politeness . . . it's obvious, she's straining at the bit. . . "Yes, I should love to, if you'll allow me . . ."

When she accompanies him to the door, shakes his hand, he senses in her the warmth, the generosity, the overflow of strength—she's ready to squander it—that come from the feeling that deliverance, freedom, are at hand . . . "Well, I'll see you very soon, you won't disturb me. So call me one day about this time. I am nearly always in. She sticks her head through the door and smiles at him archly . . . And above all, get to work, do you hear? I'm counting on you, you know. Work hard."

Astonishing how everything had taken place according to the plan he had drawn up somewhere within himself; how everything from the first moment had converged towards this, towards this disaster, this collapse . . . he is rejected, reduced in rank . . . Ah, it was magnificent, that superiority . . . but how do all these people live? . . . to think that less than two hours ago he was asking himself that. . . How can they live without that hard kernel inside them, that little compact mass, preserved secretly, that certainty, that security . . . The waiter in the café, poor man, so pervious, so soft . . . the stove is not merely an object for his eyes, for his hands, which he must attend to while waiting for the big moments that count, no, things occupy him entirely . . . And he himself, how does he live? that's what they might ask themselves, if they knew, but they're too innocent . . . the bus conductor rushing through the aisle, ringing the bell, calling out the names of the bus-stops, is pure, hard, nothing can scratch him; not a crack between his gesture and himself through which the slightest impurity might enter. Not the slightest trace of an experience of this kind. Never. In none of these lives. You have to be him, possess his exceptional skill, his cleverness, to treat yourself to such pleasures as these. The buffoon must have been amused, so self-assured there, quite at home, well-settled in complete security, to see him, like someone descending the moving steps of a Luna Park stairway, reeling, holding on tight, one foot in the air, a haggard look in his eyes . . . Good lesson he gave him . . . the important thing, you see, is not to be afraid. Watch what I do . . . And that hearty handshake to mark the nobility of all of them there, their sense of equality, even with regard to him . . . or rather, it meant—an enormous sudden flush submerges him—that hearty handshake, that look deep down into his eyes . . . Come, come, pull yourself together, be a man, hang it! Are you so impressed as all that by celebrity, by fame . . .

Gisèle, my love, my wife . . . Gisèle . . . This name is an exorcism. Keep repeating it . . . Gisèle . . . it means solace, it means security. That is what's true, that is what's healthy. They're right, all the same, with their old conventions; it's the rest that's false, so much trash. And he, idiotic, childish, playing the rebel, indulging in nerves . . . "Gisèle, I'm stupid, I don't deserve you . . . What ever would become of me if I didn't have you, tell me what I should do, Gisèle, tell me . . ." He presses her firm, round cheeks, still warm with sleep, between his two hands, under his pressure her mouth puckers and grows round in a moving little circle as naive as that made by children's mouths when they open and strain forward like that, she blinks her eyes, opens them wide so as to keep them quite open, she's speaking in her nasal, sleepy, little girl's voice . . . "Why, what's the matter, Alain? Where on earth have you been? What time is it? —Dearest, if you knew what a delight it is to come back here . . . I feel like the fox being pursued by hunters . . . you know, in that English novel . . . we always said that you were my little fox cub, but this time I'm the one who is being tracked down, I've come to seek refuge, take me in your arms . . . Do you know what I did? Do you know where I've just been? To see Germaine Lemaire . . . This time she opens wide her wonderstruck eyes . . . Believe me, I was in such a rage when I left here, I was disgraceful, forgive me . . . it was idiotic, I know . . . All at once that gave me strength, I took my courage in my two hands, I telephoned her . . . She told me to come right away . . . —You see, Alain, darling, you see what I told you, you see how mad you were . . . So what was it like? —Really, I don't know how to describe it to you, I don't know very well yet myself. Naturally, it's marvelous . . . everything is lovely . . . more so than I had imagined . . . She is extraordinary, she has a sort of majesty. —When I think that Irene told me the other day that there was nobody in the world she admired so much . . . she would give anything to see her for three minutes, to hear her talk . . . and you stayed all that time at her house . . . What did you talk about? Were you alone, or were there other people? —Yes, at first, there was that tall, lanky fellow whom I had seen one time with her . . . I pointed him out to you, once, at the movies. —Montalais? —That's right . . . Rather antipathetic, at first, but later on, he was very nice . . . He has something direct, frank about him. He seemed to know who I was . . . I like very much the way he shakes hands . . . He said he would like to see me again . . . He left almost immediately. —Tell me what you talked about. You certainly stayed a long while . . . —Yes, I was horrified to see how late it was when I left . . . But I didn't sense that time was passing. I don't know how to explain it . . . You have an extraordinary feeling of excitement with her . . . Perhaps I do, because I am so sure that she understands me . . . I let myself go . . . And yet . . . you know . . . I tell you everything . . . underneath, there is at times a sort of uneasiness . . . all at once you feel you're being watched, you have the impression, how shall I describe it, that you must always be giving her something . . . there's something she demands all the time . . . —Oh, Alain dear, that's certainly one of your ideas. —No . . . I assure you . . . that doesn't just come all by itself, fame, a reputation . . . there's a sort of unsated hunger, a need for adulation . . . you never can give her enough . . . she supervises, she takes people's measure, she must put them in their place at the slightest lapse . . . —Did she put you in your place? —No . . . imagine . . . she was friendliness itself . . . simplicity . . . but I think it would be a mistake to count on it. —Tell me, what did you say to her? —Oh, I don't know. Nothing in particular . . . As I told you, I had the impression that she understands everything . . . I told her stories, just anything at all, the things I had on my mind, I was still full of all those stories about house furnishings, the apartment . . . you know the subject doesn't matter much. —For you, darling, naturally . . . You must have been at your best, you must have been very brilliant . . . When you get started on things like that . . . She probably listened to you wide-mouthed . . . —Yes, perhaps . . . I don't know . . . But I'm going to tell you something . . . if you take away all that, the varnish, the glamour, people's opinions . . . well, the old girl herself is a bit . . . you're going to hit the ceiling . . . how shall I say . . . it's not that . . ." She puts her arms about him, rests her head on his breast, she snuggles up close to him, her laughter is like the shimmer of dewdrops, like warm, fragrant spring rain . . . "Alain, I adore you . . . I know why I love you, among other things, my darling . . . it's because of just that kind of thing, if you want to know: you're marvelous, you know. That's what I love in you, that purity, that honesty . . . and you, you really are 'that.' When I think what a state any other young man of your age would be in, anybody else, to whom Germaine Lemaire had written what she wrote you, whom she would allow to come to see her like that, with whom she would sit and talk for two hours about just anything . . . and you, you're already dissatisfied. You haven't an ounce of vanity. You dominate every situation . . . Nothing can spoil you . . ." He draws back from her and holds her at arm's length to look her straight in the eyes . . . "Gisèle, do you think so, really? You know you're the only one who gives me confidence in myself . . . I often tell myself that you are blinded . . . But just now, talking to you, I felt it: I'm the one who is right. I play her game, but I never feel that I am caught. I'm not awed by her . . . in her presence, perhaps, a little . . . that's my diffidence, my lack of confidence in myself, the slightest thing sets me up, a little flattery intoxicates me at the moment . . . but afterwards . . . no really, even at her house, I felt all the time a sort of uneasiness, something wanting . . . it's perhaps for that reason that, even in what she writes, there's something . . . at times, I wonder . . . —Oh, there, listen Alain, this time you're going too far. —No, believe me. All those things don't just come by themselves. She must have known what to do. She knows how to play her cards, believe me . . . She keeps her accounts straight, she sets up hierarchies . . . oh, yes, she does . . . she never wastes her time . . . and that's what she pays for, elsewhere . . . there is a frozen, studied side to her famous sparseness, to her severity . . . a side that's cautious . . . miserly . . . that's it. —But listen, Alain, you, why would she have written to you? Why does she ask you to come to see her like that? There she showed enthusiasm, complete disinterestedness . . . —Yes, of course, things aren't so simple . . . It's just possible that I interest her . . . it's probable . . . she wants to be influential . . . have a coterie of young people about her . . . But rest assured, she's never carried away, she never loses her bearings . . . there's something about her that's cold and a little petty . . . practical . . . she sees every little side . . . —That, darling, I don't believe . . . you have to depreciate everything, especially what belongs to you, what's given you . . . With me, you know perfectly, it's the same . . . —With you, Gisèle, my love, but how can you compare . . . You know, I'm going to tell you everything . . . But, darling, don't you believe that that's what happiness is, the only real happiness, this absolute confidence, this fusion . . . one single being . . . I don't know anymore where, I finish and you begin . . .

they're right with all their old myths . . . they've known for so long . . . When you scolded me, a while ago, about that armchair affair . . . forgive me, dearest, I went into such a rage because I knew that, in reality, you were right . . . indirectly I wanted to tell her, Germaine Lemaire, to see what she would think about it . . . —You told her about those chairs? . . . —No . . . Not exactly . . . I spoke to her about our presents . . . About the family . . . My aunt . . . I told her about how she came to tempt us with her apartment . . . The meaning of all that . . . How they try to keep us down . . . That we should have to free ourselves from it all . . . —What did she say? . . . —She seemed to be fascinated . . . Those are things she understands very well . . . And then she had a moment of inattention . . . she was called to the telephone . . . she began to think about something else . . . anyhow, I don't know, but it was disagreeable to me, the way she reacted . . . Do you know what she said? that surprised me . . . Why, go ahead, take it, take the apartment. It's darned convenient, why be embarrassed? That shocked me, it's silly, I felt humiliated . . . —But why, Alain, I don't understand . . . —I don't know . . . there was something about her tone . . . Not in what she said . . . On the contrary, she said that she herself would have done it, that you had to be egotistical, know how to take things, that it was only my due . . . but there was a sort of contempt . . . —Oh listen, Alain, you're crazy, I assure you, you make me feel desperate. There couldn't be any sort of affront in what she said to you, that's lunacy, you know it . . . On the contrary, if you want my opinion. It proves that she appreciates you. She thinks that you have rights, just as she has. It's true that you, at least, would get a little more use out of it than Aunt Berthe, a big apartment where you could have a quiet place of your own . . . You wouldn't be disturbed any more . . . You could work quietly . . . We could invite our friends . . . She, herself, one day, why not? Can you see us inviting her here . . . Your old aunt is drying up there all by herself, she'd be just as happy anywhere, rubbing her fingerprint plaques . . . It does you good to have things like that said to you. You're too decent, too conscientious . . . You are not sufficiently aware of your own worth, of what is due you. it's true that she would not have hesitated, Germaine Lemaire, I'm sure of it, she would have seized the opportunity on the wing. —Is that true? You think so? . . . He hugs her close to him . . . And I, you know me, I thought of only one thing: For her that's so much nonsense, all that, what I said there . . . At one moment, I hated her . . . It seemed to me that she hadn't believed one word of what I told her . . . that she had thought I was beating about the bush . . . There was something in the way she spoke, in her intonation . . . perhaps in the expression of her eyes . . . I don't know, really . . . a little look of seeing through things, a cunning, amused look . . . It seemed to me that she probably believed I was, in reality, dying to get it, that apartment . . . that I had an itching need for it . . . that I couldn't help talking about it and that I wanted her to approve of me . . . And then, more than anything else, at one moment . . . I had told her that I thought her place was very lovely, all those things brought back from all over everywhere, made you think of an enormous, sumptuous booty pile . . . she said . . . only you can't understand, it's nothing you can lay your finger on . . . I just felt it . . . she smiled in a certain manner as she looked about her . . . she said: But go ahead and take it, don't refuse, since that gives you such pleasure, all that, since you like that so much, pirates and conquistadors . . . she thought that impressed me, that sort of thing, that aspect of her which was the one I had imagined . . . I felt I was being ridiculed, sullied, I don't know how to explain it . . . —Darling, now we have it . . . so that's where it comes from, that haunted look, that unhappy expression . . . I've been wondering . . . now I understand . . . But Alain, you're losing your perspective. You're funny, you know. You don't realize the impression you give. Why, you are the last person in the world about whom one could think that, I can guarantee you. Germaine Lemaire would have to be stupid. And that she's not. one look at you is enough, Why do you think she appreciates you? Why do you think she sees you?"

"That's true, Gisèle . . . you must be right . . . and I must be crazy. I am crazy. I must always destroy, spoil everything. It's true that she has something generous about her . . . something warmhearted. She told me very simply what she thought. She, in my place, would certainly not have hesitated. That must have been what amused her, all those scruples, that rebelliousness . . . That's very adolescent . . ."

My son-in-law likes grated carrots. Monsieur Alain adores them. Now don't forget to make grated carrots for Monsieur Alain. Nice and tender . . . new carrots . . . Are the carrots tender enough for Monsieur Alain? He's so spoilt, you know, so fastidious. Finely chopped . . . as finely as you can . . . with that nice new gadget . . . Now . . . that certainly is tempting . . . Look, ladies, with this you get the most delicious grated carrots . . . I really must buy it. Alain will be glad, he adores them. Well seasoned . . . olive oil . . . "la Niçoise" for him, it's the only one he likes, I buy no other . . . The right proportions, he knows all about that . . . a little onion, a little garlic, parsley, salt, pepper . . . the most delicious grated carrots . . . She hands him the dish . . . "Alain, they're especially for you, you told me you adored them . . ."

One day he had had the misfortune, in a moment of abandon, a moment when he had felt relaxed, satisfied, to toss that at her casually, that secret, that revelation, and like a seed that falls on fertile soil, it had sprouted and is now growing: something enormous, an enormous oleaginous plant with shiny leaves: Alain, you like grated carrots.

Alain told me he liked grated carrots. She's lying in wait. Always ready to spring. She seized upon that, she holds that between her clenched teeth. She has caught it. She pulls . . . Dish in hand, she turns upon him a pair of gleaming eyes. But with one gesture, he disengages himself—a brief, lissome gesture with his lifted hand, a movement of his head . . . "No, thank you . . ." He's gone, there's no one left, it's an empty envelope, the old garment case off by him, a piece of which she's clenching between her teeth.

But he must not do that, he doesn't understand what he's doing . . . Being busy talking, he hasn't understood what happened, he has moments like this, when he's talking, when he's preoccupied, in which he notices nothing. He looks absentmindedly at his plate, makes an offhand, heedless gesture in the air with his hand: "No, thank you . . ." She feels like calling him to order, begging him, how had he dared . . . "Oh, listen, Alain . . ." He has belittled her mother, he has humiliated her, that makes her feel ashamed, it hurts her to see the little prefabricated smile which her mother—how well she controls herself—puts on her face then takes off right away as, noting that the disaster is complete, that one must know how to bow before fate, she sets the dish down in its place.

"But what's got in to you, Alain, see here . . . you adore them . . . Maman had them made especially for you . . . Here . . ." She's ready to brave everything, every interdict, to rush to her mother's aid. He has a horror of that, but no matter: "Here Alain, let me serve you . . ." just one of his moments of inattention . . . Now he's caught, brought back into line . . . that's the way to take them . . . she hands the dish back to her mother. Her mother, who is proud of her, sets the dish down, her mother caresses her face with a tender, grateful look . . . all men are big babies. And the two of them, allied, leagued against them, leaning towards each other . . . so much to tell each other . . . entirely absorbed . . .

But what's happening over there, between the two men, what's it about?

"Germaine Lemaire . . ." Germaine Lemaire? But why, all of a sudden? "Why, Alain, whom are you talking about?

—About Germaine Lemaire, believe it or not. —About Germaine Lemaire? —Yes, your father . . . —But . . . Papa . . . why . . ." How did he know? who told him? it was so well guarded, their treasure which belonged to them alone, holy relic preserved from impious eyes, from impure hands . . . but he's so sharp . . . The slightest word, an allusion, a too excited manner, a too clamorous show of enthusiasm . . . and he has caught the scent. . . But it was she . . . she herself, in a moment of madness . . . impossible to resist the temptation . . . when he had said: "If you want me to, I can ask the Férauds to speak to Germaine Lemaire about Alain. They know her. They are neighbors of hers." That was too much. She hadn't been able . . . her dignity demanded it, her own self-respect, her respect for her father, her regard for the truth . . . "But Papa, Alain doesn't need that. He knows her . . ." Imprudence. Madness. Shame. She had blushed right away. Perched up there, ludicrous, looking down upon them, strapping cabbage-monger, fishwife sitting in state on her float disguised as Queen of the Carnival . . . everybody was embarrassed, they had all looked elsewhere . . . she had regretted it right away.

She knew she would pay for it one day, she would lose nothing by waiting, nothing could keep her from paying, and now, suddenly, the moment has come at a time when she herself has forgotten, when she thought it had all died down . . . "Why Papa, what suddenly made you think of her? —Oh, nothing . . . an article about her in *France Soir*. I saw a picture of her . . . You can say what you want . . . he's sneering . . . she's a pretty woman . . ." He doesn't need to say more . . . "a pretty woman" . . . a short formula, but he has a well-trained, very gifted pupil, he has taught her well—there . . . she works out the formula instantly: a pretty woman, ha, ha . . . this, ladies, is your woeful situation, your tragic estate, but you must submit. It's painful . . . you're unwilling . . . you balk, don't you, hee, hee, my tender, frail little birdies? . . . But that's the way God made you, after all. You have to resign yourselves, that was nature's plan. Ah, they're not satisfied, they also want to think, to do . . . they get bored, shut in like that, ornaments, valuable objects, hothouse plants, luxury indulged in by successful men . . . is there anything you can complain of, your Mother and you? have I ever refused you anything? . . . relaxation, the warrior's rest . . . but just as soon as they try their hand at hard work . . . it's revolting to see them, the poor dears . . . I've been told . . . ah, that's a pretty sight, their equality . . . perched on scaffoldings; dragging crossties . . . the tourists are indignant. . . handling guns, disguised as males . . . Mme. Curie . . . that makes me laugh . . . nonsense . . . madness . . . old women at forty . . . faded, wrinkled, monstrous, bluestockings, objects of ridicule, of repulsion . . . look what that leads to; to the most dreadful, shameful thing that can happen to you: "This Germaine Lemaire, well, as for me . . . ha, ha, ha . . . he slaps the table hard with his hand . . . for all the money in the world, I. . ." She's trembling, her voice is trembling with indignation: "Oh, Papa, how can you . . . I'd be darn glad to look like her . . . she's more than pretty. She's beautiful. Every one says so . . . Men killed themselves . . ." He gives a little snort . . . hm, hm . . . "Men killed themselves? That's marvelous. The snobbishness of certain morons can bring them to that . . . But for me, children, there's nothing doing, I'm not taken in. I've seen her, in fact, at rather close range, your Germaine Lemaire. Believe me, she's as ugly as sin. That's perfectly obvious. —That depends on what you call beauty. For me, it's something else, real beauty . . ." She hangs on to that for dear life, to keep afloat, she feels a rage against him for pulling her down with him . . . she tries to free herself, she hits him hard . . . "If your ideal is the hairdresser's wax dummy . . . fashion plates . . ." She hates him . . . he should let go of her, let him sink, let him perish, so much the worse for him, but she's going to save herself, she is not going to give up . . . she senses that if she were to let herself go a second, well, she too, perhaps . . . might see . . . in that trash which one should despise, in those hairdresser's dummies . . . not so long ago, she herself . . . but she is not going to, he can pull as hard as he wants, in vain . . . she all but shouts: "There's another ideal of beauty, believe it or not. And not only for me, fortunately. And she corresponds to that ideal, Germaine Lemaire does, whether you like it or not. But I'm not alone in thinking that. Her head by Barut—but you haven't seen it, it doesn't interest you—that's not beautiful, I suppose? that, too, is without beauty? —Ye-es . . . his yes is a long hiss, yes . . . it's beautiful . . . of course . . . he's hissing like a snake . . . it's a nine day wonder . . . he sneers . . . I should have to be crazy to dare to say that it's hideous, that bust of Barut's. Imagine, what indignation, what an outcry . . . modern art, something new . . . imagine . . . You have to bow your head, shush . . . not a word, or else watch out . . . what would people take you for? And she too, Germaine Lemaire, what she does is all the rage for you, the avant-garde, I suppose . . . But do you know how old she is, that madcap? My age, if you want to know. Indeed she is. She's exactly one year younger than I am. Your mother's age, I read that they were born the same month, ha, ha, so they were . . ."

The most despicable reaction, barbarism, obscurantism, stupidity, the most dreadful heresy . . . he incarnates all of that, he—her own flesh and blood. She's ready to beat him, to burn him, to quarter him; "Very well, yes, she's your age, yes, she's your age. And what difference does that make? So much the worse for you . . . She's your age and she's younger than we are. For us, she points the way to the future. Whereas you . . ." She feels like weeping . . . Why doesn't someone help her, why doesn't someone come to her rescue . . . "Well really, Alain, there you sit saying nothing, you could say something, that's cowardly, Alain, what you're doing there, you know perfectly well that you agree with me, why don't you express yourself, explain yourself . . . —Oh, listen, Gisèle, calm yourself. You're ridiculous to get upset like that. . ." He presses upon her eyes, which she is unable to avert, his tough-guy, cynical, somewhat bantering gaze: do let it drop, why tire yourself. He's a poor old fogy. You can only pity him. A jealous old man . . . It hurts her. He hurts her very much . . . She can't stand this suffering . . . It's as though a scalpel were cutting into her flesh, she struggles, makes a great effort, in her turn, she presses upon him an inscrutable, icy gaze, and averts her eyes.

"Alain is right. . ." The gentle, loving mother understands nothing of all that . . . "What on earth is the matter with you, all of a sudden? What has got into you?" . . . The devoted old wife intervenes, tries to separate the combatants with her weak hands . . . "Stop, I beg of you . . . You are mad to get worked up like that. And over what, I ask you, over Germaine Lemaire's good looks, a woman as old as I am. Robert, you shouldn't. . . The children come seldom enough as it is, you miss them, you want them to come, and then when they're here, you can't resist, you simply have to tease them . . ."

King Lear, Père Goriot. His shy tenderness. His diffidence. Alone, old, deserted, unknown, left out, cast off by her, his darling daughter, his only child . . . But she loves him, he knows it . . . She will never like anything so much as to take the fine warm skin on the back of his hand between her fingers, pull it gently and watch it as it becomes detached from his flesh and remains a second in the air, forming a slight roll; smell his peculiar odor, which she recognizes right away, his nice odor of shaving cream and tobacco; run her hand over the silky, white ringlets on his neck . . . let it grow, I beg of you, don't go back to the barber's, Papa, I like you too much this way . . . How could outsiders separate them? What can all the Germaine Lemaires together do to the two of them? Usurpers. Impostors . . . She doesn't want him to let himself be dethroned. That's why she grows angry, becomes indignant, beseeches him . . . If he only wanted, he could be stronger, wiser than they: her omniscient, benign father. He would give her his approval. Bent low before him, as is proper, she would receive what would mean peace, would mean happiness: his benediction . . . "Maman is right. It's true, it's stupid, I'm crazy. Forgive me, Papa. None of that matters. Nobody cares. Only listen: I forgot about it, what with all these arguments. There's something far more interesting that I wanted to talk to you about. I have something marvelous to tell you. You know we are perhaps going to get it, Aunt Berthe's apartment . . ." He scowls even more. He is making his contemptuous, disgusted grimace: "Aunt Berthe? You must have fallen down off the wardrobe, as they say . . . That crazy old woman. Don't you see she's making fun of you. —Oh, Robert, why say that . . . that's not at all sure, with Berthe you never know . . . Her mother, immediately all excited, rushing from side to side, trying to bring them all together, clucking, her feathers all puffed up . . . Berthe is so fond of Alain, you know that. Personally, I shouldn't be surprised if they got it. Think of it . . . it would be such a good thing for them. You couldn't wish for anything better. They would be quite near us. It would be marvelous . . ." He should take a look at them, they're so handsome, so moving. Their darling daughter and her Prince Charming, heir to a powerful name, laden down with gifts . . . He should give in . . . "Certainly, Papa, you'll see, what will you bet that one day we'll get it? But that won't just happen all by itself, I realize that. There will be certain difficulties . . ." Exertion, advice, discussion. A contest to be engaged in. All of them in a huddle, closely massed here about him, protected by him . . . Fortunately, he is with them . . . "We were just going to ask you . . . What do you think, Papa? We were thinking of a three-cornered exchange. —A three-cornered exchange? How do you mean?" But he said that without looking at her, he's not yet over his grumpiness. How touching he is, goodness itself, really . . . the wrinkled, rather rough skin of his cheek, his nice soft neck . . . what a darling he is . . . "Oh, my sweet Papa, how nice you are . . . You will tell us, won't you, Papa, you know we don't know anything about those things, we just don't know. Aunt Berthe spoke to us of a three-cornered exchange. That would also depend on the proprietor. You told me . . ." He lowers his head abruptly and stares at her over his glasses: "What did I tell you? —Well, that you knew him . . . —Why of course I know him, it's Prioulet . . ."

Why not go there? Why not go look at the apartment? Right away, Alain, I should like to go now, I'm so crazy to see it . . . Do Alain, I beg of you . . . Of course not, we shan't go up . . . Aunt Berthe won't see us, she takes her afternoon nap at this time. It's just to see it from the outside . . . We'll hide, it will be amusing . . . it's just to see something, a small detail. . ." She feels so warmed up after all these wonderful plans, she would like to continue just a little bit longer, it's like a craving for sweets, for cakes, after a heavy meal. "Do, Alain, let's go . . . Let's not go home now, I just want to see something . . . the layout. . . the way it's oriented . . ." just a little peep, a greedy little lick, a nibble, the cake won't be at all spoiled . . . it's just to get a foretaste . . . it's a little tryout, a timidly outlined movement before the grand ensemble, the great exciting leaps . . . "Well, shall we go? right away . . . Oh, what a dear you are."

She makes you think of a fox cub, she looks like a young wolf, the end of her little nose points in the wind, its delicate, pink, slightly downy nostrils—the golden down of her skin—are quivering, cupidity makes her eyes shine . . . he loves that about her, her intensity, her purity, when she suddenly escapes from him, all her strength gathered in her glance—a little wild animal lying in wait for its prey. He would like to catch her, to hold her warm and silky in his hands . . . he leans towards her . . . "Darling, you are lucky, it's as you want it. Look, I'll explain it to you: the sun rises on this side; it turns, look, that way. West is over there. You'll have sun in that window nearly all day."

She feels him looking at her, she knows what he sees: she reminds him of a fox cub, a little forest animal, wild, capricious . . . He looks at her charming nose, a bit short but so delicate, so straight, freshly powdered, downy, golden . . . her eyes become darker when she stares like that at something, with such intensity . . . the blue in your eyes turns violet, your eyes are like violets . . . the tall blond lad, who looked like a Swede, had said that to her, seated beside her on the bench, resting, watching the others play . . . she had fixed her eyes on the ball in the same way—concentrated, all attention—as on that window, up there, on the one that's smaller than the others, that juts out a bit . . . her lip curls, showing her slightly protruding, very white, canine teeth . . . "There, Alain, look, that's where I'd like to have sun, in that window, there . . ." He leans towards her, he holds her close . . . "Very well, darling, you're lucky, it's as you want it . . . Look: I'll explain it to you. The sun rises on this side; it turns . . . west is over there . . ." He knows everything. Men know all that sort of thing. They're strong, intelligent. They protect you . . . it's delightful . . . She feels like snuggling up to him, she's so happy . . . "Oh, Alain, it's wonderful. That's where we'll have our studio, we'll tear down the partition . . . There where there's a window in the corner, I thought that, in front of the window . . . Yes you do . . . there, you see, the one that's been raised . . . I thought that we might make a plaster ledge, very wide, you remember, like in that house . . . —Which house, darling? —You know . . . Not at San Giminiano . . . no, I think it was near Lucques . . . We saw a tower in a village, on the hill . . . Near Lucques, yes, that was it: San Miniato, Frederic II's tower . . . Well then, just after San Miniato . . . you remember that old farm where we went in . . . There was a big, square courtyard with old paving stones and a tree, you don't remember? . . . Yes, you do . . . near a small lake . . . it reminded us of the enchanted tree we saw in Scotland . . . I made you come back to look out the window of a low-ceilinged room . . . Well, the window had a ledge, I showed it to you . . . and we could get an old bench . . . you can certainly find one . . . with short legs, sort of dumpy, an old bench all shiny with age, the sun would strike it . . . it should have a perfectly straight back . . . or rather no, no back . . . Why, you're crazy, Alain, people can see us . . . what must they think . . . —They must think that I adore you . . . that we are like two lovers . . . —That's true, that will set their minds at rest. A little while ago, I said to myself . . . didn't you? . . . that we gave the impression of two burglars, looking over the premises. Getting ready to do the job . . . We were hiding there like two criminals . . ."

"Old people should not be moved about. They're delicate, you know, old people are. It's dangerous to transplant them." These words, deposited in him, he doesn't know by whom, now, all of a sudden, the way things happen in dreams, someone is speaking them, a man whom he can barely distinguish: a vague figure in a dark overcoat; he utters them as he is leaving, walking towards the door without turning to look at him, in that soft tone, beyond blame, that priests use, in the tone indicating distance, that doctors assume, their manner of not wanting to touch upon certain things, not wanting to commit themselves, in which may be heard a tiny note of disapproval, of aversion . . . "They're delicate, you know, old people are . . ." Something that hurts very badly, a deep-cut image forming inside him, that of an old woman with white hair . . . It stands out sharply: the pain that flows into him fills up, sets off its outlines like the colored liquid that fills the tubes representing veins and arteries in certain anatomical engravings . . . the untidy white hair is hanging down on either side of a wrinkled old face the color of yellowed wax, as she comes down the blue-carpeted, white marble stairs, awkwardly lifting her stiff, skinny legs from step to step, her dull eyes have a haggard expression; her arm, her hand, with its big knotty veins, its twisted fingers, hold tight to her breast a sort of shopping bag, an old sack, with the gesture of a frightened child . . .

"Oh, that's quite ridiculous . . . there you're going a bit far . . . What burglars . . . Imagine . . . Why, for Aunt Berthe, it's a real boon to have to fix up a new apartment . . . she didn't suggest it for nothing . . . Egotistical as she is . . . She's bored if she can't be pottering about, changing door-handles . . . We are giving her work, real work, which will be sufficient to keep her busy for years . . . —You don't have to convince me, I was just thinking of what people would say . . . —Oh, that, people . . . Only, you know, I know her, it won't just happen all by itself. We, if we ask her, you know perfectly . . . But what we should do . . ."

He has a curious sensation, as though he were taking off from the ground, as though he were losing his specific gravity . . . "What we should do is to get someone to act for us . . . —Get someone to act for us? But who, Alain? —Oh, I don't know . . . —Oh, Alain, I have an idea . . . Suppose we ask your father to go and speak to her? —Of course, of course . . . —I could ask your father, if you don't feel like doing it yourself . . . —Of course, you can ask my father . . . But suppose Aunt Berthe refuses . . ." Unreal gestures, as though relieved. All alone. In the silence of night . . . Whispering . . . Where did you put the knife? the ropes? Bring the shovel . . . He has taken off, he's rising . . . Alone. All ties are severed. Human beings are far away . . . he is floating along, released from gravitation. Alone. Free. Slight dizziness. Nausea . . . Why no, he's not afraid; he's strong . . . "Suppose she refuses . . . You know she hasn't the right, you know if we wanted to . . . Your father knows the owner . . . Look at me, Gisèle . . ."

He takes her by the neck, he forces her to turn her head towards him and he looks deep into her eyes . . . "Gisèle . . . you hear me. He sets his jaw. We are a pair of gangsters . . . Decent people will be afraid of us . . . He grits his teeth, rolls his eyes like the murderers in the silent films . . . We're going to rob old women. Their swanky apartments are ours. And the parties we'll give . . . He's coming down. He lands. He's on solid ground once more. The crowd greets him like a conquering hero. People surround him, applaud him . . . Parties, Gisèle dear . . . they'll come running . . . only too flattered . . . Fiestas, my friends."

THERE'S A SORT of radiance that emanates from him, like a fluid, it flows towards you from his narrow eyes, from his Buddha-like smile, from his silence . . . she doesn't know what it is . . . that's his charm . . . he is charming: "Your father-in-law has charm, don't you think so? I think he has something, I don't know . . . I think he's very attractive . . . Oh, he must have broken many a heart, in the old days . . ." They should blow on it, on the spot where they burned her, without meaning to, perhaps, and right away the pain will go away . . . they should make just one move . . . they should acquiesce, if only by a slight nod of the head . . . don't they think he must have been like Alain thirty years ago? Alain will become like him, probably, as he grows older, he has the same smile at times . . . but they don't budge. And the burn festers, the wound spreads . . . But that famous charm, after all, which people are always talking about, that charm of his, what is it, when you look more closely . . . if anything, it's something a bit crafty, a bit disturbing . . . "Oh, in reality, no, Alain is not so much like him as all that. They're very different. It's his mother, especially, that Alain takes after. Poor woman, I'm sure things must not always have been very gay, I pity her . . ." it's something dubious, and also frightening . . . a secret connivance, a collusion . . . A sort of disdain: other people are poor innocent creatures who are unaware that, for him, they are puppets, nonentities. Intruders. Though men possess every grace and every gift, though women spread before him the science, the beauty, the pomp of Byzantine empresses, he will give them no more than cold admiration, pay them merely somewhat absentminded, slightly exasperated, almost hostile homage: all that is nothing, that's not what matters, that's of no interest, those people are a waste of time . . . What matters is that tiny thing, that mysterious gleam, that sparkle, that hidden, secret jewel . . . he discerns it anywhere, it shines, it scintillates timidly in the most wretched little slattern, in the saddest little monkey-face . . . he possesses a sorcerer's wand, a dowser's rod which permits him to discover it, a powerful searchlight which peers into them, which seeks, but what does it hope to find? . . . One is afraid, one feels like hiding . . . One would like to help him, to guide him . . . Is it that? An elf, a mysterious being, a delicate dancing flame? . . . But they need not fear, he is never wrong. It's there in them, whatever they do, he sees it . . . At times he's amused, he laughs to himself when they try to shine, show off, spread themselves, start discussing great ideas before him, become clumsily involved, grow excited, stick their necks out imprudently, then are obliged to hurriedly turn back . . . a powerful opponent forces them to withdraw, they abandon their ground, furious, red in the face, they sulk . . . he likes to watch them . . . how comical they are, what does it matter, what is it worth, all this knowledge with which one imagines they are overwhelmed, this reasoning power, it's hardly good enough to lay at their feet, to be trampled on by their dainty little feet . . . they possess what cannot be acquired, what no one can take from them. People may try to attack them . . . "Oh, she's a little ninny, laziness itself . . ." they can say that to him, he won't even deign to discuss it with them, all they'll get will be to occupy the field of his vision for a few seconds before they are driven from it forever: they are indeed what he thought they were, poor brutes, robots . . . insensitive, blind. He alone, despite all appearances, all obstacles, he—strong, virile, independent, can open up a path and discover . . . it's there . . . he leans over tenderly, it's his, deep in their eyes his gaze caresses it and they feel themselves living more intensely . . . it's his thing, his creation . . . in their most secret recess his possession, it trembles, flutters gently—life itself, the very source of life, in them, they possess it . . . something sacred, precious, something he will never want to speak about, diffidence keeps him from doing so, respect . . . "She's nice, my daughter-in-law," that's all he says, but she feels that, with him, she can let herself go, she can take any liberties she wants . . . she can let the words come out just any way . . . "Well, I wanted to talk to you . . . Alain would never know how . . . I said: I'm not afraid . . ." She laughs and he encourages her, on her cheeks she feels the warm, dry cushion of his fingers. "What is it you are not afraid of, my child? —Well, to ask you . . . Alain's afraid of you, you know . . ." His nod expresses indulgent, tender good nature: "Really, Alain's afraid of me? That's something new, it seems to me. When did you invent that? —No, I assure you, it's true. But I said: I'm going to speak to your father. It's about Aunt Berthe. She suggested . . . Oh, yes she did, I assure you, she came herself to talk to us about it . . . So we said to ourselves . . . you, she's so fond of you. She listens to you. It would be wonderful for us to have that apartment. You know where we are now, it's all right for the time being, but it's really too small. We can't invite anybody . . ."

It's as though he had become, all of a sudden, steadier, heavier, as though something, a precipitate, had formed inside him and fallen to the bottom. He leans back, puckers his eyelids and looks at her. A piercing, hard look. She knows what he sees: she feels her own face congeal under this gaze. A sly, voracious expression appears, she feels it, on her own features, in her eyes, she has the glazed eye of a bird of prey, of a small buzzard, all its claws tensed . . . She turns her head . . . "Oh, you know, personally, what I say, it's not for me . . ." But he stares at her pitilessly: come on there, no fuss, you've pretended enough . . . they're all alike, the dear little Madames, he knows them, that's why they get married, parties, invitations, stupid daydreaming, special little dishes, she's going to make a moron, a society dummy out of him, he has already been sufficiently dulled, sufficiently demeaned, humiliated by those people, spending too much time with them, letting himself be set up in an apartment furnished by them, deteriorating, easy life, Capuan delights . . . It's too unjust, it's wrong . . . How he loathes her at this moment. But he has hated her from the beginning . . . jealous, really, that's it . . . Defend herself, repulse him, he should let go of her . . . "Oh, personally, what I'm telling you, it's above all for Alain. He can't work when I'm at home. Even though I make no noise . . . It would do him a world of good . . ." Words are forming, they come crowding . . . Yes, Alain is humiliated, demeaned, and for once he has the opportunity, before my parents, to pull himself up a bit, to contribute something on his side, you won't move . . . you've never lifted a finger . . . you washed your hands of him at the very beginning . . . all you've done was to put spokes in our wheel . . . but he's your son, after all, it's not up to me to beg you, it's up to you to help me . . . you know better than I do . . . she restrains, stops all that and only allows the carefully molded words to come out, words she chooses cautiously: "It would do Alain good to be able to invite people to the house. He needs . . . You know Alain . . ." He looks elsewhere, stares at an object situated very far off, his lips sketch the ghost of a slightly bitter, resigned smile. "Ah, you think so? So I know Alain well?" The word Alain on his lips is all damp, as though impregnated with the tender odor of milk, the tart odor of wet diapers . . . salivas . . . smearings . . . Napoleon running his forefinger dipped in wine, over the face of his son and heir, bouncing him on his knees, playing doggy on all fours . . . dimples, laughter, tickling, tell it again, Papa . . . up a little earlier every day to take him to school . . . problems . . . leaving his friends, I must get home early this evening, Alain has a test tomorrow . . . boring vacations spent in little out-of-the-way spots . . . Alain needs salt air, sea air . . . I was dotty about him . . . all these scraps he has thrown at her, she sees them collected together inside him, tied in a tight bunch with, on the tag, the one name he has just spoken: Alain . . . And she took it all away from him . . . usurper . . . kidnapper of little children . . . old woman all in black, pale of face, claw-like hands, glazed, staring eyes of a maniac, lying in wait for innocent babes making mud pies in public parks, carrying off his little boy, rocking him hard to keep him quiet, whispering to him to calm him, so no one will hear him cry, call out . . . has she ever really loved, really rocked his child? . . .

Shame and rage make her blush. Nothing to lose now. Between ourselves, between us old people who know a lot of things, who are acquainted with life, no consideration, shall we? no emotion. Kidnapper? He must be joking . . . the little darling, between ourselves . . . he might have kept him . . . a newborn infant, it's true, a baby, puny, weak . . . a capricious brat . . . the truth long repressed, the horrible reality she has been trampling under foot frees itself, swells, she feels a lump in her throat. . . always hanging on to her skirts, she must continually be giving him a lift, reassuring him, consoling him, Germaine Lemaire, his latest obsession . . . other people's opinions . . . continually throwing himself into her arms, when he needs protection . . . poor, frail little chap who trembles if you flick your finger at him . . . Is this worthwhile? Do you think I really have talent? Why certainly, my darling . . . you are the cleverest, the most intelligent of all

. . . Drawing off her sap like that . . . Sucking her life away . . . "Yes, you know him as well as I do. You know how he needs to be reassured, upheld . . ." She feels that everything inside him is moving and changing place, she has made a shrewd thrust, he stiffens all of a sudden, in his heavy jaws, his fixed gaze staring straight in front of him, there is virile, courageous resignation, he reminds one of a gore besmeared bull as it lowers its head and faces the matador: "That's true. You're right. And you think that it will suffice to change apartments . . . No, Gisèle dear, neither you nor I will succeed in changing him. People are what they are . . . His voice hoarsens . . . He was like that already when he was knee-high to a grasshopper, when he was no bigger than that . . . I tried everything, believe me. But nothing can give him confidence in himself. He's terribly diffident, Alain, uneasy . . . That's his nature, he's like that, so there you are." His voice is hollow, he lowers his eyes, she has the impression that the blows he is giving her in return quicken, at the same time, his own suffering, but it can't be helped, since he wanted it, he must keep on until the end . . . "No, when all's said and done, it's an immense joke, education. At your age, I too believed in it. But the raw material is what it is . . . You can't change it. You'll see, when you have children of your own . . ."

There was a sort of tenderness in his voice, just now, as he spoke those last words. Tenderness and pity . . . It's the fate of them all . . . eternally sacrificed . . . wretched victims . . . Mary Stuart, Marie Antoinette . . . lovely princesses who set poets, warriors to dreaming . . . abandoned in the hands of mere boys . . . He lays his hands on her shoulders: "There now, Gisèle dear, do you really want it as much as that? I can really do something towards your happiness?" Gentle and strong. Courageous. A bit disillusioned. He is the worthy companion that fate should have given her . . . "I'll speak to my sister about it, if you think that would be of any use . . . I'll admit I don't much like to do it . . . I believe it's just so much trouble for nothing . . . However, if you want . . ." A real man and a real woman, that's what they are now, confronting each other, looking each other straight in the eyes. An affectionate light filtrates from his narrow eyes, from his smile . . . it's incredible, the amount of charm he has . . . "You're an angel. I adore you. It's very sporting of you. I'll go and tell Alain. He'll be glad."

"Your father is a dear. You know Alain, I adore him. He's going to see Aunt Berthe. He's going to speak to her, he agreed . . . —Going to see Aunt Berthe? This instant? He agreed. Like a little saint. I'll go to see Aunt Berthe. Without further ado . . . Did he say anything else? Nothing, nothing, what you call nothing? —Oh, Alain don't act silly, now Alain don't you act crazy, you hurt me, I assure you. Stop that, Alain, you frighten me. Stop making those faces, listen . . . —Not a word, not a tiny bite. Tenderly the wolf licked the gentle little lamb, that had come very sweetly, of its own accord . . ."

"Oh, Alain, you shouldn't, your father adores you, I assure you, he's touching."

"Yes. I adore him, too. But that's not the question. So, not a bite? Not the slightest imprint of his teeth? He controlled himself? Oh, shame upon you for lying. How mean of you to tell all that bosh to your own true love, to your very best pal . . . But why hide it, since I always know everything. A lynx-eyed clairvoyant, that's your little Alain. Is there anyone more intelligent? More perspicacious? So, just a few little knocks . . . Ah, everything has to be earned in life, hasn't it, we get nothing for nothing here below, that's how it is . . . A few little educational cuffs. It's never too late. No opportunity should ever be lost."

"Oh, there you're completely wrong. It's just the contrary . . . he told me that nothing could ever change people."

"Why how silly of me, how unpardonable, idiotic, crazy,

moronic . . . Of course, what was I thinking of? Of course. I didn't get it. What's the use of the apartment? All that is nothing. We can't change our lives. That would be too convenient, wouldn't it? People remain what they are. That's it, hurrah! I'm burning . . . it's that . . . and that hurt you, my mad darling, my love, my little elf . . . The old grandmother looked at you too sternly with her wolf's eyes. Ogres, all these old people. If you let them, they would eat up tender little children. But fortunately, I'm here. Come darling, let me take you in my arms. Come and sit here close beside me, we're safe, you know, when we snuggle up like that to each other . . . Why, Gisèle, what's the matter? You're crying?"

"No, Alain, I love you. You are my own true love."

An air of happy surprise. An air of unconstraint, of warm, gracious ease. The words form just any way, they gush forth, transparent and light, gleaming bubbles that rise up into a pure sky and vanish, without trace . . . "Ah, fancy that, I really am delighted, what luck to meet you, it's been so long . . . You see us, my father and me, hunting about . . . It's a book which I must have, very hard to find . . . How very glad I am . . . But true enough, you don't know each other . . . May I present . . . My father . . . Madame Germaine Lemaire . . ." Clear, well-pitched voice. Glance in which there hovers a modest gleam of filial devotion, of quiet pride . . . "My father . . ." And right away his father . . . the slightest sign of affection touches him . . . the shy embarrassed smile when he had seen the printed dedication in the middle of the blank page: *To my father* . . . And yet what could be more natural, more usual . . . but he's not spoilt . . . He had leaned over heavily, his back slightly stooped, his very white, gleaming hair, a bit tousled, one lock, as always, hanging down on his forehead . . . The image, while it is forming, lacerates, burns, as though engraved in his flesh . . . he had lowered his head and looked for a long while without speaking, at the blank page, and in the middle: *To my father*, in small print, resting one finger, as he does to see better, on the metal bridge that joins the lenses of his glasses . . . he had raised his hand in a caressing gesture and let it drop right away—one of those signs between them, infrequent, astonishing, like the flashes of light that come to us from distant stars, disclosing mysterious combustions . . .

"My father . . ." with a hardly perceptible note of affectionate pride, and his father, right away, moved, malleable, letting himself be modeled, would have bent over, just enough, with dignity, then straightened up again, pleasant, vivacious . . . You know Alain Guimiez's father is really charming. He seems so sensitive, so intelligent. They seem so fond of each other . . .

"Madame Germaine Lemaire . . ." The heavy gusts of wind that drive before them in the dust the leaflets handed out on every street corner by shrill-voiced hawkers, and set the streamers of half-torn posters flapping do not reach them. Not a breath from the outside causes the slender flame that rises solitary, erect, to flicker before that name: Germaine Lemaire.

No one bends an inch too low, or draws himself up the tiniest bit too high before this noble-faced woman, with the calm, direct gaze . . . Why, she's still very handsome, Germaine Lemaire, you had never told me that . . . and so simple. One has the impression of having known her for a long time. A courageous woman, there's no denying, who must have worked hard all her life, and so direct, such a decent sort. She opens wide her limpid eyes, with a broad gesture she holds out her strong hand: "I'm glad to know you, Monsieur, I'm so fond of your son." Happy smiles . . . looks filled with friendliness . . . exquisite scene . . . delightful comedy, entrancingly acted by such well-matched partners.

And but for almost nothing—just a certain movement on his part, this charming spectacle would have taken place, to the joy of his soul and of his eyes. But it's not a mere nothing that is wanting, it's innocence, purity, goodness, pride, it's all that together that he would have had to possess. Yet, no, sainthood itself would not have permitted him, at the very outset, to make this little movement. Nothing in the world could have—the odds were so evidently fixed in advance, the roles prepared a long time ago, the scene outlined so many times in his mind's eye, prefigured, glimpsed in a flash, experienced in striking summaries—nothing could have prevented that, instead of the happy surprise, the air of warm unconstraint, there should appear on his face and at once meet the gaze of his father standing opposite him, on the other side of the counter, an expression of fear, of distraction, when she appeared—but through what ill-luck, through what unforeseeable blow of fate, just at that moment, on that particular day—on the other side of the glass door to the bookshop. His father watches him a bit surprised and, turning to follow the direction of his glance, sensing something already—it was all prepared, this too, carved in deep-set letters a long time ago—his father sees coming towards them along the aisle, between the tables piled with books and reviews which she is sweeping with her wide, black silk mantilla, a large, strangely got-up woman with roughhewn features, looking like a secondhand clothes dealer, or an out-of-date actress, dressed in outlandish garb. She holds out her hand in a broad gesture by which she seeks to express, which expresses, one feels it, in her own eyes, regal simplicity . . . And be abashed, panicky, dragged and hurled there in front of them, in a ridiculous pose, pushed on stage by means of kicks . . . Go on, what are you waiting for? It's your turn to play . . . reeling, stammering, in a voice that flits and knocks about: "True, you haven't met . . . May I . . . my father . . . Madame Germaine Lemaire . . ." And right away, what he had foreseen, the half-smile, the fierce gleam in the narrow eyes, under the heavy lids, that reaction which he perceives on the part of his father, a quick, silent displacement, as though something were coming apart, then became recomposed otherwise, assumed another form: "Ah, so that's it . . ."

He's an insect pinned to a cork plaque, he's a corpse

laid out on the dissecting table and his father, adjusting his glasses, is leaning over him. Yes, that was it, the diagnosis was correct, everything functioned exactly as might have been expected when one was familiar with the patient's organism, when one had always been able to observe him so closely, to study, to remember, from birth, all his little diseases, all his most insignificant aches and pains . . . His father could not have mistaken it for a single moment: so that was the meaning of that haggard, dazed look, all of a sudden . . . Imagine, Mme. Germaine Lemaire entered, and the wretched upstart, ashamed, trembling, what is she going to see? surmise? think? won't she be disappointed, shocked? will they be polite enough? deferential enough? . . . Nothing is too good for other people, for this idiotic female, not a line of what she writes will remain, thirty years from now no one will remember her name, and he knows it perfectly, you can bet, the little snob, not so dumb as all that, but little does he care, that will do for old fogies, what they sneeringly call "immortal values, masterpieces . . ." life is too short, they're all in a hurry, nobody's eternal, quick, bestir oneself, kowtowing and flattery, infinite precautions, anxiously following the progress in her of each word, of each nuance . . . Never enough respect . . . But with one's father, one is not so considerate . . . all I'm good for is that, to pay for the art books he'll show her, which he'll make her admire, lay on her knees . . . shall I hold it for you, it's not too heavy? while he turns towards her, staring at her face, the motionless shining eyes of a dog who has found the scent, on the lookout for the slightest movement of interest, of satisfaction, awaiting patiently the moment when he must turn the page for her . . . but I, his father, once he has made use of me, quick, I can disappear, it would be so convenient if he could get rid of me, but as it happens, this time bad luck has intervened, we were taken by surprise . . . a cruel blow of fate . . . we must try to put a good face on things . . . "My father . . ." since it has to be done . . . how can you hide this large protuberance, this enormous embarrassing appendix which pulls you back, interferes with your movements . . . a coconut tree, of course that would be perfect, only the trouble is, that it's a bit too early, I'm still alive and kicking and young, hang it, and, thank heavens, independent . . . "May I present . . . Madame Germaine Lemaire . . ." And that manner . . . that look . . . Can you believe it, the young scamp, his ears need a good boxing, holds inspection, am I well enough dressed? clean hands and collar, get into your best bib and tucker, my friend, you're going to be introduced . . . He does me the honor . . . to me . . . I don't give a rap for his Germaine Lemaires, I never did strive, the way he does, out of pure snobbishness . . . That marquis, that time at Aix-les-Bains, and yet we were friends, he wanted absolutely . . . but it was I, as soon as we got back to Paris, who didn't want to . . . that society set . . . I myself cut things short . . . but he, in my place, the little good-for-nothing.

All of that swirling about, overlapping in disorderly fashion . . . But he knows all about these tiny particles in movement, having observed them countless times. He has isolated them from other particles with which they had formed other, very different, systems, he knows them well. Now they are rising, cropping out, they form a fine deposit on his father's face, a thin smooth layer which gives him a set, frozen look. And immediately she assumes her empress manner, her high-pitched voice, her peculiar accent, a sort of imitation English accent, and that tone which she also uses at times, too pointedly polite . . . "I'm very happy to meet you, Monsieur, I must congratulate you, you have a charming son. And you know, he has a lot of talent . . ." The tiny particles become more excited, fall into a panic . . . She's trying to teach him a lesson, him, his father, that's really the limit . . . she's taking advantage of this opportunity—she's waited a long time for it—to hold him there before her, stiff with timidity, congealed with fright, with respect, an unworthy father . . . The poor martyred child has complained to her, quite obviously . . . great mind misunderstood, unrecognized genius, crushed by his petty surroundings, pearl on the dung-heap . . . She takes his defense, she dares . . . against him, his father, who has given the best years of his life, who has sacrificed everything to attain . . . to what, I ask you . . . and at the cost of what effort . . . why even now he is constantly obliged to carry this little genius both arms outstretched . . . quite recently, in fact . . . poor fool, if she knew . . . it's even funny . . . But they need a lesson, the lady and her fancy-man . . .

His eyes glued to his father's face, he is waiting. About the narrow lips the fine deposit has become set, scarcely moves. The delicate lips are stretching . . . "I am, indeed, very proud. So apparently he's to become our great critic? A future Sainte-Beuve? . . ."

He's been ridiculed, jeered at, debased. All is lost, destroyed. Disappear. Never see her again. Furthermore, he won't see her again, whether he wants to or not. She raises her head, laughing, contempt gleams in the depths of her eyes . . . "Oh, Sainte-Beuve, I couldn't say. And besides, why Sainte-Beuve, do you like him so much as that?"

She cannot allow this sneering. Down dog. She must defend her caste, her position. As for him, she abandons him. Little mongrel puppy. She had been mistaken. She's going to stop committing herself . . . She turns away absentmindedly, dismissing them forever, both of them, she turns towards the salesgirl . . . "Ah, Mademoiselle, here's what I'm looking for. Would you, by any chance, have, in the 'Two Sirens' edition . . . They have no more hold over her. They no longer have access to her. They are a mere incident, a brief diversion which she thrusts aside, forgets. They're not worth her wasting the tiniest bit of her time, not worth her pausing a single second on the route she has chosen for herself, and which she is pursuing so brilliantly, forging ahead, all sails to the wind, soon a hardly visible dot for them, far out at sea, then disappearing forever.

That was how it had to happen, quite inanely, quite simply, at the most unexpected moment. He had anticipated, foreseen it so clearly, he had so dreaded it, that now he feels a sort of relief. This time, it's all finished, the doubts, the fears, the efforts are finished; the pitiable contortions intended to amuse her, to detain her just a second longer, just this one more time, to obtain one more vague promise, one wretched reprieve, one hope. No more will he come fawning, groping for something in her that he can catch hold of, cling to. No more, drawn back into some far distant past—occasionally a sensation of dizziness came over him, a sense of remoteness, of strangeness, when he was with her, talking to her—no more will he feel himself falling into the depths of he knew not which barbarous ages, an abject sycophant doing his utmost in shame and in fear, at the table of a cruel tyrant. Large doses. Never too large. They never get enough. Her manner that time, with her head thrown back, her mouth half open, a bit flushed, misty-eyed, the day of the *vernissage*, in the back room, amidst the paintings—a bit greasy, a bit soft, another one of her young protégés—when he fed her those tasty bits, those sweet bits . . . "Your ears must have burned . . . Jean-Luc and I talked about you until five in the morning . . ." Delicately cascading laughter which she herself hears ring out like the "fresh, crystal-pure laughter of a young girl": "About me? Until five in the morning? But what on earth did you say? —Well, I thought that I was mad, but Jean-Luc is even madder than I am."

Jean-Luc is mad. See what havoc. You are a scorching wind. You are a simoom, a typhoon. Nothing in your path resists you, our spirits waver, sink, we're all mad. Jean-Luc is mad. Look, the poor fellow has been carried off. It hurts us, whom a similar fate awaits, to see him, his clothing all torn, he had rolled in the dust, I look, a bit ashamed, at the poor struggling nude body, at my own wretched double . . .

"He told me: If I stopped seeing her, I think I should kill myself. It has become an obsession with me . . . I think I need to be treated . . ." How pitiful, how ridiculous, look, I am stronger, I can still hold my own. Seated now beside you, I look at him. We look at him. We smile a bit, both of us. How can we resist . . . "You know it has really become an obsession with Jean-Luc. He told me: I only live now for that, for those brief moments, of expectation, then, of remembering . . ."

She drinks it in, a flower drinking the dew, its petals opening to the sun: "But I give him so little . . . Unfortunately, I have so little time . . . —But you don't realize . . . It's very simple, he told me, word for word: I owe her everything, without her I shouldn't do a thing. My entire life depends on her. If she were to show the slightest impatience, frown ever so slightly . . . that way she has, you know . . ."

She opens wide eyes that sparkle and scintillate with joyous excitement . . . "But what way?"

I am seated beside you. I am observing you. I have succeeded in slipping up very close, there where nobody enters. Outside, the anxious multitude is waiting. I am alone in the awe-inspiring lair, I must take advantage of this moment. Take the risk, at the peril of my life . . . I am going to see what nobody can see . . . I advance, trembling, through a dark maze . . .

"Oh, you have a way that cannot be mistaken by anyone who knows you, a way of showing people when they no longer interest you . . ." There it is, the door's going to open a bit, I'm going to come nearer, and the monster will be captured, bound hand and foot, led on leash . . . the danger, the ceaseless anguish will be averted for all time . . . "One suddenly has the impression, no one gives this impression the way you do . . ."

She smiles, with that smile she has in such moments, a smile that is enchanted at the spectacle of herself: a miracle, an inexhaustible mine of pleasant surprises. Her wonder knows no bounds, a pampered child who discovers in his stocking, hanging in front of the fireplace, this, and this too, a fresh gift from heaven . . . "Indeed, I didn't know that, I'm unaware of it . . ."

Now he's quite near . . . one step more . . . he's trembling . . . "No one gives the impression the way you do that, all of a sudden, people cease to exist for you, that never again, no matter what they do, can they exist for you . . ." One step more . . . "The unfortunate creature to whom that happens, has no recourse. You probably never go back on your decision . . ." The door opens halfway . . . he leaps up . . . "You do it quite unconsciously, it comes naturally to you . . ." A frightful roar. He gives a leap backward. He has gone too fast, too far . . .

She frowns, her eyes examine him closely . . . "I didn't know that I was so ill-natured as that . . . —Ill-natured? You ill-natured? But you never do it on purpose, heavens, you absolutely do not realize it . . . You are kind, on the contrary, very kind —Kind? She's still frowning. Kind? I believe no one has ever yet told me . . ." Safe. Only watch out. "Yes. Kind—very firmly—kind. Even though the word may not be to your liking. And we said it too, that night, when we were talking about you, when you were with us . . . we couldn't leave each other . . . Kind. You have genuine kindness. The only sort that is really effectual. Don't laugh. I know something about it. I can talk. But that's what is so frightning: all that we accept from you and which we risk losing at any moment. With Jean-Luc, it's a feeling—he told me that—almost of panic . . ."

He's advancing again, pushing in front of him, for protection, the inanimate body of his friend, he comes as near as he can, taking constant precautions, the danger is terrible . . .

All her unleashed watchdogs scent something. Tyranny? cowardice? abuse of power? an exacerbated sense of the hierarchies? stinginess? pettiness? When she's wholly nothing but humanity, but an innate feeling of equality, always far in the lead of all progress, divine simplicity . . . suffering just anybody to come unto her, wasting her precious, fruitful time on these pygmies . . . She has a disappointed little pout, which immediately disappears: "Well, I can see that you indulged in psychological analyses at my expense . . ." The bite tears into his flesh, he runs away, screaming with pain, the entire pack is upon him: "I who introduced you to each other, thinking it would help you . . . And that's how you pass your time . . ." —No, mistress, no, have pity, don't sell me, don't put me in irons, don't have my eyes put out, please deign to call off your dogs, I beg of you, spare me just one moment more . . . "No, don't be angry . . . Allow me to explain . . . That's what's so frightening . . . You begin by giving people every chance, you give them immense credit . . . They feel that they lose it through their own fault, that you drop them wittingly . . . It's a sentence that includes everything about them, that goes very far, it's that which people dread . . ."

She relaxes. An almost fond indulgence spreads out from her glance . . . "To hear you tell it, one would think that I am some sort of *Atlantide* heroine. But nobody is less to be dreaded than I am." She has a little air of exhilaration, she's waiting, he feels it, straining towards him . . . "Oh, that's not so, dread-inspiring, you certainly are . . ." Come on, no matter if he loses, he must seize this opportunity, he must dare: "Shall I tell you the truth? Well, I'm terribly afraid of you. I'm like Jean-Luc. I'm always afraid of disappointing you, of boring you . . . I haven't yet understood how you could have paid any attention to me. When I think of all the brilliant, gifted people, geniuses . . ." She leans towards him, her eyes are sparkling, her lips are apart . . . But a high-pitched voice may be heard . . . "Ah! Maine dear, so there you are, we were looking for you. We're waiting for you . . ." Tiny pink hat saucily worn, hard eyes which stare at him, pierce him through, set him straight: Come, come, Monsieur, we're in a public place, behave yourself, pull yourself together . . . They must have all been there in one corner for some time, watching him: "Who is that fellow? I admire Maine. She certainly has patience . . . —Oh, I don't know, a newcomer, her latest crush. Look at him, he's a scream." And a wave, the same wave, broke over them, while they observed him silently, the same wave passed over them, in which there was mingled a bit of discomfort, of embarrassment, of pity, a bit of contempt, of surprise, and a large amount of satisfaction . . . to think that they themselves could have, with less luck, less force . . . oh, no, how can one . . . brr . . . delightful little thrill . . . they watched his feverish gestures, his shining eyes, his pose . . . leaning too far forward . . . losing his head, forgetting where he is, thinking he's alone with her in limbo, in the seventh heaven . . . dialogue between kindred spirits . . . forgetting that he's in a picture gallery, on the opening day, and that he's surrounded by people . . .

But she too, he has succeeded in doing that, she too, has forgotten . . . that's where her genius lies, it's from this that she derives her strength, from the attention, the importance, which, all of a sudden, she is able to give to just anything, to just anybody, raising them up for a second from out of nothingness . . . But the others out there, poor little brutes that they are, don't understand . . . "Maine is too kind, too weak with all those people, they take advantage of her, it's outrageous . . . She must be rescued . . . Come on, I'm going in there. —My dear Maine, you know we're waiting for you, besides, they're about to close . . . We are the last ones . . . —Oh, dear me, you see, you made me forget about time . . ." She nods in their direction: she's ready. She's coming. They should wait one second more . . . And she turns back to him. He feels her gaze, brimming with regret and nostalgia, settle on his face, dwell upon his eyes, flow into him . . . They're caught, encircled, they're surrounded by foreigners, barbarians, who are going to separate them, she clasps his hand in hers, she holds on to it for another brief second, while they drag her away . . .

And one fine day—as was to be expected—just this one false move. In fact, if he had prepared it all himself, organized the stage directions, designed the scenery, set everything in readiness, on purpose, so as to be obliged to make it, that move which started the whole thing, he would have acted no differently . . . He must really be mad, he must be completely crazy—he feels like kicking himself till it hurts—to have taken his father there, to the very place she herself had spoken of . . . "Why, that's my favorite bookshop," she had said that to him, and from that moment on, for a long time, he had not gone there without hesitating, fearful, hopeful, smoothing his hair in front of the glass door, assuming an appropriate expression, letting his glance wander about, seeking refuge at the counter in the back room . . . It had become a privileged, sacred spot, one that was propitious to miracles . . . she might appear at any moment, she might come while he was reading, to take up her stand silently beside him . . . they would look at things together . . . and this, have you read this, do you know about this? leafing haphazardly . . . what do you think of it? a word, a laugh suffices, they understand each other so well, they're on the same side, they can't leave each other now, they're so rare, such moments as these . . . And what are you going to do now? . . . Suppose I break it? . . . Oh, do, I beg of you . . . It doesn't matter, after all, we only live once . . . All obstacles are swept away, all barriers are down, happiness in a powerful wave overspreads everything . . . But she had never appeared, and little by little the hallowed spot had become once more the convenient shop he had long been acquainted with, which he could enter without taking any precautions, with just any face, in any state of mind, dressed any way, and with just anybody. No, there he was going too far. His father was not just anybody. To have brought his father there, even though the risk of her coming had become remote, reduced to almost nothing, that had been tempting a cruel fate.

But he hadn't tempted fate. Everything had been determined ahead of time. His father had been nothing but the tool of fate. A perfect, ideal tool, the most effective to be had. His presence alone had sufficed to unleash the disaster. Everything had suddenly become clear: the imposture, the fraud. Like the gentleman burglar whose photograph the hostess notices, while he is strolling through her drawing-rooms, on the front page of the newspaper she is carelessly folding, with shaven head and striped prison shirt, she had suddenly seen what he was, he himself, in reality, a youngster in short breeches whom his father was holding by the hand, a frightful little fellow, weedy, silly, sly, boasting . . . "Do you know, Papa, what the great writer, Germaine Lemaire, told me? Do you know what she said about me?"

That's still too presumptuous. That would still be too much to expect, any astonishment on her part, any loathing. She probably had felt nothing as strong as that. At the most, a vague discomfort, a sensation which she hadn't even taken the trouble to analyze. If one day she could be forced, at the same time that she made an effort to be very clear-sighted, very sincere, as sincere as possible, to tell what she had felt at the moment when, with that air of relentless coldness—the air of a judge who dons his magistrate's cap before reading the death sentence—she had turned to the salesgirl, shaking them from her, his father and him, like so much dust, she would probably say quite simply, that what she had felt was that she had been there wasting her time, it's awful to know so many people, they spring up every moment from everywhere, obsequious, anxious, hanging on, looks that cling to you, hands outstretched, there's no way to wind up, one would like to satisfy everybody, they'll be so desperate if you get rid of them, but you have to harden yourself, arm yourself, against pity, time is short, there's so much work overdue, we're not here to amuse ourselves . . . But she won't even say that. She surely wouldn't remember anything. The motions she had made were simple reflexes commanded by her instinct. Her strength is to give it full rein, to let herself be guided by that instinct which, with her, is so flexible, so sure, it must give her the impression that she is never wrong. And besides, even if she were wrong, what would it matter?

She doesn't care a rap about justice. She never passes judgment. He, for her, was nothing but a whim, a source of amusement: a stone she picked up and threw into the water to watch it skip. A few ripples, a gentle splash. It has disappeared. She'll take another pebble.

And he feels a slight excitement, like a glimmer of hope, of happiness. Perhaps, just the same, the day will come, even several years from now, when mention of his name before her—he suddenly feels proud and as though wonderstruck—will open a tiny pigeonhole in her memory, encumbered by so many names, by the entire universe, a pigeonhole in which he is enclosed for all time, she will look pensively into far-distant space: "Alain Guimiez . . . Let's see . . . I lost sight of him long ago. What ever became of him? He had a certain talent. It seems to me that he was working on something, a thesis, what was it about, anyway? . . . Yes, he was very shy, timorous, always a bit excited, *bizarre*, a strange chap . . ."

TWENTY-FIVE YEARS of effort, of struggle, have been of no avail, there's nothing to be done about it, people do not change: he feels the same helpless rage that used to upset him so much when, like some avid, malevolent animal, she wormed her way into his nest, took his little one from him . . . and in what a state he would find the child later . . . what on earth is this little rich boy getup, some more of Aunt Berthe's presents. He used to feel like pulling them off him, the cap, the gloves, the little necktie, the new shoes, shaking him to rid him of all those sly cravings, that timid cunning she had caused to germinate, proliferate in him, to wipe off from that overstuffed, papa's-boy face its look of superiority, of obtuse satisfaction . . . But he was obliged to smile, to acquiesce, to admire, she was the more powerful, all the forces of nature, all the compulsion with which society weighs upon the recalcitrant, the unadapted, were leagued together with her against him, an unnatural father, filled with ridiculous prejudices, with preconceived, preposterous notions, with "Principles" . . . I ask you . . . that poor little motherless child needed coddling, a man doesn't understand such things . . . poor little angel, he so loves a little spoiling, sweets, ah, the little rascal, greedy as a pussycat, and vain . . . worse than a girl. . . how comical he could be, so proud, he would look at himself in every mirror, his suit was extremely becoming, he was too cute, pretty as a picture, in his little cap, with his hair well combed, slicked back . . . She never relaxed her pressure. She had the blind power of a force of nature, and he continued to struggle the way the Dutch do against the inrushing waters, yielding ground, building dikes farther on: virile, instructive games, moral talks, botany scrapbooks, visits to museums, butterfly collections, serious man-to-man conversations, contempt for facile delights, highminded curiosity, pure contemplation . . . but the irresistible tide permeated everything, the ground was porous, quickly became saturated. Soft, spongy soil, muddy, which he worked unceasingly, which he tried to improve according to the most highly perfected modern methods, with the richest composts, the latest fertilizers . . . which he drained, turned up, turned over, weeded, hoed, planted . . .

This time, everything gave way all of a sudden. She had only to come in, sit down, twitching the sharp end of her nose as though she were testing the wind, look about her in a distressed manner . . . "Why my dear children, you really have a tiny place. What you should have is a place like mine." And right away, they're entirely permeated; swollen, heavy; cupidity oozes from them and overflows in long, excited, secret talks . . . "How can we do it? —Why, speak to your father. —To my father? You don't mean that . . . certainly not . . . Complete madness. Just the thing not to do. No, Gisèle dear, there's no question of my going, I myself, to speak to my father, that's impossible. I shan't breathe a word to him about it, on the contrary. But you, Gisèle, believe me, that would be just the thing . . ."

Yes indeed, that was just the thing. Very well played, very clever . . . All the good people, all the mothers in France, all the fathers in the world assembled about him, listened with emotion to the innocent girl's words: "I was sure that you would not refuse to help us . . . You are so kind . . ." Soft, cool hand laid on his hand . . . Smooth, firm lips on the dry skin of his cheek . . . and that look of tender confidence, that air of expecting this from him alone . . . he alone possessed the strength, the power to give her this, this joy, this happiness . . . and he had let himself be taken in, he had surrendered.

And now here he is, all made up, a greasy coating sticks to his skin, they've painted his face to have this foolish look of a loving father, a doting father-in-law, they've disguised him as a nice plump old graybeard . . . he feels himself being pushed, all pomaded, along clean, empty streets, opening well-oiled doors, advancing without effort over thick carpets, enveloped by emollient heat, borne aloft by the elevator, gliding on its regularly greased cylinders . . . holding an obedient, resigned finger on the doorbell, and it gives a little ring . . . He hears velvety footsteps . . .

She's crouching there in the back of her lair, the guardian of strange rites, high priestess of a religion which he loathes, which he is afraid of, continually polishing the objects of her cult. Her excited fanatic's eye keeps scrutinizing the polished surfaces which no speck of dust, no sacrilegious breath may tarnish . . .

In a second, these eyes that nothing escapes, are going to alight on him, examine him, and then, right away, as though she had cast a spell over him, he's going to feel his clothes wrinkle, lose their trimness, beneath her gaze . . . why doesn't he have his suits taken more often to the cleaner's, why doesn't he have the spots and shine removed, have them pressed, re-pressed? . . . How is it possible that he has not ordered a new suit? He needs brushing, there are ashes on his waistcoat, there's dust in the fold of his trousers . . . His cheeks are badly shaven . . . why doesn't he use better blades? a really good shaving cream? he should have put on a clean shirt, the cuffs . . . the collar . . . he runs an anxious hand through his hair, he quickly adjusts his tie, when the chain on the other side of the door begins to rattle, and a cracked, hesitant voice . . . the frightened voice of lonely old women, the distrustful, hostile voice of avaricious old coupon-clippers for whom cunning assassins lie in wait on silent stairways, fake salesmen coming to sell brushes, washing machines, fake inspectors coming to read their gas meters . . . a voice that is quite changed, which he hardly recognizes, asks "Who is it? —It's me, your brother, it's Pierre . . ." He hears a sort of peeping noise, a happy stirring about, a quick click, the light, cheerful noise of a chain, the door opens . . . "Ah, so it's you . . ." He had forgotten that look beneath the worn, made-up lids, a kindly look welling with fond emotion . . . "So it's you, Pierre . . . Why, of course not, you're not disturbing me . . . I'm delighted to see you, you come so rarely . . . But let's see, let me look at you, let me see a bit how you're looking. Why, you're looking fine, I must say, you know you really are a wonder . . . you don't change at all, you'll live to be a hundred, you'll be like Grandma Bouniouls . . . —Grandma Bouniouls . . . no, my dear Berthe, I don't think so, I think, if anything, that I have aged considerably recently . . ." While she goes ahead of him through the entrance hall, the parlor, he is unable to take his eyes from the frail back of her neck, the little livid hollow between the two prominent sinews, a bit hollower still . . . a very vulnerable spot, innocently exposed, into which the assassin's knife could plunge without meeting any resistance . . . He feels like leaving, how could he have agreed? . . . She runs a caressing hand along his arm . . . "Come now, do sit down, sit there, why don't you . . . you look a bit uncomfortable . . ." He blushes, he bends down to hide his face, he leans over, he stares at the corner of the rug which he has turned up in passing, he takes it in his fingers, he must compose himself, gain time . . . There, he turns it back, lays it flat, that's done, the harm is repaired. She looks at him in a suspicious manner and as though she were slightly put out. "Come now . . . that doesn't matter . . . Do leave it. . ." There is a note of sad reproach in her voice

. . . and he drops the rug, straightens up right away, a bit ill at ease: he has offended, wounded her, she must think he wanted to rub her nose in her own little manias, go her one better to make fun of her . . . she must think he's petty, impure, incapable for once, for a single moment, of casting, scattering to the winds, in a burst of confidence, of generosity, those scraps of her, those tiny insignificant bits which, for so long he amassed, allowing nothing to pass unnoticed; incapable, just one single time, of sweeping all that aside and seeing her entirely as she is: sincere, pure, generous, capable, herself, of forgetting everything in a moment of tenderness, of surrender . . .

But she's wrong, he's not so mean, not so stupid . . . he sees her like that, he too, he knows what she can be like, how she is, he knows her better than she thinks . . . He is unable to wait any longer, unable to sustain another second the look she continues to direct straight at his eyes, he doesn't want with her—besides, whom would he be fooling?—to have recourse to petty little dodges, to little underhand tricks . . . "Listen, Berthe dear . . . It's this . . . He clears his throat. . . This is what I came for . . . I hate terribly to talk to you about it. . . but I prefer to do it right away . . . Gisèle came to ask me . . . The children say . . ." But it's her own fault, after all, why be so upset, she's the one, after all, it was she, with her own hands, who prepared it all, it's her own fault that he should be driven to doing what he's doing now . . . so much the worse for her, as we make our bed so must we lie in it, let her straighten it out with them now . . . "It seems that you promised to let them have your apartment . . ."

He expected it, he dreaded it . . . it was bound to happen, he had blown too hard . . . the faint little flame that had lighted up in her when he came in, that had trembled weakly, has now relapsed, lain down, died . . . inside her, it's dark again, as before, as always . . . her poor drawn face under its makeup . . . her eyes in which no light shines . . . if only he could revive, rekindle it . . . it was true that he had felt happy when he had seen her a little while ago, that he is happy to be here, he doesn't see her often enough, what a mess, we are stupidly neglectful of the people we like best, we think that it's enough to know they exist, we feel so sure of them . . . she's like a part of himself, she must know that, she's all that he has left of his childhood, of their parents, they are alone both of them now, for always, two elderly orphans, he feels like stroking the thin silky film of her very fine hair, like mama's hair, real down . . . they are indestructible between them, those ties, they're stronger than everything else, more to be counted on, even, than those that bind you to your children . . . "Those little monsters have got that into their heads now, you set them all agog . . . that's all they dream about . . . Aunt Berthe offered, she promised us . . . You spoil them too much . . . you know perfectly what they're like . . . Oh, if they could put us out, take our places . . . they ask nothing better . . . you should never have done it. But now that they're all excited about it, they asked me . . . What can I do, I'm like you, too weak . . . I agreed to come and talk to you about it. I hate very much to do it . . . But Gisèle came and begged me . . . Alain, of course, didn't dare, he was afraid I might get angry, he knows me, but she—I thought you were mad—she explained that you felt your apartment was too much for you, that you would like to get something smaller, arrange an exchange . . . in any case, I agreed to talk to you about it, although it's not easy, you know that. You know what horror I have of mixing into things like that." Not the slightest light in her, everything is extinguished. The sparkling showers of tenderness, of confidence, that he sends flying from his words, from his eyes, from his smile, crackle in vain against the asbestos curtain that she has lowered between her and him. It's finished now.

She had let herself be taken in for a second, but she recovered herself right away . . . It was easy—she's been in training for a long time—to be alone again as before, for her, that's the way things are, it's her natural state, this calm, this emptiness inside her, this chill . . . She looks at him with an inscrutable, hard, smooth expression that repulses him and keeps him at a distance; she gives a little sniff, as she wiggles the end of her nose—a brief little noise, energetic, disillusioned, just a little contemptuous . . . "Yes, I know, I did say that to them . . . Their flat seemed so small to me . . . and for me here, this is much too big. But, as a matter of fact, I don't see very well how . . . where should I go with all of these things? . . . all this furniture, these memories? . . . I couldn't be separated from them, they mean a lot to me . . . And then, I'm accustomed to this house, this neighborhood . . . At our age, you know very well, it's not easy to transplant oneself . . ." She smiles to herself, to an image inside herself which she is contemplating: "Ah, of course, they liked the idea . . . she moves her lips greedily as though before an appetizing dish . . . the little devils . . . they were all excited . . . They like that, luxury, comfort, handsome things, nice furniture . . . Alain especially, he takes after me . . ."

Serves him right, it's what he deserves, he brought it on himself. He himself, and he knows it, came, humiliating himself, denying his faith, to bow down cravenly before the idols she adores. She has contempt for him now, what's surprising about that? She makes no bones about it, she sprawls on him, crushes him with all her weight, wallows . . . "That day, when I went to see them, they were all excited about a Louis XV *bergère* . . . Alain was furious. Imagine, Gisèle's mother wanted them to take instead some heavy leather easy chairs . . . So it was Gisèle who came to see you? She gives him a rakish look, she has a little teasing smile . . . Alain didn't dare? You know he is still afraid of you . . . the way he used to be, you remember . . ." She opens big childlike eyes, leans towards him, shakes her finger, whispers: "Above all, Aunt Berthe, don't say anything to Papa . . . don't tell him we went to the pastry shop . . . Ah, he hasn't changed . . . How comical he is! ha, ha, ha . . . But by the way, what about Gisèle's parents? I thought her father had all kinds of possibilities, that he even owned some apartment houses . . . that should be easy for him. He might bestir himself a bit, he might, don't you think so?" He shakes his head like an ox chasing flies . . . "That I know nothing about . . . His voice is low, hoarse . . . perhaps . . . I don't know . . ." He would like to escape, but she holds on to him: "You don't know? Well, you should. I thought . . . I was told when they got married that Gisèle's parents, later . . . It's certainly the least they can do, between ourselves, don't you think . . ." He would like to leap up, jostle her, flee, but he can't. He's there before her, heavy, dull, bloated, deformed, sore, like someone with dropsy, a man suffering from elephantiasis . . . whereas she . . . ah, naturally, she has never known those famous joys, he was so proud, once: I have a son . . . she must have had the impression, and she hadn't been wrong, that he wanted to shame her a bit for her uselessness, that he felt pity for her . . . she had suffered now and then, he knows that, she had regretted at times . . . but also, what compensations . . . she fluttered about him, slender, light, free, unconcerned, occasionally alighting haphazardly—she had difficulty in choosing—on just any spot of the swollen, sensitive part of him—the slightest touch hurt him—pressing, scratching: "Well, tell me about Alain. His sleepless nights? His test papers? His laziness? His lies? His adenoids? And what about his nails? Have you thought of putting gloves on him? What did the doctor say? How is he getting along with the brace on his teeth? . . . And his girl friend . . . Ah, my poor fellow . . .

And this marriage, are you pleased with it?" She leans towards him, very close: "Listen, between ourselves, since we're on the subject, don't you think that, in reality, Gisèle . . . understand me, I like her very much, she's very sweet, but are you sure that she's exactly the kind of girl to suit Alain?" He makes a gesture with his hand as though to brush her aside, drive her away, he gives a sort of moan, mm . . . mm . . . She laughs and lays her hand on his arm: "It's never finished, is it? . . . little children, little cares, as they say, big children . . ." He makes an effort, stands up: "You know, I think I must be going . . . —You must go, already? What an idea . . . You'll make me think that all you came for was to talk to me about that. It's been so long since we saw each other. That little old brother of mine . . . Her eyes mellow . . . The fact is, you know, time is passing, and fast, at that, faster and faster, there's not so much time left, eh, we're getting old . . . Come on, now, I want you to taste my plum brandy, you'll tell me what you think of it. Or would you prefer if I made you a good cup of tea, just the way you like it, boiling hot, strong . . ."

THERE, IN FRONT of the newsstand, those narrow shoulders, slightly stooped, under the wrinkled jacket, that very black, very straight hair, that puny neck . . . it's he, it's the chap with the big apelike body, who kept swinging back and forth, seated on the rug in front of the fire, his long thin hands clasping his crossed ankles . . . it's the queen's jester, the favorite . . . his long, bony hand on the end of his long arm stretches out, lays the money on the saucer, picks up a newspaper . . . he's about to turn round . . . there, he has turned, to make his way through the crowd, he pushes aside those who were waiting behind him, he walks on . . . his glance is about to alight . . . Impossible to face that . . . Flee . . . Hide . . . No, there's nothing to do but to stay there, not move. In a moment, everything will finally be clear. Doubt will no longer be possible: he knows everything, the jester does, he's privy to all the conspiracies, all the secrets. He knows who is going to fall into disgrace, who is to be banished, dispossessed, slain . . . In a fine stream, it has gushed forth from her and flowed into him as, leaning towards her, he exchanged signs, looks, with her, before other people, perceptible only to them; in a sparkling, leaping, joyous cascade, it flowed from her and spread through him while he sat there at her feet, his head lifted towards her, his neck stretched forward, his ears cocked: "Ah, you know, I met young Alain Guimiez the other day, in a bookshop . . . He was with his father . . ." he threw his head back, he gave a pointed laugh, showing his big teeth . . . she leaned towards him, tapped him lightly on the back, she laughed too . . . "Be quiet, there, you loon . . . That's true, of course, you're right . . . Ah, they're impossible . . . What's got into them? Did I run after well-known writers at their age? . . . But they . . ." She leaned over farther, quite close, she whispered something horrible, something frightening into his ear . . . it spread out everywhere inside him, he's entirely impregnated with it, it's in him now, like the substance litmus paper is soaked with, in a second it's going to change color . . . he's going to be transformed . . . His face is going to become set, his eyes, which suddenly look like smooth, empty shells, are going to grow motionless, look elsewhere . . . but you mustn't run away, you must have the courage to stay there, stand right in front of him, bar his path . . . Now his eyes have that attentive, blank expression of a soldier when he looks at the man he has been ordered to shoot, backed up against the wall opposite him, when he shoulders arms, takes aim . . . Only a miracle . . . But something moved, wavered in those eyes, it's as though a soft friendly light had been lighted, the entire long, apelike face relaxes, wrinkles, a broad, friendly grin cleaves it in two . . . the miracle has taken place . . . the long, bony hand stretches forward . . . "Well, well, Guimiez . . . I didn't recognize you . . . What's become of you? We never see you. Maine was wondering the other day . . . She was going to telephone you . . ."

Everything is happening the way it does in dreams, but this is reality, there will be no awakening . . . All his gestures are leisurely, skillful, well performed, his strength has increased tenfold, the maddest, most extravagant deeds become quite simple and natural . . . "I'm glad to see you too, I was wondering if I shouldn't telephone . . . But perhaps you have a moment . . . How about sitting down for a little while? —Certainly. I'd be glad to. Yes, if you want, let's sit here . . . —Yes, here. Fine. It's very pleasant here . . ." Very pleasant, anywhere in heaven, between close friends, between old pals

. . . you meet unexpectedly, take in all the bistros, go to each other's rooms without warning, stretch out on the couch . . . Go on working, old boy . . . don't mind me, I'm going to read a bit . . . Not at all, I had finished . . . Ah, it's not going so well today . . . And you, what have you been up to? . . . By the way, shall we go to Maine's this evening? Who's going to be there? Oh, nothing. Nobody. A lot of tiresome people. Suppose we don't go? How about staying here for a good talk, what do you say? . . . Why not . . . let's not go . . . It's so nice here . . . Sated, full up, safely settled in a place to which access had seemed impossible, at the very heart, in the holy of holies . . . But there are no more holy of holies, no more sacred places, no more magic, no more mirages for the thirsty, no more unsatisfied desires . . . Ah, this is nice . . . Curled up in security, stretched out on the couch, knees in the air, legs crossed, waving one foot, chatting, smoking . . . Leaning towards each other across bistro tables . . . "Let's see, what is that? So it's out? The *New Era*? Is that the latest number?". . . Anything that comes to your mind . . . you can say whatever you want . . . no more tests, no more exams, here you're among peers, surrounded with confidence, respect, you can show yourself as you are, free, independent. . . strong-minded . . . Oh, Guimiez is priceless . . . Oh, he's marvelous, Guimiez . . . What originality, what temperament . . . "Yes, it's the *New Era* . . . But I'm disappointed. I don't like it . . . I was told by I forget whom, that it was interesting . . . quite new. Well, in my opinion, it's timid, obscure . . . 'would-be' new . . ."

On the good old pal's attentive face there's a faint something, like a smile immediately repressed, an expression of amused surprise has crept into his eyes, it's as though he were withdrawing a bit, the better to see, and then he changes the direction of his glance, lets it rest on the review, stretches out his long hand and seizes it avidly, in a gesture that is almost brutal . . . "Let's have a look, I haven't read it yet, let's see . . ." he leafs through it with impatient fingers, he starts to read, much absorbed, nodding approval here and there, then raising his head to stare in front of him at a distant object visible only to him, which his eyes, as though tightened up and grown sharply pointed underneath lids puckered with effort, would appear to be perforating . . . Finally, he turns his head, his rather cold glance expresses astonishment . . . "Well, see here, it's not so bad. No, indeed, you're wrong, it's not so bad as all that. I see there's something by Brissand which is not bad at all even . . . After all, you can't discover a Shakespeare or a Stendhal every month . . ." He looks attentively at the poor guileless creature, the ignoramus . . . where on earth does he come from? what a spoilt child he is . . . has he never had to struggle, this gentle dreamer far from reality, this provincial hardly aware of city customs, this great hulking peasant . . . "No, indeed, occasionally those fellows have some good ideas . . . Maine was very much interested in their movement at one time . . . And then she fell out with them, I forget why . . ."

So there. There's been a misdeal. It wasn't that. At least, not exactly that. But there's no need to get panicky. It was something else, that's all. Something very nice, too. Not that sort of "unbuttoned" comradeship, certainly. You don't sprawl on couches with your legs in the air, holding forth on whatever comes into your mind. But it's still very acceptable, very creditable. More than your wildest hopes. Only the chosen are allowed to enter. You're between pals, between companions, between friends. But order reigns here, discipline. You must have a sense of decorum. You have to think before you speak. There are subjects which are taboo, there are shared creeds. You don't attack just anybody that way without thinking, you don't indulge in idle talk. But this doesn't mean exclusion? certainly not, isn't that so? It's just a warning, a reprimand? . . .

"Oh, you know, what I say . . . I didn't read it very carefully . . . I realize that I always have a tendency to be too positive, too partial . . . —Of course . . . hearty, protective laughter . . . I assure you, you are wrong . . . Well, you'll see, you'll get over being so uncompromising . . . When you've been in the swim of things a certain time, like myself, you become more tolerant . . . —Yes, that I can believe, I understand . . . But you said a little while ago . . . But Germaine Lemaire . . . you said that she had fallen out . . . Is it true, what they say, that she's quick to fall out with people? . . . —Maine? Oh, as for that, I believe . . . Oh, she doesn't let herself be burdened with scruples. If a person bores her to death, she lets him drop. He sweeps the air with a broad, easy gesture of the hand. Everything that interferes with her, she sends packing. She overwhelms everything that crosses her path. Maine, she's a force of nature. Have you ever noticed her teeth? Big, powerful, there's nothing she couldn't crunch. Ha, ha, ha . . . The teeth of an ogress. An appetite for life . . . She devours everything. Insatiable. I always said that Maine was a type from another century, a Renaissance character: Queen Elizabeth of England . . . Cesare Borgia . . . She thinks she can do anything she pleases. She feels outside the common norm. Outside the petty moral rules that are made to fit little people . . ." For a second they contemplate silently this enormous effigy, this hugely proportioned statue. Overwhelming. Amazing. "Yes, Maine is tremendous . . . She can do things . . . his eyes moisten, a sort of bantering has crept into his tone . . . It's with other women, especially, that she can be terrible: and with what savagery, what contempt . . . In fact, she never invites them to anything. She hasn't a single woman friend. A few awestruck young women protégées of hers, who show her their manuscripts. But try to give high praise to another woman before her, even though it be to Mme. de Lafayette or to Emily Brontë . . . she becomes screamingly funny. Did you never watch her? She immediately has a frown, here, between the eyes, which become glazed, pale, transparent . . . I adore her when she gets like that . . . —Yes, that's true, so do I. At times, she has something impressive about her . . . Indeed, my admiration for her is . . . And has been for a long time. But she always frightened me a little, even from a distance, before I knew her . . . I had to screw up my courage the first time I wrote to her . . . This will seem idiotic to you, but since we're on the subject . . . You know her so much better than I do . . . I don't know whether things are going well between her and me just now. The last time I saw her, I was with my father . . . It was in a bookshop, we were looking for some book . . . My father's not always easy to get along with. He's a bit brusque at times, he can be very unsociable; actually, I believe he's rather shy. In any case, I had the impression . . . Did she, perhaps, say anything to you about it? . . . —Ah, no . . . She didn't say anything to me . . . But you know, I think you're imagining things . . . There's nothing to get upset about . . . When I say she lets people drop for mere trifles, it's a manner of speaking . . . I don't know what your father is like, but it would surprise me if he had displeased her in any way . . . You see Maine doesn't observe people very closely . . . Yes, it is surprising . . . I know nobody who is so often wrong as she is . . . No, she knows how much you admire her . . . And that's what matters above all else to her. She must have thought that your father was awed . . . You see, for Maine, people are mirrors. They are foils. In reality, she doesn't care a rap about people . . . What principally matters to her is herself, she alone . . ."

He seems to have become gentler, drawn closer, there's something intimate, almost fraternal in his tone . . . Is this a prudent probe? A discreet sign? An appeal? It will have to be answered, the temptation is great. Why not take the risk, try one's luck . . . "But if she's like that, as you say, so self-centered . . . isn't that, for a writer . . . ?" Here is a pledge. It's dangerous to give it without being entirely certain, but no matter, one shouldn't hesitate any longer. The suddenly recovered taste of freedom produces a burst of insanely rash words . . . "Quite frankly, isn't that a failing which can become rather serious . . . A real shortcoming . . ." Chin up. The enormous statue is going to fall from its pedestal with a great hollow noise, roll on the ground, break into pieces . . . There'll be no more statue . . . The prison gates will open . . . One must dare . . . for the sake of dignity, for the sake of truth . . . "Don't you think that it's because of that that there is, in her work . . . something . . ." The poor insane creature feels a horror-struck gaze leveled at his face: "What, for instance?" The alert has been given. The observation posts are searching the darkness. The hounds are yelping. There's a sound of hurried footsteps, of machine-guns rattling: "What have you to say against her, against her, too?" Nothing. It's over. Order has been restored. Back to your cages, back to your jails, back in rank. Nose to the wall. Who moved? No one. Beat drums: "She's a very great female, is Germaine Lemaire."

Isn't Mme. Germaine Lemaire our Madame Tussaud?" Like the leucocytes, like the antibodies that a healthy organism produces for its defense as soon as a harmful microbe has entered into it, ripples of laughter, of joking, had burst out . . . Did you see that, in today's *Literary Echoes*? It's incredible . . . on the first page, with a big heading . . . Just the same, they didn't dare to put it right on top, it's hidden, a bit shamefacedly . . . People may possess all sorts of courage, they are a tiny bit frightened just the same, isn't that true, when they give these little blows below the belt . . ." Coated with flattery, riddled with scoffing . . . "But who could have done that? —Why, you haven't seen it?—Maine is our Madame Tussaud! —It's not possible? Who did it? —That little Levalliant fellow, so aptly named . . . —The itch of failure is driving him wild . . . Did you read that last book of his? —Very clever little chap, he'll go far . . . he's trying to get out of the old grooves, he's right, to avoid the beaten tracks . . . it's the secret of success . . . Maine—our Madame Tussaud. That's marvelous. He deserves a good mark. I take off my hat to him, he'll go far. —Our Madame Tussaud . . . You're always our Madame something. Maine is our banner. Our great national figure, Germaine Lemaire. —A professor of literature at the University of Lyons, a remarkable fellow in fact, said that to me the other day: Germaine Lemaire consoles me for our disasters, Monsieur, she proves to me that we have lost nothing of our genius."

Swallowed, digested, entirely assimilated, destroyed, what still remained of it? . . . "Do you want me to deal with this little good-for-nothing for you, Maine? Shall I give a good kick to his lucubrations? Shall I silence this puling? It would be so easy . . . such fun . . ."

She had bowed her heavily crowned head in a curve traced by noble resignation, she had felt a delicate, pensive smile flit across her face: "No, don't bother, why? It's very useful, on the contrary, all that . . . things straighten themselves out . . . things must take their course . . ."

"Isn't Madame Germaine Lemaire our Madame Tussaud?" It's there, in what she has just written. In the same way that the end of a bit of horsehair sticks out of a smooth well-stuffed mattress, it sticks out from the firm, smooth, creaseless sentence, upon which she has rested a second, lulled by its harmony, its soothing cadence . . . It was from this that it shot forth and stung her: Madame Tussaud. And in that gesture, in this dialogue . . . One almost hears your characters speak . . . One sees them so clearly, they're so alive . . . but in that very appearance of resemblance . . . couldn't there be? . . . What's got in to her? . . . Why, that's where her genius lies, to be able to give such a vivid impression of reality; her supple, sinewy sentences encompass each thing with precaution, without bruising it, leaving intact all its prolongations, all that is in the background . . . they leave it its density, they respect its blanks, its shade-filled corners . . . Her ever-obedient style, when brought to the point of incandescence, can, if need be, slowly coerce a hard resistant matter, and again, it barely grazes—a breath, a quiver, the brush of a wing that skims over things without bending their soft down . . . "Really, I believe that I can now do almost anything I want with words"—she can dare to say that . . . But it's there. There, precisely, in this ease, this satisfaction, this joy: it's in this great perfection: Madame Tussaud.

But then, everything she loved, all the treasures that have always been entrusted to her keeping, to hers, that of the predestined child, and which she gathered, kept safe within herself with such great reverence, such great fervor . . . faces, gestures, words, shades of feeling, clouds, the color of the sky, trees and their leaves, their swaying tops, flowers, birds, flocks, the sand on beaches, the dust of roads, wheat fields, straw stacks in the sun, stones, the beds of brooks, the crest of hills in the distance, the undulating line of old roofs, houses, church towers, streets, cities, rivers, seas, all sounds, all shapes, all colors, contained this poison, gave forth this lethal perfume: Madame Tussaud.

It's a hallucination, a mirage caused by her fatigue, she's been overworking, she can't pull herself together, it will blow over . . . there, within reach of her hand, in the row of works that grows longer with the passing years, at the cost of what sacrifice, what effort . . . in this little book, her favorite, she's going to find the oft-quoted pages . . . she, herself, each time that she rereads them, is surprised . . . how was I able to do that? . . . they contain the incantation that will liberate her from this spell that has been cast over her, the amulet that will avert from her the evil eye . . .

How lifeless it is. Not a tremor. Nowhere. Not a hint of life. Nothing. Everything is congealed. Congealed. Congealed. Congealed. Congealed. Completely congealed. Frozen. A slightly shiny, waxlike coating covers it all. A thin layer of shiny varnish on cardboard. Masks of painted wax. Shiny wax. A thin varnish . . . It seems to her that someone from the outside, in a monotonous, insistent tone, continually repeating the same thing, the same simple words, the way a hypnotist does, is directing her sensations . . . She doesn't want . . . It's not true . . . It's not what she really feels . . . She feels that here is life . . . reality . . . and here already, it's forming, growing, is that familiar sensation of delight, of happiness . . . here is life, recaptured, it causes these fine, pure forms to vibrate gently . . . Yet no . . . nothing vibrates . . . Nothing . . . They are plaster casts. Copies. No sensation of happiness. Not the slightest sign of life. It was an illusion. It was autosuggestion. It's all empty. Hollow. Hollow. Hollow. Entirely hollow. Nothingness. The hollowness inside a painted wax mold.

It's all dead. Dead. Dead. Dead. A dead star. She's alone. No recourse. No relief from anyone. She's pursuing her way in solitude beset with terror. She's alone on an extinguished star. Life is elsewhere . . .

In the same way that a woman abandoned among the ruins of her bombed-out house, stares dazedly, amidst the rubble, at just anything, the most commonplace object, an old twisted fork, the battered old lid of a pewter coffeepot, picks it up without knowing why, and with a mechanical gesture, starts to rub it, she stares blankly, in the middle of the unfinished page, at a sentence, a word, in which something . . . just what is it? the tense of the verb is not right . . . no, that's not it . . . maybe this verb is not the right one . . . which one then? a word assumes faint form . . . she is straining . . . Her mind is like the motor of a car whose battery is dead and which, at the first turn of the crank, throbs, gives a start, begins to run again.

Gathering all her tensed strength, her gaze avid, straining, she is seeking . . . she has found. Just the right word. Made especially to measure. Extremely well-cut. Inserted there jauntily like the little bow of ribbon, the feather, that a milliner with genius knows how to stick on a hat, with a quick, offhand gesture, and which gives to everything she touches that inimitable air, that smart look, that style.

Her practiced eye inspects, ferrets about, nothing escapes

her. Her strength increases tenfold, deploys, she has a sensation, which she knows well, of perfect ease, of freedom. No obstacle can stop her. She's afraid of nothing. She's indifferent to scruples. She braves injunctions. She takes what suits her wherever she likes. Her powerful muscles lift lead. Like all good workmen she is able to use the most rudimentary, the crudest tools. The softest, most thankless matter becomes firm, dense, under her modeling. Anything goes down with her enormous, wolfish appetite.

How could she have allowed herself for a single instant to be afraid of those anemic creatures, with their frightened eyes and halting gestures? Their weak, extremely delicate stomachs can't stand good red meat, tasty pates made from the best, tested recipes. This food is too rich for them, it turns their stomachs.

They eat only insipid, sterilized, pasteurized, dietetic foods, which they prepare with infinite care and precaution—they are so afraid, they're obliged to deprive themselves of all that is good, healthy, invigorating. They'll end by letting themselves die of starvation. Their work is pale, drab, withered, shriveled, congealed. Not a breath of life in it. It's there that everything is dead. Dead, dead, dead . . .

There's a knock at the door: three light taps and the door opens slowly. Through the narrow opening, the long, familiar, slightly apelike head appears, the very deep-set little black eyes are beaming, the thick lips curl, stretch into a broad grin, showing all the teeth . . . "Now there, what did I tell you? . . . And there we were whispering, we were afraid to interrupt the lady's inspiration . . . Come on Maine, confess, you'll get an indulgence for it . . . You weren't doing anything . . . You weren't even thinking about anything . . . I saw you . . . Ah, such laziness . . . it's shameful . . . But do come now, at least . . .

We're all three of us here. Lucette and Jacques are here too. We've been waiting for you now for an hour. Lucette's wild . . ." It's irritating and, at the same time, agreeable, she likes to feel these little nibbles of their irritated gums, these little nicks that it amuses them to give her with their still rather soft nails . . . "Tss . . . Tss . . . she shakes her head in a scolding manner, while her fond glance brims with indulgence . . . Tss . . . Tss . . . Very well, I'll stop now, let's go . . . I've done enough for today. I'm coming. Let me straighten my papers and I'll be right with you . . ."

Their laughter, their idle jesting, their perfectly dosed familiarity, cleanse the air of heady scents. After all the effort, the excitement, the depression, the overheating, it's as refreshing as a bath that's just the right temperature, rather cool and mixed with astringent essences. She stretches, immerses herself . . . "My poor dears, what a day . . . I've a stiff wrist, I've a headache . . . I feel like going out, let's do something, whatever you want, go anywhere, but let's go out, I can't stand to stay shut up any longer . . . Lucette, think of something, instead of sitting there sulking . . . —But we can't go out, Maine, we're stuck . . . I'm furious, I've had enough . . . For two hours I've been here doing nothing, I'm dying of hunger . . . And the house is empty, I've looked everywhere, there's not so much as a crust of bread, and it's impossible to stick your nose out of doors, we're stuck, there are two men on watch downstairs . . . it's your fault, too, Maine, you should have given stricter orders . . . Now we're cornered, they've settled themselves across the street, in the bistro, and they've brought a camera with them . . . no matter how often the concierge tells them that you're not here, they won't give up, they're going to stay there all night . . . I've had enough. Enough."

Something filters from the childish anger that shakes this

curly doll's head, from the spoilt little girl's pout, from the obstinate, shallow expression . . . something which awakens that mixture of contempt and admiration felt by a father who, after humble beginnings, has worked hard all his life, surmounted all difficulties, suffered all affronts, for a fashionable son who knows how to spend his money with disdainful bounty . . .

But it's not only that . . . something else, which she doesn't perceive very clearly, emanates from this sulky off-handedness . . . something indefinable . . . a quality . . . which she had sensed in them from the first moment, because of which, but without putting it into words, of course, guided by her instinct, she had chosen them all and gathered them round her—people are amazed, at times, they can't understand—because of which, among all those who would have been so willing, who had many generally appreciated virtues, she had selected them, precisely these particular ones, apparently so unprepossessing that she has to force them on people (and that's not disagreeable, either, quite the contrary, this opportunity that they furnish her to prove to herself, and to flaunt before all the curious, envious eyes, her sovereign freedom, her power) . . . there's something in their capricious child's anger, in their exasperation, in their overfed, overstuffed disgust, which is necessary to her, indispensable . . . she couldn't get along without it . . . it produces upon her the same salutary, but imperfectly understood effects as are produced on the human organism by certain bacteria . . . It seems to her that everything coming from the outside—but it's never mentioned here, between them, by tacit agreement, out of a feeling of embarrassment, of delicacy, and indeed, how should they mention it?—that enormous stream, carrying along with it so many impurities, swollen with all the cupidity, all the nostalgias, the compromises, intrigues, envy, her abashed feeling even now, when she occasionally senses that others have noticed her anxious, angling look, the fluster which she never entirely succeeds in dominating before the slightest word of praise or disparagement, at the simple mention of her name, all that is stopped, filtered, through this rage, this sulky child's grimace: not a trace of it comes through, not the slightest bit, no, nothing but a perfectly decanted, distilled substance, it can be analyzed, not even an undeterminable trace remains of the vain satisfaction that fame gives, of the adulterated, petty joy that victory or revenge over her enemies might give her, no, indifference, perfect detachment, pure as the water from certain springs, like the light that is cast by a clear sky, radiant as the rays of the disk that God causes to shine about the heads of those, innocent in heart, whom he has chosen to spread his word, to sing his praises . . . She drops down, overcome, on to the couch . . . "Will this never end, are we never to have any peace . . . Damn it, how tiresome they can be . . . Jacques, dear, I beg of you, get us out of it, tell them they're wasting their time, tell them anything you want . . . that I've gone just anywhere, put them on a false scent . . ." But here, all at once, there has just crept into the tone in which she said this, and they have all noticed it, it has penetrated them without any one of them having wanted or dared to admit it to himself—or perhaps he does dare, but between them never a word, it's to hide this perhaps that they put on these airs of disgust—it had appeared . . . just a trace, a shadow, like the shadow of the fine hair on the end of a little demon's ears: a secret satisfaction . . .

It has entered into him and is growing in him—the contentment of being here, all shut up in the ark, all banded together, united, all those who deserved to be gathered together, saved, while against the watertight hull of the precious vessel, there break the constantly rising waters of envy, of curiosity, he is filled with it, and they all know it, it circulates through his entire body, in his bearing, his manner, in each of his movements, like the blood that flows into the tiniest artery, as, rising to the heights that his role demands of him, he opens the door and says: "Yes, I'll go and speak to them, I'll try to get them to leave . . . Yes, right away. I'll go down."

"Meanwhile, René's going to tell you something funny. He made us laugh so hard, a little while ago. Go on, René, tell her . . . —No, really, I don't see why that amused them so much, there's nothing to get excited about. I told it to them to pass the time. It's simply that I met Guimiez the other day . . . She feels herself retracting a bit, hardening . . . —Indeed, and what's he been doing? . . . something which she does her best to overcome creeps into the tone of her voice . . . What's he up to? —Well, it just happened that the other day he spoke to me . . . I was buying a newspaper . . . He had an odd look about him, he was all upset, quite pale . . . He asked me to have a drink with him . . . I felt that it was to tell me something in particular . . . And I was right. We hadn't been seated five minutes when he began to talk to me about you . . . He told me he had met you . . . in a bookshop, I believe . . . with his father . . . that it hadn't gone well . . . that you hadn't liked his father . . . I didn't understand very well why . . ."

"Our future Sainte-Beuve . . ." that ironic smile, the scoffing light that glimmered in the narrow eyes . . . But she is inured, she's been hardened for a long time now . . . she feels no more repugnance than a doctor examining a wound, when the stench of their rancor, of their envy, reaches her nostrils, when she is besmirched by their spurts of familiarity, their humility, their insolence, the need they have of revenging themselves at little cost—they're so ungifted, so commonplace, so lazy . . .

Only this time what issued from the narrow eyes, what could be detected in the mocking tone, had traversed, shattered, the thick shell of indifference, of slightly pitying disdain behind which she feels protected and from the vantage point of which, ordinarily, she can enjoy herself watching them, in perfect safety. She had suddenly felt herself exposed, blushing, trembling before this gaze from which there poured onto her, covering her, the cold spite, the contempt, of a man who has been pampered, gratified, for many years, with grace, youth and beauty, the distaste of a fastidious connoisseur for a woman . . . but she didn't look like a woman, she was a shapeless, unnamable something, a frightful monster, hair all disheveled, a few forlorn locks, she was aware of them, hanging down in back, she hadn't dared lift her hand to push them up under her hat, she had felt flabby, gray, greasy, as though she needed washing . . . that pitiless glance had run to earth in her a failing, the most serious of all, a crime, a sacrilege . . . a terrible sentence threatened her, she had tried to defend herself with the means at her disposal, but the struggle was an unequal one, the man had won, she had fled, wounded . . . And the other one, beside him, the man-cub, with that look of a young animal whose father had trained him to lie in wait, to choose his prey, seeing it all, he too. She had hated them . . .

"Now Maine, don't make such a disgusted face . . . I assure you, that lad is very attached to you, he admires you, he adores you. He praises you to the skies . . . He appeared to be sick over it, he made me feel sorry for him. I should have brought him to see you, if I had dared . . . I consoled him as best I could . . ."

So it was not that, it was nothing—her imagination, a nightmare, and it has vanished. The familiar, reassuring, soothing world is there, surrounding her once more. A delightful feeling of relief, of release, bursts from her in a rippling stream

. . . "Not at all, what's got into the boy, I didn't think anything at all. I can't say that I found his father exciting . . . but more than anything else, I had no time, I was in a hurry . . . People imagine that you can always be at their beck and call, they're really funny . . ."

But another time she'll have to be careful. She must watch herself. Try to understand. Each time she must make the effort to tilt over towards them. And from there, from their side, see herself: each gesture she makes projecting in them gigantic shadows, her most insignificant utterances reverberating deep down inside them. Their frailty and her own strength are so great—this should never be forgotten, she must take every possible precaution: a single thoughtless movement, however slight, can shatter them . . . A single movement on her part. . .

She has that strange sensation, which comes over her at times, which she has experienced already, as a child, the impression of losing her ordinary sense of dimensions, of proportions, and of growing huge—a giant in seven-league boots which allow him to walk over rivers, bridges, houses—she can lift up this insignificant existence . . . deviate the course of a fate, transform utter wretchedness into supreme joy . . . she is stirred by generous excitement . . . "Oh, I have an idea . . . why don't we all go to his house this evening? —Whose house? —Why, Alain Guimiez's . . . Let's do, it will be fun . . . Why no, just like that, quite simply . . . It will be very amusing to drop in on him suddenly . . . Jacques dear, do you know what we're going to do? —Maine's mad . . . —Not at all, you'll see . . . They've gone? Are we free? . . . So let's call him up . . . Quick . . . You do it, René . . . I'll give you the number . . . Tell him that we are in his neighborhood, that we're going to stop by his house after dinner, just for a moment. . . Come on, don't look so flabbergasted . . . be a sport . . ."

It's too much at one time, he didn't ask for all that, it's too abrupt, too sudden, he would have needed to prepare himself a bit—just a few seconds of composure—but the enormous tidal wave knocked him over, he's rolling about, blinded, deafened, trying to regain a foothold, he shakes hands somewhat at random, he doesn't catch their names . . . "Good evening . . . delighted . . . Good evening . . . Why, not at all, come in . . . No, you're not disturbing me . . . Certainly not, what an idea, you know quite well that I am very glad . . ." His smile is edgy, constrained, he feels this, his voice is badly pitched . . . he offers them seats, clumsily displaces an easy chair, he all but knocks over a small center table which, calmly, skillfully, they catch just in time, set straight again, all his gestures are jerky, awkward, his eyes must have a feverish light in them . . . "Just now, when you telephoned . . ." they must have been amused, they surely spoke about it, it was so ludicrous . . . "I didn't understand, I didn't quite take in . . ." it's best to tell them the whole thing, show them . . . "it was a surprise, I was so far from expecting it, I mistook you for an old pal of mine . . ." They know, they've seen it all; his amazement, his humility, not believing his ears . . . "Who? Germaine Lemaire? Oh, listen here . . . that doesn't take with me . . . Why not the Pope?" Did he say that? . . . Yes, he said it, he hears his own idiotic laughter: "Come on, old boy, drop it, don't try so hard . . . Why not the Pope?" and the surprised tone of the dry voice at the other end of the wire . . . "Hello . . . Can you hear me? Is this Alain Guimiez?"

Yes, show them everything, it's better so, they will perhaps feel pity, be a little embarrassed to see it exhibited, they'll turn their eyes away, they themselves will try to hide it, to forget it . . . that's the only way to foil this cruel trick that a facetious fate has played on him . . . these are tricks that it plays only on him, this is not the first time, something similar, already . . . but where? when did it happen? he doesn't remember, it's not the moment to try . . . he must present them immediately with all the relevant evidence, explain it all to them, confess: I was so surprised I seemed to recognize the voice of a friend . . . go all the way: I thought he was playing a trick on me, it's quite like him, I've often spoken to him about you . . . Why hesitate, since they know everything . . . Now it's a matter of limiting the damage, of saving what can still be saved, he'd better hurry, quick, undress and leave in their hands this old rag, this grotesque clown's costume he's got up in, they can do with it what they want—it's an old skin which he has sloughed off, like them, he's going to hold it up with the tips of his fingers, examine it in a disgusted, pitying manner . . .

But he can't do it, he hasn't the nerve. Impossible to run this risk, to trust them, he'll be apprehended, snatched up entirely by them, he, his rags, his nakedness, they have no mercy, no pity, they've proved this to him each time he has tried to rely on them . . . it's better to speculate on their absentmindedness, their inadvertence, conceal, hide everything he can, they have perhaps noticed nothing, understood nothing, it may have rolled off them, it has perhaps already faded out, they are so ignorant of such things as these, that are so remote from them—people accustomed to life in the open, who can't understand that he should be suffocated, upset, the way a child whose constitution has always been accustomed to the shut-in atmosphere of a dark tenement cannot stand the out-of-doors, the light of the sun . . .

It would have been better for him if he had remained locked in, steeping in the lukewarm, slightly nauseous liquid of his loneliness, his forlornness . . . It was so he would not have to leave it that he had played that mean trick on himself: the outside air frightened him . . . "Why not the Pope?" He said that to try to ward them off, he realizes now, it was surely to make them flee that he had said it: "Oh, drop it . . . Why not the Pope?" in that waggish tone . . . But he hadn't put them off, he had got them rather a little more excited, they made haste, they came running, they're settling down everywhere, sniffing . . . their eager, sly looks are creeping about, worming their way in . . . they are like dogs that smell in every corner to discover the prey they're going to carry away between their teeth and which, in a little while, they will lay, all warm and quivering, at the feet of their mistress . . . she will lean over . . . approving little pat, caressing glance . . . "Ah, when was that? where? How funny . . . I didn't notice . . ." greedy-eyed, she will relish in advance the tasty meal to be devoured later once she's comfortably settled at home with them under the table . . .

She lays her hand on the desk . . . "Is this what you work on? —Yes, it's there, nearly always. —Ah, you prefer that, to have your back to the window, and sit facing the wall?" She looks at him attentively, and this flatters him, she must sense it, she does it on purpose, looking at him in this attentive way, filled with regard, she doesn't like to do things halfway: if you do things, isn't it so? they should be done well . . . it's so delightful to be able to burst in upon one of these confined little existences and throw it into confusion, transform it all of a sudden, for a long time to come . . . He would like to turn away, frown, but the words she has just spoken, the sound of these words—like the famous tinkle of the little bell that induces salivation in Pavlov's dogs—makes his eyes beam, stretches his lips into a flattered smile, he opens his mouth, hesitates a second . . . "Yes, I like it better, to work with my face to the wall . . . it's more . . ." He suddenly has a sensation of walking on something that is swinging under his feet, it's like a narrow footbridge thrown across a raging torrent, and upon which, while all the others grouped on the opposite bank, stop talking, watch him, he is advancing. One false move and he'll fall. He feels about cautiously with his foot . . . "Yes, my back to the window—it's more convenient . . ." Fine. That was just the right move; "Convenient" was well chosen, just modest enough, a bit negligent . . . Really, he's doing very well. They all take heart again . . . "It's more convenient . . . for concentrating . . ." Watch out, there, danger ahead, a too forceful, too sudden, clumsy movement is causing him to bear down a bit too heavily, tip over a little too much to one side . . . they're all watching him, amused, he tries to advance one step more, but he sways, he's going to fall . . . it can't be helped, let them make fun of him, let them laugh, but there's no other way to do it . . . "Oh, you know, for me . . . he stoops down, bends over . . . it's very hard you know, for me, to concentrate my thoughts . . . he kneels down . . . Everything distracts my attention, the slightest thing suffices . . . I don't know whether you too . . . But I . . ." towards them, nearer, they should help him, on all fours, it's so pitiable, he's crawling . . . She tilts her head to one side, smiles at him . . . "Yes, I too, I was like you: a bare wall in front of me—that was all . . . They watch him while she helps him land near them on the other bank, pick himself up, suddenly grow calm, confident, he stands up, looks at her delightedly . . . "Ah, you too, you had to have that?"

A current passes from them to him, he feels their benevolent gaze upon him, he nods towards them, he waves his arms . . . "Come over here . . . you're not comfortable there, come sit nearer the fire, here, you'll be more comfortable . . ." They settle down with a satisfied air, they look about them . . . good-nature, congeniality, flow from their eyes . . . "By Jove, that's very nice, that's a lovely piece you have there, that Louis XV *bergère*, it's really quite beautiful. . . —I had understood you to be talking about some awful leather easy chairs . . . —Yes, I was, but they just happened to be connected with this *bergère*. The easy chairs . . . you see . . ." Let them know it . . . they can know everything, see everything, he'll hide nothing from them, everything that's his belongs to them, aren't they his comrades, his friends, he's ready to share everything with them, to pool everything . . . "you see, I had told Germaine Lemaire that my family was determined to force two unspeakable easy chairs on me . . . You know . . . the English club chair type . . . it was a long story . . ."

But it's still so narrow, the opening between them and him, the door they're holding ajar, how can he get all that in through there, all that enormous, heavy, cumbersome pile, he doesn't know how to undertake it, where to start . . . again he feels them watching his clumsy movements with a sort of pitying amazement, while he pushes and drags as best he can . . . "Families, you know what they're like . . . their tastes, the things they try their best to foist upon you . . ." But it can't be done, it's stuck somewhere, it's jammed, it won't go through . . . he makes a gesture of helplessness, of resignation, and she looks at him, she seems almost shocked . . . "What's the matter with him? What's he after, anyway? For whom is he making these efforts? Not for them, after all, that would be ridiculous, they don't need all of that. They're not so spoilt. A few crumbs from the table at which she, their mistress, is seated with him, her guest, would have satisfied them quite well . . . Why is he wasting his time like that? She stops him with a little impatient gesture of the hand, turns away from them, thrusts them aside, she leans towards him . . . "Tell me, rather . . . what did you do? . . ."

"No, why don't you let him continue his story? Do, Maine, let him, I want him to tell us . . . Why did he refuse them, the easy chairs? I should have preferred them, nice leather armchairs, they're better than all these old *bergères*. You can sink down, ploof, the way you do at the movies . . . you can even go to sleep . . ." The thick, rather flabby lips pucker into a spoilt child's sulky pout, the large curly head wags with an air of capricious obstinacy . . . "Leather easy chairs—I think they're much nicer, don't you?"

Ploof! all at once everything is upset. A chess-player who, in the midst of a close game is obliged to look on while his host's little girl knocks over all the chessmen with one teasing blow of her little fist on the board, would make the grimace that he feels appear on his face now, would wear this same tense smile, torn between a desire to see the mother administer a good licking, or himself wring the infernal brat's neck, and that of putting an end to the stream of brokenhearted embarrassment that flows from the mother, he's fairly doused with it, he would like to wipe it off . . . Why no, not at all . . . No, indeed, it's nothing, poor child, she doesn't realize . . . don't scold her . . . it doesn't matter . . . don't mention it, forget it . . . But he senses that there's something else as well on his face, something anxious and slightly obsequious, which recalls the expression affected by the devoted retainers in old-time plays, when their heedless, fashionable young masters spoke vulgarly, or used coarse, indecent language in their presence: the much embarrassed lackey—this meant a real convulsion, a real upheaval in his well-regulated world, which was orderly, tidy, polished—the faithful servant smiled . . . tickled in spite of himself, how could one resist . . . that's what happens when our masters, even in fun, lower themselves, let down their barriers . . . and a note of obsequiousness crept into his smile, to hide his discomfort, his bewilderment, to obtain forgiveness for his familiarity . . . our young master is certainly witty . . . oh, what things he can say, but he's surely fooling, His Grace is joking . . . His Grace is having fun . . . "Club chairs, like those in movie houses, you're not talking seriously? . . ." It's certain, it's perfectly obvious, they all saw quite clearly that outraged, scandalized look, the tense, anxious, obsequious smile . . . she frowns, gives a disapproving nod, how provoking they are, really, they're impossible . . . she tries to call them to order . . . "Do be quiet . . . Please don't listen to them, they say just anything at all. Lucette would certainly not like to have movie-seats in her house either. Of course not, Lucette, why do you say that?" She turns a severe look upon the enfant terrible: will you be quiet, you don't come out with such things as that before these people, those are jokes we indulge in among ourselves . . . but not before him, what can you expect, the poor boy, that shocks him terribly, he doesn't understand . . . "Lucette is ridiculous, don't listen to her."

But they are hard to keep in hand, they begin to fidget, grow impatient, inattentive, they're lounging about, their eyes are sliding, rolling, sprawling over the prints on the wall, over the awful wallpaper . . . "Oh that, that's nothing, don't look at it . . . Yes, it was a present . . . it's ugly, isn't it? . . . But how can you refuse?" With a disdainful gesture, they turn a few pages of a book lying on the table . . . "So you're reading that . . . do you like it? . . ." Something is beginning to accumulate, something that resembles a very thick vapor . . . a single word on his part, he feels it, a single gesture, the one he should make, but he doesn't dare, a single move towards the sideboard . . . you must have something to drink, what am I thinking about . . . and right away, as when a cold object is introduced into an atmosphere saturated with humidity in which the steam is about to condense, drops are going to form . . . Oh, no, not for me, in any case, it's too late . . . they're going to run, come streaming down . . . it's late, we can't, we ought to leave, we must leave . . .

But that noise, that long, uninterrupted throb, growing increasingly louder . . . it's the elevator coming up, now it's passing the first floor . . . in a few seconds, they'll hear the click of the iron gate, a key being slipped into the lock . . . the door will open and she will come in, stop on the threshold, dumbfounded, a statue . . . if he could only run to meet her halfway, warn her, prepare her . . . but take care, they're watching him, they're wondering what's got into him all of a sudden . . . Why nothing, absolutely nothing, he turns his head like someone whose ear is cocked, he holds up one finger: "I hear the elevator, that must be my wife coming home . . . she's going to get a surprise, she'll be glad . . ." She's going to look at them wide-eyed, mouth agape . . . Her coat with the big checks . . . but it was exactly for that reason that she had chosen it, there was no dissuading her, it was that naive, unsophisticated look she had liked, and in fact, if you looked at it from a certain angle . . . But a few drops, let fall by their glance, by that sort of reagent which they have within themselves, will bring out immediately the slightly embarrassing, slightly vulgar aspects of the big showy design, of the coarsely woven cloth, of the gesture she's going to make to smooth her hair, an uneasy, timid, abashed gesture . . . he always feels like stopping her . . . but that kind of thing . . . even with the persons closest to us, we don't dare . . . He's going to feel her stuck, welded to him like a Siamese twin, he's going to double in size, form with her and spread before their view an enormous, heavy mass whose movements he will be unable to direct, in which they will be able to plant their gaze, their sting . . . but the throb continues, the elevator has passed their floor, it mounts still higher, goes on its way . . . What a relief, what security . . . He's alone again, slender, light, free of movement, alive and supple, he can escape, dodge . . . But they're beginning to fidget, they look at one another . . . "Well, I believe that we . . . it's quite late . . . I've got to be going . . . yes . . . I think we must . . . we just dropped in, some other time . . ." It was that movement of distraction on his part, that brief absence, that uneasy silence—this time, that was what had brought the atmosphere, which was saturated with the vapors of boredom, of being at loose ends, of irritation, of disappointment, of a feeling of emptiness, of inanity, of a complete mess, to its point of condensation . . . the drops sprinkle him . . . he rises too, a bit quickly, perhaps, he's in a hurry, he too, for it to end, he prefers that, he's worn out, they should go, he draws himself up—did they notice it?—with an air of relief.

But as it happens, they didn't notice anything . . . It is not the overflow of happiness brought on by approaching release that causes this torrent of friendliness to well up in their faces and pour generously over him . . . he can't be mistaken, he feels it, come, come, one must dare to let oneself go a bit, give in to this sensation, why believe that they are so narrow-minded, so insensitive, people are more perspicacious, more clear-sighted than we think, they have been able to see what there is in him, way down deep, underneath the thick layers of his bungling, of his pretending they have seen, they know, what he really is, they are surrounding him, they shake his hand, the esteem they feel for him wells up towards him, from the look they plunge deep into his eyes . . . "We must get together again soon, and for a longer time . . . You call me . . . No, you call . . . Whenever you want. —Fine. Yes. And you'll come again? Only, it's so small here, it's rather tight quarters but perhaps we're going to move . . . it will be bigger, quite differently furnished . . . —Ah, so you did it, your aunt gave in? . . . —How charming! you haven't forgotten . . . No, my aunt has not agreed, not yet, but it may go through, there's hope. —So much the better, you must go after it, not be afraid . . . Remember: the conquistadors." Her hand resting on the stair rail, she turns her head towards him, she bestows upon him, one last time, her friendly, almost tender face . . . "I'll help you furnish it, I adore that. We'll go to the Flea Market . . . Yes, I do too, that's my passion, how we understand each other . . ."

THE THREAT IS growing, there's been a succession of disquieting signs . . . In the dust of one of the footpaths leading to the ranch unfamiliar tracks of big bare feet have been seen. The faithful dog was found stretched out in the middle of the courtyard, his eyes glazed and a trickle of blood running from his half-open mouth . . . And then, nothing more. A ponderous calm. People continue to go through their everyday motions, as though nothing has happened. No one speaks, they are all hiding their fear. One evening, a servant disappears . . . A few days later, in a clearing not far from the house, his barely recognizable body, mutilated, scalped, pierced through with enormous, multicolored arrows, is found tied to a tree . . . And once more, the torpid, false tranquility in which anguish ripens. People move about with effort, as though the air, grown thicker, soaked with terror, impeded their movements. Little by little, in the woods surrounding the house, may be heard the sound of rustling, of crackling, through the thicket, one seems to see dark, nude bodies moving, painted faces, gold bracelets gleaming, cruel eyes spying.

She doesn't recall which Indian stories, read long ago, when she was a child, have left in her—the way water cuts a groove in tender limestone—a bed, a furrow, that has remained, empty for a long time. Between its banks, following their contours, wed to their form, flows what she has been sensing for some time now . . . the same old fright, her childhood fright, when the first threatening sign appeared, when suddenly she saw, under the reassuring, familiar aspect of her little brother, of her good old Pierrot, with his mischievous eyes, his shrewd glance, his nice, slightly timid, slightly childish smile, you're the image of Papa when you smile like that . . . when she recognized the enemy, a messenger sent as a scout by the enemy to look over the ground, prepare the attack . . . "Well, Berthe dear . . . I wanted to speak to you . . . It's about this apartment . . ." Something a bit crafty has appeared in the line of his mouth, has crept into the receding contour of his chin . . . "Pierre is deep," the old English woman who gave them lessons had said that about him to a friend when he was only five or six years old, their grandmother, who hated priests, had nicknamed him "the shaveling" . . . his voice was hollow, a little hoarse . . . "You know me, Berthe dear, you know quite well that I hate to do it, but after all, it's your fault too, you never should have . . . I know . . . I'm like you, too weak . . . Stupid . . . I always let myself be taken in . . . Of course you're right . . . We understand each other. I'm going to tell them you don't want to . . . And above all, Berthe dear, don't worry, there's no sense in it . . . Oh, Alain is terrible when he gets started, you know him . . . There's nothing you can do, he has things about him that are not from our side of the family, they come from the other side, you know, from the Delarues . . . that savage egoism, sometimes . . . With me too, if you knew . . ." She looked at the too delicate skin of his slightly bloated hands, his fingers, which he had difficulty in bending, awkwardly holding the slender handle of the tea-cup, the heavy folds of his neck which had grown thicker, his slightly threadbare suit, his badly ironed collar . . . the traitor, the enemy, had vanished . . . She saw seated opposite her an old man, lonely like herself, neglected, her brother, her good old Pierrot . . . She felt sad when they separated and he, too, seemed moved when he kissed her goodbye, when he patted her cheek in the entrance-hall, when he looked at her, his heavy hand resting on the door-latch . . . "Well, I'll be going . . . and above all, don't worry, Berthe dear . . . I'm going to tell those little rascals, they'll understand . . . I'll see you soon . . . I'll come again. And this time it won't be to bother you. It's idiotic, time is going by, it's true, you're right, there's not so much left . . ." She felt like coddling him the way she used to do, hugging up close to him.

But as soon as she was left alone, the image which, for a moment, had been erased, reappeared, the kind, very affectionate brother was again metamorphosed: he was hurrying, surely . . . Before he had reached the street door, all trace of her emotion of a few moments earlier had disappeared—the furrow left in us by reactions of this sort often vanishes very quickly, as soon as we're alone again—he was rushing over there to tell them, he's so volatile, so vacillating, sways with every wind . . . They were waiting for him, impatiently . . . So what did she say, Aunt Berthe? —Well, children, there's nothing doing. She didn't go along. I warned you, I was certain. I know her pretty well, believe me. Cranky. Egoistic. Her things, you know . . . Her comfort. The entire world can perish . . . The story of the bicycle she wouldn't lend, the candy she hid away. That must have been included, he hadn't failed to tell them all that . . .

At enemy headquarters, they listen attentively to this report, weigh all the arguments presented, make calculations, draw up plans . . .

And then, in that false quietude, that ponderous silence, again this sign, this sheet of paper she has just found, twice folded, slipped under her door while she was out. Each word written in his good, firm, clear handwriting gives notice that danger is about to return . . . Another, more forceful attack has been launched . . . "Dear Aunt Berthe, what a shame not to have found you in . . . I wanted to speak to you . . . I'll come back tomorrow. Lots of love and kisses. Your crazy Alain." Pitiless, obstinate, cunning, smooth-tongued, winning, asking forgiveness ahead of time for what no force on earth will be able to stop him from doing: your crazy Alain . . . that avid light he used to have in his eyes, when he managed, and she, the idiot, thought it was touching, he was so funny, ah, the cute little scamp, to lead her—what a playactor—to the merry-go-round, the toyshop . . . the light that shone in his eyes, that day, at their place, when she had committed that piece of folly . . . what had come over her? she herself had been amazed, at the time . . . what demon had egged her on? what morbid impulse . . . not at all . . . what will she imagine next? she had just wanted—they provoke this need in her—to tease them a bit . . . She had had a feeling of tenderness for them, they were so young, so touching, they were so affectionate, seeing to it that she was comfortable, showing her things . . . it was so small, their place . . . she had had a generous impulse . . . she had yielded to the inclination that takes hold of her at times to play the fairy godmother . . . to the desire which, even now, at her age, seizes her occasionally, to scatter everything to the winds, to be released, free, for a moment she had felt light, rejuvenated . . . why not, after all. . . "Not at all, children, it's not mad . . . I do . . . I do . . ." She had taken the game seriously . . . they couldn't get over it . . . But she's afraid, suddenly something makes her very frightened . . . a look exchanged between them . . . no, they hadn't exchanged a single look . . . they were very decent, filled with solicitude . . . it's something rather, that was too quick, too immediate in that surprised manner of theirs, in their delight . . . as though everything had been ready inside them for a long time . . . the words she had spoken fell like a fruit they had watched ripen . . . They were calculating . . . waiting . . . watching her . . . cruel eyes concealed all round her were spying on her

. . . ominous rustlings, whispers . . . five rooms for her alone . . . a useless old woman . . . shut up there all alone . . . never entertains, never . . . for her alone . . . If that isn't a shame, if that isn't disgraceful, and here are these young people, her own nephew, her only heir . . . the canny smile that the old lady in the black picture-hat had worn, on the very day of the wedding, her shrill, thin voice . . . "And where are they going to live, this young couple? Not with you? Ah, I thought . . . I was told it was so spacious . . ." She had drawn herself up, bristling, immediately furious: "With me? I don't know who could have told you that. . . what sort of an idea is that . . . at their age, I was living in a garret, a tenement . . . and I didn't complain, it meant independence, it meant happiness . . . But these days . . . she feels like shouting . . . I'm entitled to be left alone, I've got a right to live in peace . . ." The old lady had acquiesced with a smile of bogus understanding, bogus good humor . . . "Of course . . . I should say you have!" But there's nothing you can do about it. . . They're stubborn . . . Their vice is going to tighten . . .

There's the doorbell. What is it? Who is it? What's that? What's it about? Why it's the door. Which door? Why, the door she ordered, the door she had had taken back to be repaired . . . it had been spoiled, there were holes, marks, but they don't show any more, it has all been fixed, they've planed it, sand-papered it, polished it . . . they've brought it back. It's there on the landing. They should go now, they should leave her alone . . . this is really not the moment, she feels like driving them away. But there they are, impassible, inexorable, the blind tools of a mocking fate. They lift the door by holding it between their widely stretched arms, they turn it, to make it go in . . . the mechanism has been set in motion, it's working, there's nothing to be done about it, she herself set it going, there's no way now to stop it, she acquiesces, she nods yes . . . oh, very well . . . oh, yes . . . she clears the way for them, draws aside everything that might be in their way, the tables, the chairs, she guides them . . . come this way, it's more convenient . . . they speak a few brief words under their breath . . . Watch out . . . easy now . . . a little lower . . . No, not there . . . you'll knock it . . . There now, go ahead, there, that's right, you've got it . . . their gestures are very prudent, they advance by setting their feet down gently on the polished floor . . . They remind you of pallbearers carrying respectfully, cautiously, a heavy, solid oak coffin. With one movement, they slowly lift the door up then lower it, letting the hooks slip on to the hinges. They try the handle. They step back a bit, look at the door with satisfaction: "There now, I think, this time, it will be all right." But the solid oak door has a piteous look surrounded by these thin, too light-colored walls . . . It looks like the pretentious imaginings of an incompetent decorator . . . She feels trembling inside her, very much weakened, the last ebbing of forgotten emotions, a slight disquiet, a weak, barely alive exasperation . . . But what is she thinking about? What does anything mean to her? Everything is done for, in any case. She has nothing more to lose. She can look reality in the face . . . she feels a taste of bitterness in her mouth . . . "I must say, I think it's awful. In this setting . . . With these glass doors . . . It would have been better to leave the old door . . ." But what has got into her head? She's like that old cousin of theirs who was choosing her last resting-place in the cemetery: I believe I like this one best, it has a nicer view . . . it's still a family joke, a gem which the heirs hand down to one another . . . But why laugh? It's so hard to leap suddenly outside one's familiar world and measure up to certain events. She has forgotten . . . What was I thinking about? . . . "Oh, it doesn't matter. Unimportant. It's quite all right like that. Yes it is, I assure you. Thank you. You are perhaps right. This is perhaps one of my bad days. And then, what's done is done, isn't that so, we're not going to begin to change everything again, there would be no reason to stop, ever . . ." Her voice is faint, as though deflated, it's perhaps what people mean by a toneless voice . . . she turns towards them an impassive expression, she is smiling at them . . . she feels that she is like a woman threatened by a ruffian hidden behind a curtain, who makes an effort not to show anything, answers the telephone, talks to a visitor who, having dropped in to see her for a few moments, is about to leave, unaware of the danger. Divided like this, with part of herself turned towards the invisible enemy, she accompanies them to the door. Her voice seems to be calm: "So then, the only thing that remains to be done will be to put up the curtain rod . . ." But she can contain herself no longer, if they would only go, quickly . . . "That doesn't matter, it will be swept up, do leave it the way it is, it's quite all right like that. Very well. Thank you." They should leave her alone—they can do nothing for her—face to face with the enemy.

She's done for. Impossible to struggle. They've got her in their power, she's going to give in . . . When she had her attack, as she lay there suffocating, a submissive, guilty, grateful look raised towards the face leaning over her . . . "You were lucky, believe me, that I should have heard you call . . . Because you've got such a big place . . . Nobody can hear a thing . . . Fortunately, I was on the stairs . . . Aren't you afraid? . . . Because at our age . . . you shouldn't live here alone any longer . . . Ah, such is life, you know when you're no longer so young . . . She had struggled: "Me? You must be joking, I'd rather die . . . you don't know me . . . I've got to have my quiet . . ." That satisfied, idiotic smile of theirs, their self-assured, implacable, exasperating manner, the look of destiny, of fatality itself . . . "Yes, yes, we say that, but one day you'll come to it, you won't have the energy to keep all that for yourself . . . it requires too much care, you should have something smaller . . . You'll turn it over to your nephew . . . they need space, young people do, and you'll be so glad to do something for them, to watch little children growing up about you . . ." She had felt like biting, why on earth don't they let go of her, in her fear, in her rage, in her weakness, she had given them clumsy blows which had hurt her—hideous old woman with her unkempt gray hair hanging about her over-red face, making ludicrous gestures, skinny old witch with her dried up entrails . . . "I'll never do it, you don't know me . . . I say we have only one life to live, I've never asked for anything . . . all I want is for people to leave me damned well in peace . . ." losing face, forgetting all sense of propriety, all dignity. They smiled and wagged their big, flabby fingers: her powerless rage, her awkward squirmings amused them no end . . . "You'll do it one day, of your own accord, come, come, you'll see . . ." Loathsome pressure . . .

She stiffens, pulls herself together . . . Well, they'll see. Let them try. No more shouting, no more fidgeting. Motionless, sunk into herself, heavy, calm, she waits for them like an aged wild boar when it turns and sits facing the pack.

WATCH OUT, YOU loon, what's got into him, watch out, he's going to knock everything over, he's going to hurt me, he's going to muss my hair, she draws aside, pushes him lightly from her, the way she used to do, when he was a child, when he would come rushing in like that, when he dashed towards her and kissed her so hard, but he can contain himself no longer, he feels like hugging her, like lifting her up and swinging her around with him, come on, Aunt Berthe, let's rejoice together, let's be happy . . . "We've got the most unheard-of luck . . . It's extraordinary, what has happened . . . A real miracle. An amazing coincidence . . . We can arrange an exchange with the man who lives next to the Brétés. Right on the same floor . . . He is leaving Paris . . . He wants a small *pied-à-terre* in our neighborhood . . . And his place is really marvelous. A real find. Two large light rooms on the first floor, giving on to a big courtyard with a tree . . . a linden tree . . . It's in perfect condition . . . In a lovely old house . . . There are some big closets . . . A storeroom that could be made into a bathroom . . . For us, obviously, it's too small . . . In a short time, we should have to start all over again . . . But for you, Aunt Berthe, we thought . . . You absolutely must see it."

She remains silent. She's in one of her grumpy moods, her face is heavy, set, her eyes have an inscrutable, obstinate expression. But one should not be discouraged. He leans towards her, lays his hand on her hand, which is clutching the arm of the chair, he feels that he has all the patience of a good schoolmaster who is trying to explain a problem to a recalcitrant, not very gifted child, come now, let's keep trying, we'll get it, let's try starting all over again somewhat differently: "Listen to me, Aunt Berthe. Let's talk seriously. This is a unique opportunity. It will never occur again. It would be absurd for you to refuse. Remember when you had those suffocation spells . . . The Brétés . . . You know how nice they are . . . they'll be right near you, on the same floor. Here you live in two rooms, the three others are of no use to you, you say yourself that you never set foot in them. It's for you, what I'm saying. For us, of course, you know what it would mean. But for you too, Aunt Berthe, believe me. Sooner or later, you'll be obliged to make a change . . ."

She says nothing. She keeps her eyes leveled on him.

But that look of hers doesn't frighten him any more. The time is long passed since that look, like searchlights peering into the darkness to discover the fugitive, made him stand stock-still, completely dazzled, he had felt he was done for—no salvation, he was caught: a low, wretched, repugnant creature . . .

Now he is protected, now something arises which comes between that look and him—a picture, that of a dark mass, of a very indistinctly outlined figure which is moving beside him on a garden walk . . . He knows who it is, of course, he could answer right away, if he were asked: it's Berthier. But in his mind, he speaks no name. What sort of face did Berthier have? And the face would be there immediately: a pink-cheeked face, with a snub nose, large, rather thick mouth, big clear, innocent eyes. Who was Berthier? Berthier was his chum at the *lycée*. Which *lycée*? Lakanal. What was he like, what impression did he make, this Berthier fellow? He was a shy, self-effacing lad, he seemed, at times, to be a bit bewildered. M. Lamiel, the philosophy professor, had said to him in a moment of anger: You're an idiot. But he was very sensitive, he had certain divinatory powers. What were the two of you doing on that walk? We were crossing the Luxembourg gardens, going to take the train at the Port-Royal station, to go back to the *lycée*. We had just had lunch with Aunt Berthe. She had stuffed us with all those tasty little dishes she serves, we felt a bit drowsy, a bit congested. The weather was hot, the path was sunny. All that and many other images, other more precise, detailed bits of information are there, just behind, all ready, like filing cards placed one in back of the other in a filing cabinet. But these cards, he doesn't take them out, he doesn't need to at this moment, he knows generally, if somewhat vaguely, what they contain, and that suffices for him; what he takes out now, is the figure with the indistinct outlines walking beside him on the path, he only hears its voice, no, not even its voice, just the words that the nearly vanished figure spoke. It stopped suddenly on the path, it said: "You know, your aunt is hard. She's contemptuous." Like that. For no reason whatsoever, just a simple statement. Dumbfounded: "My aunt? Contemptuous? Hard? My aunt? —Yes. Hard. She has a contemptuous manner." The words resounded the way the rescuers' pickaxes resound in the ears of a trapped miner. He was released. Saved. Embraces. Tears of joy. People were flocking about him. Your aunt is hard. She's contemptuous. It's a fact. That's how she is. That's her nature. Now he need only call out. Immediately they come running from every side. She's surrounded, captured, a large crowd gathered about her is looking at her, people are pointing at her, look: she's hard. Contemptuous.

He turns a calm, severe, gaze upon her: "There's no use looking at me like that, Aunt Berthe. What I just said has nothing offensive about it. You would make a mistake to refuse. It would be bad for you and not nice for us, I assure you. There would be no sense in it. I don't ask you to say yes right away, but at least go and look at it, that won't commit you in any way . . . Well, say something, after all . . ."

"I have nothing to say, Alain, you know that. I've already said it to your father. I don't even need to look at it. It's all decided."

Heavy. Inert. All shrunk into herself. Enormous motionless mass lying across his path. He would like to dislodge it, give it a good punch and kick it hard, to make it move . . . "Why of course . . . his voice is hissing like a blowpipe that's trying to perforate a thick, steel wall . . . Of course. How stupid of me . . . Poor fool that I am . . . Of course you're not willing. Not even to go to see it. That was to be expected, it's enough to ask something of you—and it's all over, there's nothing doing, you can't give in. It's like the day I asked you for that friend of mine, that was no joke, he was starving . . . Of your own accord, you might perhaps have helped him, but it's seeing somebody . . . However, you know I'm going to warn you, you haven't the right. Fortunately, there are laws . . ." He's not alone, everybody will stand by him, all decent people are on his side. Parasites that choke everything that's supposed to grow, everything that wants to live, that absorb to no purpose all the new sap that's rising, should be pulled up by the roots . . . "You know it's against the law, you know you haven't the right . . . His voice is trembling with rage, with indignation . . . You haven't the right to do that. . . The law itself protects . . . at present, when there are so many young people, the law, you hear me, forbids you . . ."

She appears to be reviving a bit. She nods her head slowly, with raised eyebrows, and a bantering, almost amused look: "Ah, indeed?"

He feels himself being swept, carried, borne far away, farther and farther, drifting towards strange, terrifying regions which he had glimpsed already, a long time ago, when he was still quite young, little more than a child . . .

Escaped prisoners, members of the resistance, Jews hiding under false names, were lolling in the sun, chatting on village squares, seated about fountains, drinking together in bistros, as though nothing had happened, cunning, disquieting prey, cunningly forcing the others, the pure who had done nothing, the strong who had nothing to fear from anybody, into loathsome complicity, drawing them into their debasement, defying the law, disrupting order, until one fine morning, a man got up—after all someone had to take it upon himself to do it—and hurried, slinking along the walls, to denounce them.

A great heavy mass is weighing upon him, ramming him, he is suffocating, he wants to live, he's struggling . . . "Very well, you'll see, you won't be able to remain here, you'll be forced . . . He knocks as hard as he can . . . You'll be forced . . . My father-in-law, his rage deafens him, he perceives his own words as though they came from far off . . . he knows your landlord . . . he'll tell him, I'm going to ask him . . ." As he hurries towards the door, he hears her finally shout, very loudly: "Go ahead, do it. You're quite capable of it. It wouldn't surprise me if you did."

AND THE GUIMIEZES, what's the news of them?"

She brandishes that under their noses and throws it into their midst . . .

Come, come, why are they hesitating? Whom are they trying to deceive? She knows very well that they were only waiting for this moment. Everybody was bored to death during the preliminaries, during all that insipid gossip . . . Everybody had had enough of chewing on nothing, nibbling . . . It was getting to be nauseating . . .

But the Guimiezes, now they're a treat . . . What could be more consistent than the Guimiezes . . . what could be more appetizing? There's something about the Guimiezes that they alone have . . . an exquisite quality . . . a bouquet . . . what are we waiting for?

So come on, then, let them get going, they're really funny—afraid, timid, both a bit ashamed and tempted. Somebody should make the first move, after all, they should bestir themselves a bit, it's high time . . . "Well, then, what about the Guimiezes? It seems to me that it's a long time since we heard anything of them."

But what is the meaning of that tone, of that jesting note in her voice, that roguish look in her dimples, in her eyes? Whom is she making fun of, they wonder . . . You might think—can you imagine that . . . only, what nerve on her part, what lack of perception—that she has thrown that to them and is standing a bit apart, that she's amusing herself getting them all excited, so she can watch them tremble and wriggle—like an avid pack, her pack?—impatient to grab the juicy morsels . . . Immediately all their muscles relax; they shrug their shoulders languidly, raise their eyebrows; a thin varnish of indifference veils their eyes . . . "Who? the Guimiezes? But why, all of a sudden? —Oh, as far as I'm concerned, you know, the Guimiezes . . . I scarcely know them . . . They interest you, though, don't they? She blushes slightly . . . They fascinate you, don't they, the Guimiezes? . . ."

But that one, over there, no prudence, no sense of dignity restrains her . . . She has already begun to be mildly excited . . . They realize that she's suffering . . . It's boiling up in her, bloating her . . . It's weighing, tingling . . . "Go ahead, Fernande, go on, you're dying to tell it . . . Now, then . . . tell us . . . what do you know? What's new in the Guimiez household?"

She would really like to snub them, they irritate her with their condescending, disdainful, slightly disgusted manner, comfortably ensconced there like lords and ladies seated with crossed legs, impatiently wagging the toes of their finely shod feet, letting their gloved hands hang negligently down, hands that hold the silk purses they're going to throw her later, to her, the old streetwalker, the procuress, who knows their secret hankerings, who knows how to flatter their baser instincts . . . What has she unearthed for them this time? What's she going to show them now? She should hurry, she's making them waste their time . . . Where is that gem of hers? Come, come, she should show it to them . . .

But something greater than herself forces her to make this sacrifice, to agree to let herself be rigged up in this wretched disguise (in the same way, a secret agent, to serve his country, willingly submits to every sort of humiliation and insult, while he is concealed under the garments of a pariah), something which she recognizes by her feeling of intense excitement, it is almost one of exaltation, by the cheering warmth that rises to her cheeks, to her forehead . . . The love of truth, of justice, the thirst for knowledge, the generous desire to give, to share, even with them, break down all the dikes inside her, overcome the last pockets of resistance, uplift her, heedless of everything, she leaps into their midst . . . "Well, yes, believe me, I heard some pretty things about them . . . They're a nice pair, the Guimiezes are. Do you know what they did, in connection with the story about that apartment? Their aunt's? They're trying to take it forcibly. The poor woman is like a hunted animal . . . She told the Delarues that her nephew was threatening to have her put out . . . It's disgraceful . . ."

The chair creaks under his too heavy, elderly man's body, as he leans over, raises his big, hairy hand and slaps it down flat on the table with a triumphant bang. His jowls are shaking with slightly false, spiteful laughter . . . "Ho-ho-ho . . . I was sure of it, sooner or later, that was bound to happen. I always predicted it, I knew it. They've made a little scoundrel out of him. There you have the result of that ridiculous upbringing, mollycoddling, nothing could be discussed before that child . . . Everything was impure, you always risked corrupting the little angel, his father used to tremble . . . he made me stop, I remember, I was talking about I forget what, it was absolutely harmless, you can believe me . . . his father blushed . . . Oh, no . . . afterwards, not before the child . . . He kept an eye on everything . . . And that idiot of an aunt spoiled him, stuffed him in secret, to make him like her . . . The result, I always predicted it: Alain wears his ego in a sling, and he's running wild . . . When he wants something, nothing can stop him, there's nothing he wouldn't do. In fact, they're all like that, all that young generation, she, he's not an exception . . ."

"A lapsus! hee, hee, you made a lapsus."

"What lapsus, my dear lady?"

"Why, you said 'she' in speaking of Alain . . . sharp little voice like a mouse's squeak . . . Yes, you did . . . little laugh . . . I heard it . . . you said . . ."

"No, I said 'he.'"

"You said 'she'. . . Without realizing it . . ."

Ah, he'll see, that bumptious gentleman . . . She feels upset by his great hulking laughter. The satisfaction, the self-confidence with which he delivers his platitudinous remarks irritates her. Fortunately, she possesses something with which to protect herself, a real treasure similar to those that divers bring up from the bottom of the seas and which she has brought up after endless trials and endeavors, endless dangerous, painful, consternated incursions into the suddenly yawning abyss of her unconscious . . . It's about all she was able to collect, it's all she has kept, but she has no regrets—it's like something magic, a talisman: it confers a power upon the persons who possess it that is not shared by common mortals, and it places other people at their mercy.

Nothing is more amusing than to see them—like ostriches, with their heads hidden under their wings and their buttocks pointing upwards, displaying with touching naïveté, in her presence, that which best gives them away: a word spoken in place of another and immediately made good, but it's too late, she has heard, an apparently harmless gesture, an object they've lost, the simple fact of forgetting, the most innocent of little gifts and which they think they have chosen haphazardly, a liking they have shown, at times disarmingly ignorant and oblivious, and right away, thanks to her magic power, she catches them, there's no use for them to struggle . . . how red he is, that very self-satisfied gentleman, he's fidgeting, he protests, he almost splutters with rage . . . "I did not say 'she,' I'm certain of it . . . But when all is said and done, let us suppose that I did say it, what is there to it, anyway . . ."

Who is that crazy female . . . What she needed was not to be psychoanalyzed, that made her crazier than she was before, she should have been locked up, she's insufferable . . . and not only crazy, stupid, spiteful . . . What was she after? She's watching him with her delighted, idiotic smile . . . They all look at him as though they were accessory to something she has done to him, but which he doesn't see—some ridiculous joke . . . like an April-fool fish that she's pinned on his back and which they all see, highly amused, swinging harder and harder, while he struggles to catch hold of it . . . "What's it all about, any how? I said 'she', very well, let's admit it, and then what, what about it? What crazy thing will you invent next, that what? . . . he's about to catch it, it's there, they're all watching him, he's going to take hold of it . . . that I think Alain is . . . so what next, what is there more ridiculous . . . there now, he's got it, he pulls it off, he's holding it in his hands . . . Ah, it's that too perhaps, that, without realizing it, I'm in love with Alain? Well, I consider that Alain is a perfectly virile young man, believe it or not . . . And as for myself, my dear lady, until I was past fifty years old . . . no, really, it's too idiotic . . ." So here's how I treat your cardboard fish, now watch, it's torn up, and I'm scattering the pieces to the four winds.

But how enraged he is, how he resists . . . "I was teasing you, you know that . . . Calm down . . . We all have in us . . . See here, who hasn't . . . it's well known . . . No, seriously . . . What I do think, though, is that Alain . . . You know what the symbol of the apartment means . . . Alain is an orphan, he's been deprived of his mother since he was a little boy . . . I realize that his aunt replaced her, but for just that reason . . ."

That's too much . . . They all protest at one time . . . They have shown great patience, they weren't averse to this suspense, these shilly-shallyings, these bits of byplay that prepare and increase, at the same time that they defer, enjoyment . . . But there she's gone too far, she risks jeopardizing everything, arresting their momentum for good . . . "Oh, no . . . from every side come groaning voices . . . No, I beg of you, we've had enough of psychoanalysis, enough of psychology, they're not interesting . . . What we want are the facts . . . Go ahead, Fernande, don't let any one interrupt you, tell us, after all, that's very serious, what you were saying, it's almost unbelievable . . . The Guimiezes dared? Alain dared to threaten his aunt? Really? —He certainly did, it's just as I say . . . The poor woman told it herself to the Delarues . . . It's outrageous, she's simply sick over it . . . Madame Delarue told me that it's pathetic to see her . . . she's grown old, thin . . . And no wonder . . . Would you believe it . . . They all lean forward . . . Would you believe that it's even worse than that . . . Gisèle's father knows their aunt's landlord . . . —And so? —So Alain went to see her. He made a horrible scene. He told her that if she didn't give in, they would speak to the landlord . . . She hasn't the right . . ." They give horrified, delighted little shouts, they feel like holding each other tight and closing their eyes, as though they were sliding on a toboggan . . . oh, that makes you dizzy . . . oh, gee, that scares me, whoo, how awful! . . . Why, that's really foul. . . Can you believe it? . . . If my little Marcel should ever . . . Alain Guimiez, a well-brought-up boy like that . . . Oh, yes he was, no matter what you say, his father brought him up very well . . . Behave like a good-for-nothing . . . "A good-for-nothing? I think the word is too kind . . . You haven't yet heard the best part . . . the poor woman had a telephone call supposedly from the owner's agent, who told her, just in passing, that she was occupying an apartment that was too big for her, and she recognized her nephew's voice . . . —Is that possible? —She's sure of it. And you know what I myself think? . . . She's very nervous, rather delicate . . . At one time she had several serious breakdowns . . . What they're trying to do, I'm going to tell you . . . If they were trying to drive her crazy, well, that wouldn't surprise me."

They experience a strange sensation, as though they were chewing on those seeds the Indians take, peyote seeds, or smoking hashish . . . the picture that appears before them resembles somewhat that reflected by deforming mirrors in street-fairs . . . A curious, grotesque, slightly disturbing picture . . . They turn fascinated eyes upon it . . . It's they themselves, they recognize themselves perfectly, down to the slightest details, only queerly distended, deformed, misshapen—hideous dwarfs broader than they are long, with short legs, low foreheads; they have something extraordinarily heavy about them, shrunken up into themselves; something narrow, stubborn, brutish in their sly, criminal faces . . . But they have only to turn their eyes and there, in another mirror, there they are again, bursting out of all ordinary dimensions, endlessly stretching, growing huge, their high foreheads disappear beyond the edge of the mirror . . . Compared with these giants, the people walking about them look like children's dolls . . . For an instant, they look at themselves, almost attracted, a little frightened, but only a little, it's delightful, they know quite well that it's a game, they have only to look away, their usual mirror is there, very fortunately, to set things straight again, destroy all these disturbing illusions . . . a mirror that doesn't deform, reflects exactly the image of what they are . . . not so bad, after all, what do you think, not bad at all, even, you'll have to acknowledge it, they feel very cocky . . .

"Personally, I must admit, that's completely beyond me, I don't mean to boast . . . but with us, in my family, all that is quite unthinkable . . . I'm not even referring to the use of such methods, obviously there can be no question of that, but to try, even by means of persuasion . . . When I think how many times my mother, poor woman, and yet she lived only for her children, how many times she offered us, but never, neither my sisters nor I, should we have dared . . . —Of course, naturally, you especially, no really, I can't imagine you . . . But we're the same, although we're no saints, no models of virtue, but from that to . . . no, really, it's disgraceful, fortunately however, they're exceptions, such monsters as that . . . I'm not exaggerating, what they're doing there can kill her, they're delicate, you know, old people are . . . The stuff assassins are made of, that's what your young Guimiezes are."

"Why, you're terrible, all of you. You're downright mean. As for me, you can say what you want against the Guimiezes, I won't believe it as long as I haven't seen it with my own eyes. And even then . . . I think the Guimiezes are absolutely charming. So there. They're handsome. Intelligent. Affectionate. Alain adores his aunt and she reciprocates . . ."

The noisy, self-assured voice reverberates in their ears like a loudspeaker making announcements for the travelers in a railway station. They give a start. They sit up. What is it? What happened? Where have they been brought to? Where are they? They stare wide-eyed.

Here are the Guimiezes. A charming couple. Gisèle is seated beside Alain. Her little pink nose is bewitching. Her pretty periwinkle eyes are shining. Alain has one arm about her shoulders. His delicate features express rectitude, kindness. Aunt Berthe is seated nearby. Her face, which must once have been beautiful, her time-yellowed eyes, are turned towards

Alain. She is smiling at him. Her little wrinkled hand rests on Alain's arm in a tenderly confident manner.

But as we look at them, we feel a sort of constraint, a certain uneasiness. What is the matter with them? We should like to examine them more closely, to stretch out our hands . . . Only watch out. They're roped off. That makes no difference, we must see. We must try to touch them . . . Yes, it's surely that, one could have suspected as much. Those are wax effigies. Those are not the real Guimiezes.

Watch out. No nonsense. You're not allowed to touch the dolls. You're supposed to look at them from a distance. There are attendants everywhere. They have already directed their vacant stare at the inquisitive visitors. If they lean over the rope, if they stretch out their hands to these mock Guimiezes, the attendants will set off the alarm system. Police cars will arrive. The policemen will shake their doll-like heads: Why did you want to touch the mock Guimiezes? Answer. They don't dare answer. Was it to damage them? Were you trying to damage, to soil the mock Guimiezes? This charming couple. This doting aunt who loves them so. You were trying to destroy the Guimiezes. They were in your way. Oh, indeed. The Guimiezes were in their way. Will you tell me why? You won't? You don't dare. Very well, I'm going to tell you. You wanted to destroy them out of meanness, out of envy, out of an unhealthy need to defile, to pillage everything that is beautiful, noble, charming. They remain silent. They're afraid. They realize that all this can lead to no end of trouble. They'll be dishonored, marked for life, pointed at, ostracized, led about under the hostile gaze of crowds in an ignominious getup. Waxlike fingers will be pointed at them. There go those wretches who tried to defile, damage, destroy what is a source of joy for all decent people, the object of their contentment, of their delight, that adorable family: the Guimiezes.

They feel a guilty smile appear on their faces: "Oh, after all, you are perhaps right, here we are, all out to knife them . . . Personally, I like them very much, the Guimiezes . . . —I've always thought highly of them . . . I must admit that they're very nice, very attractive . . . —Perhaps Fernande is wrong, she may have been misled . . . —Oh, you know, in reality, all I did was to repeat what was told me. I didn't see anything myself. I was surprised too. Personally, I've never had any reason to complain of them, I always thought they were charming, the Guimiezes."

PEOPLE WHO DON'T know him misinterpret it. They mistake for diffidence, for excessive sensitiveness, that terribly embarrassed, uneasy, retiring manner he has at times, as at this moment, that toneless, slightly hoarse voice—in their eyes, it's part of his charm, people believe in him so easily—but she knows him too well: it's a feeling of annoyance, almost of rage, that he has, and which gives him that look, that voice, it's sly, shameful resentment, against anyone who takes the liberty of interfering with his comfort, of disturbing his timid, cramped bachelor's peace . . . marriage, paternity changed nothing, he was like that already, at the age of ten . . . As soon as he hears someone cry out in distress, call for help, he rolls up like a ball, pulls the covers up to his chin and turns out the lamp . . .

But she's going to shout as long as is needed, she's going to force him to overcome his lazy prudence, his egoism . . . he's in danger, he too, it also concerns him, a crime is about to be committed, a crime is being organized, and the criminal is his son, his own son, something must be done right away, he must help her, she has done all she can . . . she tried to bring the unfeeling young rascal, the poor pervert, to his senses . . . congealed, petrified, not believing her eyes . . . her darling little boy, her little Alain, do that to his "Tatie," his good old, doting auntie . . . she repulsed him with all her might, as far away as she could, she hurled back this stranger, this outsider with the face of a low schemer, to a great distance . . . she let him feel the weight of a look that she charged with an enormous load of reprobation, of contempt, hoping that he would struggle under it, that he would free himself, that he would pull himself together, quite dumbfounded: Why, Aunt Berthe, what's happening? Don't you recognize me any more? I'm still your little Alain . . . I lost my head. What was I talking about? A single decent move would have sufficed. She would have recognized him right away, she would have got back her same old Alain, so affectionate, he can be, at certain moments, so considerate, so tactful, so forgetful of self . . . no one could be more so than he . . . But he was off, he couldn't stop now, it was shame that rose up in him, it was his disgust with himself which increased his rage, his spitefulness, and caused them to swell immeasurably . . . Put up no defense, in such cases . . . not a word . . . she didn't move . . . she became more passive still, more inert, inviting his blows . . . let him go after a poor defenseless old woman, let him go farther still, to the very limit of shame, of loathing, let him hurt her, then let him hurt himself, himself too . . . the suffering will become intolerable, he'll be forced to stop . . .

Up until the very last, she had retained that hope, when he stood up, mad with rage . . . at the moment she had felt no suffering, as happens they say, sometimes, with those who receive a mortal blow, they speak a few words in a calm voice, take a few steps: Empress Elizabeth stabbed in the heart, climbing on to the boat, Caesar . . . *Et tu, Brute* . . . She retained all her clarity of mind, an astonishing amount of composure . . . Even at that very moment, when everything was tottering about her, collapsing, she had the strength to keep her heavy, icy gaze upon him, to look coolly, until the last minute, wanting to give him one more chance, at that repugnant informer's face which he was showing her to frighten her, she was able to articulate distinctly, at the same time that she reeled under the blow: "Of course, you'll speak of it, you'll do it . . . I know you" . . . still hoping that he would come to himself, that they would both wake up, that it was nothing, a nightmare . . . there now he is turning round, he has his serious, sad expression that she loves, he runs towards her, he takes her in his arms, he covers her cheeks, her hair, with kisses, as he used to do when he had been naughty . . . Oh, Aunt Berthe, I'm a monster, forgive me . . . I lost my head, I didn't realize what I was saying . . . It was that look of yours, so cold, so hostile . . . You know I adore you . . . But he didn't come back, he left, he went running down the stairs, she followed the diminishing sound of his footsteps as though she were hearing them beat in her own heart . . .

Now something unbearable is about to happen, she can't face it, it must be stopped at all cost . . . She's ready to humble herself, as she had done in the past when, losing all self-control, she ran out on the landing in her nightgown, went down a few steps, clinging, pleading . . . "I beg of you, Henri, stay with me . . . just this evening . . . Don't go out this evening, don't leave me . . ." As soon as the door was closed again, she realized that it was not because she needed to have him near her—and he didn't mistake it, he knew it—that she was driven to lower herself, to disfigure herself like that: to be alone, surrounded by silence, would be more soothing than anything else, after the scenes and the shouting, and a good detective story, which she would read curled up in her bed, would be more entertaining than those dreary remarks they exchanged by force of habit, that oppressive compulsion—no, it was something she was unable to distinguish very clearly, a strange, mute terror . . . she ran to the telephone to call his club, his café . . . she must reach him, find him, catch up with him at all cost . . . If he doesn't come back right away, something irremediable is going to happen . . . he's going to exceed a certain limit . . . he should turn back, he should come home, there's still time, he should hurry . . . one step more and it will be too late, he's about to set foot on dangerous ground where some evil fate is going to metamorphose him, she will no longer be able to recognize him, it won't be he, this strange man . . . "A bad husband, that's what he is. Henri is a very bad husband. Poor Berthe has had no luck. She made a poor choice. Hers is a poor lot, a poor marriage. And poor Berthe's nephew is a scamp. Alain behaves like a crook. He's an ungrateful wretch . . ." The nervous little boy, kind at heart, nevertheless, the nice affectionate child whom she allowed to bite at her, she being strong, generous, indulgent, inviting the furious hammering of his little fists, the spoilt, provoking, high-tempered child was to be transformed into that: a crook, an ungrateful wretch. Into something hard, inalterable, something inflexible, against which she's going to collide, against which she's going to crash. They're finished, the pecking, the biting, the embracing, the living warmth of the hand-to-hand tussle. She will be separated from him for all time by a distance that she will no longer be able to bridge.

She too, in his eyes, will be petrified—an object, a tool which he will make use of, an inert thing, delivered into his hands, which he will maneuver according to his whim . . . An unbearable sensation—like the one she's always given by a mental image that she effaces right away: her own corpse which other people are handling, transporting, above which they're talking to one another in low tones . . . and she, separated for all time, powerless as regards her own fate, she, for all time out of the picture—a feeling of horror makes her withdraw within herself . . . No, not to her, that's not possible, it won't happen to her, she won't believe it, she can't think it. . . "Listen to me, now do listen to what I'm telling you, Pierre, I beg of you . . . It's very serious, you know . . . I'm sick over it, it keeps me awake at nights . . . I ask nothing better than to believe I'm mistaken . . . But listen to me . . ."

It was to be expected. She should never have hoped for anything else from him. He hardly listens to her, he sets fascinated eyes on the corner of the rug he turned up a little while ago, as he sat down . . . Now he's leaning over, the back of his neck swells and reddens . . . he stretches out his hand, takes hold of the rug . . . She would like to take him by the collar of his coat, straighten him up, push him hard and hold him propped up against the back of his chair to make him look at her, listen to her . . . but she knows it would be of no use. Nothing now can tear him away from this turned-up corner of the rug . . . it's impossible to divert him from something that has suddenly caught his attention, in one second it becomes an obsession, a mania . . . he's a good one to make fun of her, he's much more of a crank than she is . . . Yet no, not such a crank, really, not crazy at all . . . it's at those moments when you want to force him to concentrate his attention on some precise thing that you feel deeply about, when you urge and implore him, it's then especially, that he escapes to go and settle on something else, to which he is irresistibly attracted . . . everything interests him, amuses him at those moments, when others are begging him to give a little of himself, to fall in for a second with them . . . Suddenly, at the very moment—how often this has happened—when she's complaining about something to him, confiding in him, he lays his hand on her arm . . . "How pretty that is, look, don't you agree?" She's been cut short at the height of her momentum, she's all upset, she's staggering, she can't get her footing again, while he, feeling a certain pity for her, a bit sorry to have been so abrupt, but pleased, amused—he's always indulgent towards his own misdeeds—lends her a hand . . . "So, what were you saying? Excuse me, but it was so lovely . . ." Now, after this little escapade, he's ready to make an effort. He straightens up, settles himself in his chair, folds his hands: "Yes, yes, I am,

I'm listening to you. Why yes, I hear very well. What's the matter?" That satisfaction he had just indulged in had made them lose time, but she doesn't hold it against him, there can be no question of that at present, of grievances, resentments . . . she has already forgiven, everything is forgotten, come, come, if he wants to, he can make up for lost time, but he should hurry, he should show a little good will, she's at the end of her tether, she feels the tears welling in her eyes . . . it's very serious, he should realize that . . . "It's no laughing matter . . . Alain has behaved outrageously . . ."

He draws himself up all of a sudden. He appears to be looking at something inside himself that gives him that fond, contented little smile . . . he leans backwards . . . "Ah, that confounded Alain, again, what's he done now?"

She knows, she recognizes immediately, what he's looking at inside himself with that conceited smile, the film he's showing for himself alone on his inner screen. She has seen him often, in the old days, taking the child on his knees, or squeezing his little hand when they went walking together on Sundays, showing him the pictures that he sees now: he himself grown old, grown sickly and poor, standing in the crowd, there, on the side of this street, drawing his worn overcoat about him, because of the cold, while he waits to see the handsome rider (she felt at the time what voluptuous pleasure it gave him to see shining in the child's eyes, beneath his tears of tenderness, of heartrending sorrow, flashes of pride), the intrepid conqueror, hard and strong, trailing all hearts behind him, who passes by on his chestnut steed without recognizing him, he's returning from a crusade, from long victorious campaigns, he believes he has lost, he has perhaps forgotten his old Papa, but the poor paternal heart is bathed in joy, in pride . . . Look at him . . . Ah, there's a lad for you, at least he's no softy. He's a real man, eh, my son?

Poor devil. She feels sorry for him. It was because he had enjoyed taking attitudes of this kind with their father, when they were young, that he had made of himself what he is today: a poor man who has shrunk, who has deteriorated, who has not made the most of his possibilities . . . She feels her strength returning, together with a salutary need to shake him . . . what an unwholesome attitude of weakness, of surrender . . . he's ridiculous . . . why is he behaving like a man in his dotage . . . come along there, a little dignity, a little self-respect, authority . . . after all, he should not forget his role of educator, of judge . . . the boy has behaved like a guttersnipe, he probably needs to be set straight, there's really nothing to brag about . . . he's a little good-for-nothing . . . "He came to threaten me. He wants to report me to the proprietor. He's going to have me put out. Now, once and for all, have you taken that in? . . ."

His face grows serious, he seems finally to be coming to his senses, he settles in his chair, puts his elbows on the arms, joins the tips of the fingers of both wide-open hands, the palms apart—a gesture he makes when he is thinking deeply about something. He looks at her hard . . . "What's that you're saying? What is that story, anyway? Why, see here, that's a joke . . . It doesn't hold water . . . Alain report you . . . Alain have you put out . . . You know Alain better than I do. You know perfectly well that he's the frankest, the most considerate sort of boy . . . She leans her face towards him . . . again . . . it's too delightful . . . He's very affectionate, that you know . . . And as for you, he loves you very much. That's certain, everybody knows it, he's very much attached to you . . ."

She didn't need all that, it's too much . . . life is coming back, a more intense, purified life, a life that is richer in precious possessions, in inestimable treasures . . . the ties of blood, love slowly strengthened by long sacrifice, long abnegation . . . how could she have let herself be blinded to the point where she no longer saw—but she had glimpsed it, sensed confusedly somewhere inside her, way down underneath, and that was at the most terrible moments—that scenes of this kind between them revealed, precisely, the indestructible force of their feelings, an overflow of riches which it amused them to squander . . . the very fact of this superabundant security made them feel the need to work themselves up from time to time by means of these savage contests, these cruel games . . .

But it's too early to let oneself go entirely, this upsurging of regained, restored life that accompanies convalescence, approaching recovery, must be contained. There's no hurry now, she can take all the time she wants and look fearlessly about her . . . just as an extra precaution . . . Let him examine this as well, she's not afraid to show him everything, now that she knows recovery is certain . . . There were other things too, strange symptoms . . . she realizes that it was stupid of her to worry, that she is perhaps inclined to feel persecuted, but all the same, if he would just take a look . . . of course she asks nothing better than to have been mistaken . . . "Only, how about this, there was something else, still, it wasn't only a matter of words . . . Something happened a few days ago. I had a telephone call from the landlord's agent." He gives a start, he draws aside the better to look at her: "From the agent?" His voice is a bit raucous, he frightens her . . . he's not going to let her down now? He should keep cool . . . "It wasn't exactly for that. Not about putting me out. It was about some water pipes . . . But in this connection, the agent said to me: a dressing room and a bathroom, it seems to me it's rather a lot, all that, for one person alone. And that was a few days after Alain had come and told me: You have no right to stay . . . my father-in-law knows the landlord . . . Imagine that. You can understand that it was enough to get panicky about. And it's not because of me, myself, it's to think that Alain . . ." He shakes his head exasperatedly . . . he strikes his front teeth hard with the tip of his tongue to make that disapproving, annoyed, clucking sound. "Tss . . . tss . . . you're losing your head, I assure you, that's a simple coincidence, I'll guarantee you . . . Alain is incapable of doing that. That's madness, there's no question of it, you know quite well that he says just anything when he's in a rage. If that's what's keeping you awake at nights . . ."

There now. That's all that's needed. Everything is fine. Now everything is for the best. Don't think about it any more, give in to this delightful sensation of relaxation, of calm . . . But he seems to be annoyed, disgruntled. It's one of those sudden collapses such as he often has: all of a sudden, something inside him falls to pieces, his face is downcast. He scowls, retires within himself, he must be ruminating—but what? what grievance? against whom? against her, certainly—his lip is curled in a grimace of disgust . . . she's the one who disgusts him, she feels it . . . "Tempests in a teapot, you stir up trouble over nothing . . . you see evil everywhere . . ." He grows silent, this time, he is staring fixedly in front of him . . . But that's not true, he's wrong, she can be kind, naive as a child . . . she has confidence, confidence in him, especially: a few words from him have sufficed to erase everything. She's ready to ask his pardon for having troubled him, upset him, for nothing, come, come, he should make an effort . . . she has already forgotten it all . . . they could be so happy now . . .

But the joy that effuses from her collides against this disgust of his, against this contempt, it flattens, swells, changes shape, it's a joy that assumes grotesque, bloated forms, she feels this while she is laughing with the shrill laughter of a little girl, opening eyes wide with wonder . . . "Oh, how happy I am . . . You don't know what pleasure you've given me . . . So you really think that Alain is incapable of that? Of course, it was mad to think it . . ." He shrugs his shoulders, in a fed up, impatient manner . . . "Why, of course not, it's ridiculous, there's no question of it."

She feels uplifted, impelled by something powerful and gentle—a sensation like that we experience when we're lying on a sandy beach and let ourselves be gently pushed and rolled about by the waves, our faces covered with foam, our hair full of seaweed, breathing in delightedly the smell of the ocean . . . she lets herself be borne along, it's exciting, come on, it's such fun, a bit dangerous, perhaps, but she likes that kind of danger, she's being jostled about—it's so comical—she feels washed, purified, a foamy wave has swept it all away: all the anguish, the mistakes that can never be repaired, that we must carry about with us for the rest of our lives . . . oval doors that look trashy, gloomy rooms, always closed, opening into one another, a long hotel corridor she has always detested, kitchen that's too dark, noisy neighbors . . . it's all been torn out, carried away . . . it scares you a little, but it's so exciting, bracing . . . come along, let's lend each other a hand . . . those two lovely rooms—they're right: it's exactly what she has needed for a long time—looking out on a quiet courtyard with a big tree; beautiful old floors, no more dusty, lifeless carpets, everything's going to change, the devil take all that, she's had enough of it . . . by the way, that old *bergère* you like so much, take it, Alain dear, it's yours, I don't want it . . . and the big wardrobe . . . take it, what should I do with it in the new place . . . Oh, is that true, Aunt Berthe? How kind of you! . . . Leaps of joy, strong, soft arms round her shoulders, young laughter, carefree, confident . . . all together facing the future . . . truth, wisdom lie there, in this eternally new life, in this march forward with them, hand in hand . . . she leans towards him . . . "You know how much I love Alain . . . If he had behaved differently, I should perhaps have given in. Actually, it might be the intelligent thing to do. I'd have to think about it . . ."

He turns on her a look which suddenly envelops her entirely, nothing can escape, he half closes his eyes the better to encompass her, nods his head as though weighing her in the balance . . . "Why, of course, don't I know it? But you'll surely give in. They need have no cause for anxiety. It's as good as settled." She feels that he's making an effort to contain the contemptuous rage that has crept into his voice, but he doesn't succeed, it escapes in a thin whistle . . . "You've never done otherwise than to give in to all his whims . . . You made him what he is, a rotten, spoilt child. There's nothing anybody can do now. Only, I'm going to tell you . . ."

So it's still there inside him, after so many years, as virulent as it used to be, when it frightened her so that she didn't dare take the child to a pastry shop, buy him a toy . . . the poor little fellow knew quite well that it was useless to ask his father—he was much too self-centered, too petty—the poor darling turned to her, to his Tatie . . . But that was precisely what he couldn't stand, that affection the child had for her, their joy when they went out together, the pleasure it gave her to spoil him a bit, poor little chap, always a bit sad, who had never known a mother's love . . . Now he's off, she knows that old tune, she knows perfectly, it's her fault, of course, look what she has made of him: a weakling, a good-for-nothing . . . "What Alain needs just now is not your apartment . . . The very idea is absurd, I've thought so from the start . . . But they pestered me so about it, begged me . . . I was delighted that you refused . . . I'm going to tell you, shall I, what he needs . . . Do you realize the position he's in? He would do much better, believe me, to hurry and finish his thesis and get himself named just anywhere, to just any out-of-the-way hole . . . He would at least have a regular salary, and a pension later, which is not to be sneezed at, that would be better than to live off odd jobs, by his wits, or to ask help from his parents-in-law

. . . A modest future, ah, certainly . . ." Now he's happy, he has torn them apart, they're separated, holding one in each hand, he is squeezing them tight, he turns them towards each other and forces her to look: there's the knave she was going to join up with, with whom she was going to prepare the future, walk hand in hand, ah, he's a nice one, that companion of hers, her little darling . . . a little snob, a lazy lout . . . "That marriage . . . Germaine Lemaire . . . there can be no question of living in Paris in a five-room apartment, in a swanky neighborhood . . . they should take a look at themselves . . . of passing his time fixing it up . . . he knocks them against each other . . . giving parties . . . fiestas, as they say . . . he's hurting her . . . he laughs, delighted, there now, another good knock: and rest assured, they won't be for us . . ."

He appears to be calming down—it must have relieved him to let himself go like that, or perhaps he's a bit remorseful . . . His expression becomes gentler . . . "Don't worry, Alain will certainly be forced to understand. I hope, for his sake, that it won't be too late." In the inflection of his voice, there's a note of disillusioned wisdom, of noble resignation: "Life will teach him, as it does everybody else. He'll see. And so much the better for him. It's better like that."

She waits a moment, she too is very calm now, she's taking her time: "Oh, listen, there, may I say that you paint too black a picture. You know perfectly well that it's not quite like that, you see the gloomy side of everything. To hear you talk you would think they were going to be in the streets, that they risked ending their days in the poorhouse. Even if, later on. Gisèle should have nothing—and that's not certain, either— But still, let's assume it. What about me . . ." She can't help smiling, knowing so well, as she does, what's going to happen, and at the same time, she's a little afraid and as though a bit ashamed, she doesn't know why, or for whom, whether it's for herself or for him, but it can't be helped, it's got to be done, something very powerful, which she is unable to resist, impels her . . . "What I'm going to leave him will certainly be more than the equivalent of all the pensions he might receive. It's worth much more, and you know it . . ."

He looks away, starts fidgeting in his chair, he seems on the point of writhing, like an exorcised sinner when the evil spirit is expelled from him: "It's extraordinary how like Papa you can be . . ." There's hostility in his voice . . . "I can hear him now: They're not worth a hoot, all those plans of yours, what is that compared to what I'm going to leave you . . . You make me laugh with that talk . . . he sneers, his lip curls . . . you take me back to the good old days . . . That didn't teach you a lesson what happened to that famous fortune, to those famous investments which kept poor Papa so occupied . . . you saw how it all turned out . . ."

He really makes her feel very sad, his case is even worse than she had thought . . . it's distressing, pitiable, the efforts he makes to draw people to him, to lure her, there, beside him, both in the same boat, as in the old days, poor devils whose lot was a sad one, whose start was a bad one, she—typist, he—quill-driver in a bank . . . But that, no, that's entirely finished, all that . . . hey, there, watch out, down dog . . . "Oh, see here, what connection is there? You know what father was like. How can you compare him to Henri? Henri's investments were different, they were reliable. He didn't worry about me, he always told me that . . ."

He remains silent, it is as though something in him were bowing, scraping . . . And she feels humiliated now by this defeat she has just inflicted upon him, she can't bear to see him humbled, abased like that . . . It's stupid for them to amuse themselves harrowing each other this way, come now, it's finished, quick, let him pull himself together . . . she's going to help him . . . "Listen, I wish you would tell me . . . Jardot tells me that oil stocks have gone up again. He advises me to sell now. I was just going to ask you . . . What do you advise me to do? I myself should have preferred to wait a bit longer . . . what do you think?" He shrugs his shoulders, looks away . . . "Oh, listen, you make me laugh. I don't think you need me for that . . . you know more about that than I do. Henri taught you a lot. I have no advice to give you."

It's still there inside her, the wound that has never entirely healed, and which reopens at the slightest touch . . . the hurt she felt years ago when, quite as intimidated—years of marriage had not been able to change that—as when she had been the little typist who answered the boss's ring, she half opened the door very gently: "Am I disturbing you, Henri, were you working?" Heavy, stocky body settled in its swivel chair, heavy glance from prominent eyes, staring straight ahead, somewhere in the distance. The chair pivots slowly, the ponderous glance turns toward her, dwells upon her: "What does he want now, that brother of yours? What's he after?"

He should try to make an effort. It all depends on him. He's her brother. They are of the same blood: as strong, when they want to be, as intelligent as anybody, as all the rest—all those outsiders. He should help her. It belongs to him too, after all, what she owns, it will go to his son, everything she has, it's their common property: "Jardot advises me to sell those shares now and to buy them back when the price goes down." He raises his head: "Well, isn't he smart, Jardot. What makes him think that they won't go higher still? That's stupid, what he told you there, there's no sign that the advance is about to stop. On the contrary, if you want my opinion, I think it has only just begun. If you sell, you're going to find yourself with your assets on your hands watching the market rise . . ." She loves his eyes when he gets excited: exactly their father's look, a bit hard, sharp, piercing, the slightly wily look of a peasant from good old stock—intelligent as the devil, both of them . . . If they had been willing to do what they should have . . . but in their family they're eaten up with pride, they're unsociable, independent, not the least bit ambitious . . . If they had wanted, they could have climbed high, they too . . . "But for goodness sake, Berthe, you're not going in for speculating, are you? What's got into your friend Jardot? —My friend Jardot . . ." She watches him, amused, as he sends that scamp running. Her brother is there beside her. He's smart. Let anybody try to plague her, to cheat her now . . . "That's just how it looked to me too, which is why I wanted to talk it over with you . . . I thought . . . —But see here, it's perfectly obvious, there's no need to think. There's a golden rule, I've always told you that: never relinquish a stock you're sure of . . . He leans back in his chair, looks at her almost tenderly: You know, I've already told you old Vanderbilt's secret: never sell, always buy." Yes, she remembers. As she listens to him she has a delightful sensation of well-being, of security. It's as though she were on ground that, having been devastated by a battle, had now been cleared, de-mined, leveled . . . Still a bit fearful, she proceeds: "So then, Pierre, about that other matter, about that apartment, you agree? I believe you are of my opinion . . . she looks where she's walking, sets each foot down cautiously . . . I'll have to think about it, but in principle . . . well . . . Silence. She can detect nothing. She takes another step. There, that's surely dangerous, you can still see the traces of enormous shell-holes . . . Only, what I wanted to ask you . . . just here, be careful . . . why no, it's ridiculous, there's nothing left . . . is to tell Alain. After what has happened, you understand, I don't feel like doing it. If you would tell Alain to come to see me . . ." She stops, all ears. This time, she has knocked against something, she has stumbled on something hard . . . He throws his head back, rises . . . "Well, I must be leaving. It's time . . ." and then the explosion takes place, only a very slight one . . . hardly a few scratches, a little dust . . . "No, Berthe dear, this time I'm not going to mix in it. You're both old enough. I think you'll both get along very well without me."

THAT CORNER OF the rug, there, just in front of his feet, which he turned up a little while back when he pulled his chair forward—he can't take his eyes off it: against the silky motley of the rug, this corner forms a triangle of grayish, rough texture bordered on one side by a disorderly fringe. He would like to lean over, stretch out his hand, but he doesn't dare . . . She's there just opposite him on the sofa, without having to look at her he sees her wide-open eyes, already a bit moist, imploring, he hears her voice trembling with contained anxiety, with suffering: "Listen Pierre, it's serious, I assure you, I wouldn't have made you come for nothing. You absolutely must know . . . Alain was . . . you can't imagine . . . I worry a lot . . ." No, impossible, he must control himself, it would be like that unfortunate gesture he made (she still remembers it, surely, hadn't they reproached him enough with it, it's one of those things that families never forget, it sticks to you for all time), when he lighted a cigarette immediately after having taken final leave of their grandmother, while he was still on the front steps and his poor grandmother was following him with her eyes, in tears. That would rise up in her right away. The slightest gesture, the slightest word between them, becomes swollen, encumbered, with all that he carries with him, with all that he brings to mind; she must have had the same mournful tone that she has now, when she told that to her parents . . . It makes no difference, he won't budge. But she exasperates him. He perceives in her tone, mixed with the suffering, a rather dubious note of excitement, almost a certain satisfaction . . . "Believe me . . . If I feel sick over it, it's not for myself, but for Alain. I should never have thought that he could be so horrible . . ." A tempest in a teapot, probably . . . that apartment affair again . . . He should never have mixed into it, it was stupid, he has no desire to start all over again . . . Will it never end, is he going to have to carry this load, this weight, till he dies, he's worn out, they should be looking after him now, "A son that age, that must be a great help to you . . ." A help! But he doesn't need any . . . peace . . . if people would just leave him alone, that's all he asks . . . the fringe is tangled, the triangle bulges considerably at the base then flattens out towards the summit . . . it won't take a second . . . he stretches out his hand . . . and besides, that will calm her a bit, she needs it, what are all these tragedies about, things should be held to their proper proportions . . . he seizes the corner of the rug by the fringe, lifts it up, turns it back, lays it flat . . . what a relief, how soothing, just one moment more and it will be done, the trick will be turned . . . there . . . he evens up the fringe by combing it out rapidly with his fingers, pulls himself up and settles himself in his chair . . . At last, that's done: "Yes, yes, I'm listening. Yes I do, I hear you very well. What's it all about? —But I tell you, you're not listening . . . Try to realize, after all, it's serious . . . Alain came to see me about that affair, about that exchange of apartments . . . He frightened me, I'm not joking . . . She dabs her eyes, turns her head away, her voice is choking . . . Oh! he was . . . you can't imagine . . ."

That air of a weak woman being martyrized, of a doe at bay, as soon as he sees it in her, immediately brings out in him, he doesn't know why, the big brute, the hefty, the male who sprawls about, stretches out his legs with their big muddy boots, sneers, ha! we're made like that, and my son, eh, he can hold his own, he's no softy, a real fellow, a tough guy, a rake, a petticoat-chaser, a pilferer of stingy old women, he's being very cocky, he laughs conceitedly: "Ah. that confounded Alain, what has he done now?" She blushes, her eyes narrow, their expression becomes sharp, fierce: "What has he done now? Her voice is hissing . . . Well, what he's done now, believe it or not, is to come and threaten me like some little guttersnipe, he threatened to report me to the landlord. To have me put out. That's all. Do you take that in? Do you see?" Ah, no, that he doesn't see. He's not going to see, she shouldn't count on it, his son in the prisoners' dock among the juvenile delinquents, pale, vicious little old men's faces, sly looks, callousness, mental backwardness, maladjustment, evident signs of degeneracy . . . "Are you his father? . . ." A man with eyes cast to the ground, back bowed under the burden of shame, a poor weak, overwhelmed man, walks forward while people look on with pitying contempt: "Yes, your Honor, I'm his father." He doesn't feel like amusing himself with her at this new little game, however thrilling, however exciting it may be for her—it's enough to make her voice tremble—to play the role of fate and hurl him like this, with a simple twist of the wrist, from the heights of paternal pride to the depths of opprobrium. He leans farther back, settles himself more profoundly in his chair, rests his elbows on the arms and calmly joins the tips of his fingers together . . . "Tss . . . Tss . . . What are you talking about? What kind of invention is that? Alain's going to have you put out! Alain's going to report you! What is this joke . . . And it is a joke, believe me . . . You know Alain better than I do, he's the frankest, most considerate sort of boy, and with that, affectionate as can be. You know quite well how attached he is to you . . ."

It seems to him that a sort of shedding takes place in her, suddenly she is entirely transformed, and now she appears all shy and blushing, with the purified expression of a confident, happy child. He feels moved. He looks at her . . . certainly, she'll understand . . . he has never been able to put them into words, but she knows him, him too, she knows his feelings . . . "Alain is high-tempered, you know that better than I do, he's full of whims, we've spoiled him enough . . . And you especially, with you he lets himself go . . . when he gets angry, he doesn't know what he's saying . . . Alain go and report you . . . Really, I can assure you, at times . . ." She leans towards him and says in a low voice, as though she were afraid of being overheard: "I ask nothing better than to believe what you say, you know that, you know what he means to me. Only, the point is . . . There was something else too. It wasn't just the things he said. Something happened a few days ago. I had a telephone call from the agent . . ." He gives a start, draws aside: "From the agent? —Yes, from the agent, only not exactly about that, it was about some water pipes. But in connection with that, he said: a dressing room and a bathroom, it seems to me that's rather a lot, all that, for just one person. And a few days before, Alain had come and told me: 'You know you have no right to stay, I could have you put out, my father-in-law knows the landlord.' Just imagine . . . Above all, it's to think that Alain . . ."

He feels a pain, a twinge, there's something in him that's gathering, pressing . . . it's not that, not what she has just thrust into him that hurts so much . . . that doesn't hold water, that story, it's fantastic, it's old-fashioned melodrama . . . "Tss . . . tss . . . you're losing your senses, I assure you, that's a mere coincidence, take my word for it. Alain couldn't do that, it's madness, there's no question of it. You know perfectly well that he says just anything at all when he's in a rage. If that's what keeps you awake at nights . . ." He knows what it is now, it's his old pain, his old, implacable malady, which has reappeared this time in an aggravated form, as always after a period of abatement . . . Old idiot, old fool that he is! He had thought that he was rid of it, he had felt so happy, he had reproached himself . . . what folly it is to worry . . . it's so easy to be wrong about one's children, we are so unjust, so hard to please . . . he was such a good little boy . . . his own blood . . . that affectionate smile he used to have, that little child's smile, that hand on his shoulder . . .

"Oh, well, Papa, it doesn't matter, let it drop, don't do anything more about it, things are all right as they are, I don't care a rap, you know, really, about that apartment. If Aunt Berthe hadn't spoken to us about it, we shouldn't even have given it a thought." We forget, we think we're cured, and the malady is still there, tenacious, stealthy . . . Let no one talk to him about education, what nonsense . . . there's no way of changing people's real nature, what they are, in reality, will always crop out . . . This fear, which he feels growing inside him now, is the same, he recognizes it, that was sown and made to germinate in him by old-fashioned detective novels . . . that scene, in one of them, he doesn't remember which, every time it comes back to him, he has the same little reaction of revulsion . . . An old house in London, a large room the walls of which are hung with garnet-red silk; the fire in the fireplace casts a sinister glow, a number of guests are seated about bridge tables . . . the murderer must be among them . . . the detective has placed everywhere, within reach of people's hands, all kinds of objects, strange firearms brought back from the colonies and, on a certain low chased-copper table from India, a very fine stiletto which may be used as a paper cutter, the stiletto being the murderer's favorite weapon; each one of his crimes bears his "signature." All that's needed is to watch, to wait. Finally the moment arrives. An irresistible force, something furtive, at once avid and blind, something very terrifying, horrible, makes one of the guests stretch out his hand towards the stiletto . . . Without realizing it, she has just divulged it to him, the signature—still the same—and the same blind force which, already then, made the little boy's eyes shine when they used to stand together in front of shop-windows, of pastry shops, a secret greed . . . The child had never asked him for anything, he hadn't dared . . . he would ask his doting auntie . . . "But you won't tell Papa I asked you, Papa doesn't like that, he'll be put out . . ."; this same greed, this avidity in his young wolf's shining, glassy eyes, while he was hurrying to see the old lady—but don't say anything to poor old Papa, he has his own ideas on the subject, he doesn't understand . . . It was irresistible with him, like an epileptic fit . . . the slightest obstacle exasperates his desire to the point of making him lose his head, everything must yield . . . It's the craven, the shameful exigency of the drunkard, of the drug addict.

"Oh, how happy I am . . . you don't know what pleasure you've given me . . . So you really believe it? Of course, it was mad ever to think it . . ." She opens the wide, enchanted eyes of a child, a minute more and she's going to clap her hands.

He thrusts her aside, he thrusts aside with an impatient gesture—imagine such a thing—that childish, preposterous idea . . . "Why no, for goodness sake, it's ridiculous. It's a fit of temper such as he often has. The temper of a spoilt child . . . —I, myself, ask nothing better than to believe it, you know that. You know how I love Alain. If he hadn't frightened me so, well, I don't know, after all, what I should have done. I should perhaps have given in. Actually, it might be considered, he might be right, it's perhaps the intelligent thing to do . . ."

"You would 'perhaps' have given in! . . . You say that to me, why of course, you're going to give in. They needn't worry. It's already settled . . . His suffering, his rage have reached their culminating point. All you've ever done was to give in to his idiotic whims . . . You made him what he is . . . There's nothing anyone can do now . . . just keep it up. Only, I'm going to tell you something . . . I'm going to tell you, shall I, what he needs, Alain, at the present moment. Do you realize the situation he's in? Do you see what he's come to? He'd do better to finish his thesis quickly and ask to be appointed somewhere . . . If he did that, it would already be something. If he were named to just any out-of-the-way hole, it would be preferable to playing the society game, fixing up apartments, sponging—yes, sponging—on his parents-in-law . . . the pain he feels is the same we feel when a wound is cauterized, when a gangrened limb is amputated, it has to be done, till the very end, it must be cleanly cut, this tumor, this sick flesh which is contaminating him must be torn from him, he must not allow himself to rot entirely . . . he's almost shouting, she draws back, frightened . . . that's what he needs, our Alain, if you really want to know: to think of his future . . . His parents-in-law will leave them almost nothing, all that is just so much window dressing, all that luxury, dust in your eyes . . . and it's not brilliant, his future, if you really want to know . . . I'm telling you exactly what I think . . . that marriage has stultified him, and that snobbish, silly set, that Germaine Lemaire, I've seen her, an old fake celebrity who surrounds herself with young morons like him for the sake of their adulation . . . Ah, don't talk to me about luxurious apartments . . . The future he has before him—I know what I'm saying—isn't very bright and he'll have to be satisfied with it . . . now the pain, although sharp, is beginning to diminish . . . a very modest future, meager security, a pension, a salary. He'll be lucky at that, if he succeeds in getting some sort of appointment, he hasn't his doctor's degree, as for his thesis, I don't know what it will be worth . . . if he's able to get a position as substitute, or assistant, he'll be fortunate . . . The pain is becoming duller, little by little, it appears to be calming down

. . . Don't talk to me about settling in Paris, in five rooms, in a swanky neighborhood, entertaining . . . giving parties . . . as they say . . . fiestas, as he says . . ."

No, really. After all, there's such a thing as order, thank God. As justice. Even in this world. It's still there, where it should be, everything upon which he has built his own life, in the name of which he has had the strength to overcome all obstacles: he has had to deprive himself, drudge, there have been of course hard moments, but he has never doubted, and that has been his salvation, he has never ceased to believe that there exists, in this world, a golden rule, a law to which all must submit . . . otherwise, everything totters, collapses, soft, crumbling ground on which we lose our footing . . . Order must reign, good must triumph, endeavor and work must receive their just reward, all gatecrashers must be punished . . . He's willing to suffer, to execute his own son, to offer in sacrifice, if need be what is dearest to him, his child's life . . . "Don't worry, Alain will be made to understand. I hope, for his sake, that it won't be too late. Life will teach him, as it does everybody else. He'll see. He won't act like a child forever . . . And it's better like that. Even for him, it's much better that way."

She smiles with a meager, slightly ironic and indulgent smile, she sets her upper lip and the mobile end of her nose moving first to one side, then to the other, she's looking in front of her, she seems to be figuring something out, computing . . . "Listen, permit me to tell you, there you paint too black a picture, you know perfectly well that it's not like that, you see the gloomy side of everything. To hear you talk, you might think they risked ending their days in the poorhouse. Even if Gisèle should have nothing, later on—and that's not sure, either—Still, let's assume it . . . But what about me, what I'm going to leave them is certainly more than the equivalent of all the pensions he might receive. It's much more, and you know it . . ."

I'm going to leave you . . . you're going to have . . . After my death, you need have no cause for anxiety . . . what I'm going to leave you will be more than all that . . . It's exactly the same tune, the same key . . . "It's extraordinary, at times, how like Papa you can be, I can hear him now . . . you remember when he used to say: They're not worth a hoot all those plans of yours, what is that compared to what I'm going to leave you . . ." And it's also the same sensation as in the past, when he was quite young, a frail, shy adolescent, understanding only vaguely what happened to him, not daring to rely on his impressions, but now he knows, he has understood, it's this same sensation, after so many years, after such immense changes—it reappears like those pains in amputated limbs, in bones long since knit together, as soon as the cold weather sets in—a curious sensation of suffocating . . . something heavy fell down on him, a grave-stone, the door of a vault, they are locked in, he, his child, they are walled in, buried alive, and she, seated on top of them, bearing down upon them with all her weight, handsome marble statue of herself, which she has had made and which she is gazing at in advance, with satisfaction—erected for all time on the slab decorated with brass vases, in the family vault, watching over their "rest" . . . But it's over, all that, the good old days are over, he's strong now, he knows how to defend himself against the dead, lift up heavy marble stones and solid bronze vases, demolish mortuary statues . . . He looks at her with an expression that is voluntarily amused, distant . . . delights of maturity, of old age . . . now he can amuse himself . . . he has paid his quota, generously . . . "You make me laugh with that talk . . . You take me back to the good old days . . . That didn't teach you a lesson, what happened to that famous fortune, to those famous investments which kept poor Papa so occupied . . . You saw how it all turned out . . ."

She nods her head slowly and puckers her lips with an air of disapproval as though she were looking at a child who is making faces to exasperate the grownups . . . "Oh, listen, what connection is there? You know quite well, there's nothing in common. You know what Papa was like. When he got carried away by something . . . people could do anything they wanted with him. How can you compare him to Henri. They were certainly far more reliable, Henri's investments. He always told me: if anything happens to me, I'm not worried about you." She leans towards him, lays her hand on his arm: "Listen, I wish you would tell me . . . Jardot tells me that oil stocks have gone up again. He advises me to sell now. I was just going to ask you . . . What do you think about it? I myself should have preferred to wait a bit. What do you think?"

It's comical to see her appear in this disguise: the wolf in sheep's clothing, imitating its bleating . . . advise me, I don't know, what do you think, I'm so alone, so naive, you are strong, you understand . . . please help me . . . But he sees her eyes shining, the gleam of her long teeth . . . Reliable, wary, distrustful, she can give any businessman lessons when it comes to figuring, or investments . . . No more giddiness when it's a matter of that, no more trembling, she's very well-informed, she has probably already made her decision.

It irritates him to feel her watching him slyly, waiting for the moment when, having lost all distrust, flattered, touched, he'll start to think about it, explain it to her, quite proud, generous, strong, condescending, while she, bowed, bent over double, will lead him gently, with feeble, tottering steps, to the place to which she wants to lure him, to territory over which she reigns supreme, where he'll finally be at her mercy, willing to give up those ravings of an old "idealist," of someone who is maladjusted, and submit, as she does, to the rules of common sense, of good, sound reality, walk straight, fall back into the ranks . . . He shrugs his shoulders, he has a little disillusioned, contemptuous smile . . . "Oh, listen, you make me laugh, I don't think you need me for that. You know better than I do the price of oil stocks at present. I believe I have no advice to give you . . . —Yes, of course, I know what they're worth . . . But Jardot tells me that just now the prices are inflated . . ."

Is this another trick on her part, or was he entirely mistaken and had she been really sincere from the beginning? . . . Has he been, for once, too distrustful, he wonders . . . She suddenly assumes a serious, preoccupied tone, from her manner, she's not thinking of him, but staring with the greatest attention at the object she's presenting him with . . . "Jardot advises me to sell those shares now and buy them back when they go down . . ."

Something is about to be perpetrated under his very eyes, something exasperating, unbearable, an act of blind vandalism, stupid destruction, an intolerable mess . . . that must be stopped at all cost, he feels himself blushing, his voice grows louder . . . "Isn't he smart, your friend Jardot . . . How can he tell . . . What is it that permits him to feel so sure that they won't go higher still?" Like troops the commanding general has sent to the part of the battlefield that is suddenly threatened, all his immediately mobilized strength attacks this suddenly encountered enemy, this half-wit, this criminal . . . "Jardot gives me the impression, sometimes, of being completely stupid, I assure you . . . It's completely stupid what he tells you . . . Why, just think a minute . . . there's not the slightest sign either here or in the United States, that the rise is about to stop. On the contrary, if you want my opinion, I believe it has only just begun. If you sell, you risk staying, I don't know how long, with your assets on your hands, watching prices climb . . ." The commotion, the excitement, the mobilization of all his dispersed strength, the attack he has launched against a definite objective, the power, the precision of his blows, give him a delightful sensation of self-assurance, of pride . . . He sees that she is looking at him with respect, that she is listening seriously, with close attention . . . "But for goodness sake, Berthe, you're not going in for speculation, are you . . . What's got into your friend Jardot?"

She leans towards him, she seems happy. She gives in, she's on his side. She's going to band together with him against their common enemy . . . "That's how it looked to me, too. That's why I wanted to talk it over with you . . . I thought so . . . —But see here, it's perfectly obvious. There's no need to think. There's a golden rule, I've always said it: never give up a stock you're sure of . . ." The enemy has fled, abandoning his positions, the ground is cleared, it's a walk-away for the two of them now, side by side, across the reconquered land, she looks at him fondly, he laughs gaily . . . "You know old Vanderbilt's secret . . ." Yes, she remembers. He had told it to her. She laughs with an affectionate, trusting sort of laugh. His good old sister. His friend. Together, hand in hand . . .

He feels entirely relaxed, he would like to let himself go. Life can be sweet. He has a mania for taking things too tragically, for always walking on stilts, perched on high-minded principles . . . It's that morbid love of his—the result of an old habit—for unrest, suffering . . . It's as though he were stiff from having remained so long in uncomfortable positions . . . it's good to relax a bit—his legs and arms are numb . . . to stretch himself . . . why not, after all, what harm is there in it, what difference does it make? The good old earth trod by people with practical sense, with common sense, feels nice and solid under his feet, like one of those beautiful, thick-set English lawns that have been mown for centuries and trampled upon by so many generations . . . Alain's future is assured . . . Well, then, so much the better . . . No need to worry any more. His role of father ended long ago. He must learn finally to keep his distance, remain detached. It's high time . . . All that concerns him no longer. He's done his duty. There's nothing more to be done. The task is completed. There's no effort that could change things now. And it's very well as it is, it's perfect. He has a sense of well-being in all his limbs as he stretches himself . . . an exquisite sensation of lightness, an old hankering, which he had forgotten, for freedom, for insouciance . . . Free at last, relieved. Let them do whatever they want . . . She's watching him, she would appear to have understood, she seems pleased, soothed, she too, she lays her hand on his shoulder . . . "So, then, Pierre, about Alain, do you agree? I think you share my opinion. I'll have to think about it. In principle, I don't say no. I'll have to see. Only, what I shall ask you to do is to tell Alain. After what happened, you understand, I don't feel like doing it . . . If you would just tell Alain that I'm thinking it over. That he should come to see me . . ." He draws away from her a bit, he rises, readjusts the crease in his trousers, throws his elbows back to bring his shoulder blades closer together, frees his neck from his collar, it's good to feel this cracking, and his neck and back so straight. "Ah, no, Berthe dear, as for that, it's finished, I'm not going to get mixed up in it. I think you're both of you big enough. You'll get along very well without me."

No, QUITE EVIDENTLY, it would be better to leave it. More than anything, it's that line, there, the contours of the arm, of the shoulder . . . no doubt about it, there's something there that's a bit affected, a bit weak . . . and just as soon as you've recognized it, it spreads to all the rest, as always happens, it contaminates, infects everything else. The whole thing appears to be from a very late epoch, the copy of a copy. But what a heartbreak . . . You can look a long time before you'll find a head like this one . . . and the other arm, the hang of the pleats, the child's body . . . what tender grace, and what strength, what modesty . . . it fairly vibrates, it's alive . . . "That's very lovely, by Jove, quite astonishing . . . where did you find it? You know it's really a rare piece . . . They're going to walk all round it, very excited, they're going to come nearer, lean over, pucker their eyelids, readjust their glasses . . . Do you know what it reminds me of? Of those marvelous Gothic statues of the Loire School . . ." He will lower his eyes modestly: "Oh! I ran across it quite by chance . . . I noticed it while I was out walking one day, in a little secondhand shop . . ." They will shake their heads, they will purse their lips. "Well, well . . ." But he will be obliged to suppress his pride, his satisfaction, the danger will still be present, each second more threatening, he will have to lie in wait, keep watch . . . a single move, a very slight shift of their eyes, which they will turn a few degrees to one side, and their glance will alight, will settle there, on that shoulder, that arm . . . he will have to try to forestall them, so as to prepare them, to coax them, beg their indulgence . . .

"Yes, only there, I know, it's questionable, isn't it? I know . . . It's so much less good than the rest—don't you agree with me?—that I wondered if it had not been added, and yet . . ." They are going to examine it more closely: "Not at all, you can't see it . . . —I hesitated to take it . . . that worried me . . ." and they will reassure him, amusedly, somewhat condescendingly . . . "Yes, there, certainly . . . But you would have made a mistake. It's very nice, all the same." Never will he be able to relax his vigilance. Constantly, behind his back, their discreetly prospecting glance will graze it imperceptibly, then turn aside right away, a little flame will light up in the depths of their eyes: Well, well, so that's the discriminating connoisseur, the great expert, so that's it, that's his much-vaunted taste, why he knows nothing about it, poor Alain, nothing . . . "Did you notice on his mantel that Virgin with Child? . . . That's fake Renaissance, or I know nothing about it . . . Who ever heard of putting a thing like that in one's house." No, he must resist temptation. There will be no vulnerable spot on which they can strike him, make a hole in him, through which they can empty him and amuse themselves gulping him down whole with one swallow, as one gulps an egg, leaving nothing of him except a fragile shell . . .

"So you're interested in Renaissance things?" Alert. Commotion. While he was there warding off God knows what imaginary attacks, trying to steer clear of the traps laid by an invented adversary, the enemy, the real, the only deadly one, was spying on him . . . Now the enemy has pounced upon him. He feels his heavy hand on his shoulders, his loud, rollicking laughter flowing down over him. He gathers all his courage, turns round—that's it, all right, there he is in front of him, heavily set on his widespread legs; the pockets of his worn overcoat, stuffed with magazines, with newspapers, enlarge his girth; the thick, powerful neck, traversed by a great roll of flesh, emerges from an open collar; a faded, battered hat is pushed back on his head; full lips grown soft from chewing countless cigarette butts, slit the big, jovial face from ear to ear. Replete satisfaction gleams, as usual, in the depths of the sharp little eyes: "They're apparently very much sought after, eh, Renaissance things, just now?"

To the rescue, my companions. My real friends. All who speak the same language, who are of the same blood. All those, whom I was dreading, who would have hovered about with curiosity, with respect . . . stand by me. Let's forget our internal struggles, our criminal wars between brothers. Let us stand together against the common enemy. The barbarian is at our gates. Our entire scale of values is threatened. Everything that makes life worthwhile for us is going to be scoffed at, destroyed. While we were arguing about the sex of the angels, the savage Turk was laying siege to Byzantium. All our virgins, whether of early or late epochs, will be trampled upon by the feet of his horses . . . We must hide everything that is sacred, hide our treasures from his gaze, from his impious hands . . . "Renaissance things, very much sought after? Ah . . . really, I didn't know that, you are better informed than I am . . . Why no . . . I didn't even think of it. I was looking to see if I could find some furniture . . . A table and some chairs are what I'm looking for. The period doesn't matter . . . I'm not very particular. What I need is furniture. I've just moved. —Ah! so you're moving . . ."

Disaster. Madness. In his disorderly haste, in his confusion, he has opened a breach through which the enemy will come surging, it seems to him that he already hears the deafening noise of chariots, galloping horses, barbarian shouts . . . "Ah! So you're moving! And where are you going to live?" He will run, throw down his arms, take shameful flight. . .

"I'm going . . . we're going to live . . . yes . . . in my aunt's apartment . . . he will throw himself at the other's feet, plead for mercy . . . We're going to move . . . to Passy . . ." The enemy will be pitiless. He can hear now his fierce laughter . . . "To Passy? So you're moving to a swanky neighborhood?" He's captured, bound, he's being dragged behind the victor's chariot, his clothes torn, face down in the dust, laughed at, booed at . . . Well, how about that, to a swanky neighborhood . . . He's going to settle in Passy, in his aunt's apartment . . . How about those bourgeois leanings . . . that spoilt child. That little snob. Influential friends. Silver plate and entertaining. How about it . . . But the adversary doesn't make a move, doesn't so much as look at the open breach. There's no need even to try to fill it in . . . And yet it would be better to stop it up quickly, with whatever is at hand, he picks up just anything . . . "Yes, we're changing apartments . . . that is to say, my aunt had had about enough of hers. It was too big. So she decided to exchange with us . . . Well, not exactly with us . . ." Useless endeavors. Vain alarms. Nothing about the enemy's movements would indicate that an attack is in preparation. On his side, all is calm, peaceful; smoke is rising reassuringly from his bivouacs . . . "Is that so, well that's fine, I should say it is, in these times that's great luck . . . And your work, how's that coming along? Your thesis? I saw Dastier the other day, he told me it had progressed considerably. When do you expect to finish it?" Not a trace of envy in him. Not the slightest thirst for conquest, for destruction—he doesn't need that, obviously . . . he lets others live as they want. He seems so invulnerable, so powerful.

Ensconced in some little attic room, furnished with a torn couch with the stuffing coming out, a plain deal table, old packing cases piled high with books, pamphlets, papers, he turns his clear, cool gaze upon the world. Upon these beings who dash excitedly about, driven by passions that are childish, vain. At present his gaze is turned upon this thing that is wriggling there in front of him, upon this young Alain Guimiez . . . a very nice lad, dissatisfied, anxious . . . a very pure product of his class: a young bourgeois intellectual married to a spoilt little girl like himself. But what's to be done about that? They are as they are. Neither better nor worse than others would be in their place. They can do nothing about it, poor children. They're caught in the mechanism. Squirrels going round and round in their golden cage. From time to time, probably, making touching efforts to escape. But too weak to break the bars. Help would have to come from the outside; everything would have to be smashed: an immense upheaval. But that's not going to happen today. And meanwhile, they have to be taken as they are, helped even—why not?—if need be . . . "Ah, already? It will be finished by next May? You've got that far? —Yes, it's nearly finished. It'll be none too soon. Given the length of time . . . I'm impatient now to get through with it and do something else more interesting. I've really had enough of it . . ." Yes, he has had enough of it. Enough of all these pretenses. Enough of feeling himself slipping, clutching at things that give way, enough of this wretched seeking which leaves him more unsated, more indigent than before. Enough of apartments, of Gothic statues, of friends whose very names cause to bend, then straighten up in people, something flexible, something as light as grass which is beaten down for an instant by a breath of wind, then rises up instantly and reaches towards the sun. To leave all that. To change his skin. To change his life. To be seated, he too, on the peaks where a bracing wind blows. To drink at its very spring, a water that nothing can pollute. To be allowed to share in this certainty, this security. To watch from a distance the gyrations of these creatures similar to what he himself was, wretched, anxious . . .

He tries to come a little closer. He bows respectfully and lays at the feet of him whom he begs to be allowed to follow, to redeem himself, to save himself, all that he can give him, a very modest offering, a mere trifle, he can find nothing else . . . "I wonder if you saw, if you read the article about you in last month's *Sources* . . . In connection with your essay on Husserl? —No, I didn't see it, I don't know . . ." He doesn't even glance at what has just been brought him. His face retains the smiling impassibility of a Buddha: "You know one doesn't see everything. It's been years since I subscribed to a clipping service. Well, good-bye . . ." Oh, no, don't leave me . . . Everything about me is wavering and trembling, I'm beyond my depth . . . One moment more . . . Don't let go of me . . . "I'm glad to have seen you. I should like so much to have a talk with you. I should like to have your advice. I've been working on an article . . . I should like to show you . . ." But the smooth, dry fingers have loosened their hold, they are slipping, trying to free themselves . . . "Why, certainly, I ask nothing better. Only, just at present, I'm a bit rushed . . . Proofs of a book that's coming out to be corrected . . . and the *agrégation* papers which are due any day now. But do give me your address. I'm not sure that I have it. He feels in his pocket, takes out a notebook. Let's see . . . Alain Guimiez . . . He looks up, all of a sudden . . . By the way, what about Germaine Lemaire? What's become of her? Do you ever see her? It's a long time since I've seen her . . . She gives me a feeling of remorse . . . Every time I see her, she chides me a bit. I keep promising myself to go to see her. To telephone her . . ."

Everything is crumbling . . . everything that he has so skillfully, so patiently constructed, at the cost of constant, anxious endeavor . . . each detail, however minute, worked out with apprehensive care . . . Little rustic bouquets cautiously chosen . . . no, not that, just these poppies, the cornflowers, some big daisies, perhaps . . . no, she won't like that . . . that might spoil it . . . rare editions unearthed for her alone, to see her lay one hand on top of the other, look at him wide-eyed . . . "Oh, that's too lovely . . . You're mad, really . . . Where on earth did you find that?" Notes torn up a hundred times before they achieved that free, spontaneous, spare tone . . . Impulses, movements, restrained by male diffidence and which, at times, while she looked on with an enchanted, melting expression, made him rear up, strong and graceful, like a thoroughbred . . . Caresses that must be continually reinvented, varied, improved upon to satisfy an aging, weary vanity which a too insistent touch leaves cold but which, at times, is delightfully titillated by the lightest of contacts, yet how unexpected, how exquisite . . . "You're funny, really . . . Me? . . . the gray eyes are wide with astonishment . . . Me? You think so? No one ever told me that . . . It's strange . . . You're the first . . ." This understanding with him alone, this complicity against all the others, against this particular one, this ponderous philosopher who understands next to nothing about art . . . "A milliner, don't you agree? . . . Yes, he agreed . . . A milliner, a dress-designer, is more genuinely creative, has more originality, more imagination . . ."

Loathsome playacting. Filthy lie. Treachery . . . The other chap need only appear on the scene, heavy, self-sufficient, easing his thick neck, well ballasted on his widespread short legs, and right away she will hasten towards him, submissive, plaintive, gentleness itself, humbly begging . . . "When? When are you coming to see me? You're a brute, you're a wretch. You always promise . . . This time, I'm going to take you up on it. Next Sunday. You can't? Then when? Oh, you're impossible . . . Well, telephone me . . . Whenever you want, any day, I go out so little, you know, I'm in all day . . ."

Everything she had shown to him was just so much

trumpery, a poor imitation, no one but he would have mistaken it. . . . All those smiles for him alone, that secret understanding, those gestures that had seemed so spontaneous to him, little pats on the shoulder, looks of genuine friendship . . . "We must see each other oftener . . ." that was the dose she gave him coldly, his injection: he suffered so, poor thing, he had to be relieved. But not a bit more than what he had a right to. To each one his due, each one in his place. Nothing would ever permit him to graduate from the category of her charity poor, whom she cared for, who were objects of her solicitude (all kinds of signs gave indication of their station—and he had always known it, he had guessed it, but he had weakly pretended not to know it—certain days when they're not admitted, certain things that aren't said to them: telephone me whenever you want . . . I'm always in . . . it would of course be too dangerous to put such temptations in the way of these wretched starvelings, they must be kept in their place, at a certain distance, one must never yield, never permit oneself to be incited to pity, otherwise what liberties would they not take?), never, no matter what effort he made, would he graduate from this class of the poor and needy to that of the mighty, of her peers.

He's shattered, done for. Now he's like a little boat with a thin, fragile bottom that a big ship has run into, ripped open, he's bursting on all sides, he's about to sink . . .

"When you see Germaine Lemaire, remember me to her. Tell her that I haven't forgotten her. I must get in touch with her. But there's so little time . . . And then, I must admit to you . . . It's funny . . . I'm always a bit bored at her house . . ." The enormous, thick, reinforced hull of the big liner, of the battleship, barges ahead, crushing everything . . . "And yet she's not stupid, intelligent even, if you like, but I don't know why, she bores me . . ." A huge explosion reduces everything to a powder, all at once . . . "And then her vanity . . . She thinks she's a little too Germaine Lemaire, ha-ha-ha . . . But she's a good sort, really . . . ha-ha . . ." Everything sinks, everything is engulfed, while the big liner goes on its way . . . It must not have received the slightest shock. There must not be the slightest trace, the tiniest scratch, on its beautiful, shining hull . . .

He must let this sensation wear off . . . As though the ground were giving way beneath him . . . this vague nausea . . . before estimating the extent of the disaster . . . While he walks mechanically along, without knowing exactly where he's going, on the pavement behind him, he hears hurried footsteps . . . "Hey, there, Guimiez . . ." The big face is red, the voice a bit breathless . . . "Tell me, Guimiez . . . One thing more . . . It just occurred to me, I forgot to ask you when you mentioned it: that article about me, it's in which issue of *Sources*? Who wrote it, do you remember?" The smile he had been wearing so heroically a few moments earlier, when everything had flown to pieces, has not yet disappeared from his face: in his confusion, he has forgotten it, and the smile is still there, fortunately, ready-to-wear . . . "Yes, certainly, I remember. It was in last month's issue."

Oh, Maine, what a lovely thing . . . It's enchanting . . He takes the delicate amphora by both of its handles and holds it up in the air, with outstretched arms, he half-closes his eyes the better to see it, sets it cautiously on the mantelpiece . . . "There . . . we must put it here, it's just the place . . . It will be the principle ornament of the living room . . ." He steps back, fondles its neck, its handles, its sides . . . he turns it round a bit . . . "Like that, it's perfect . . . You can see the reflection of that glorious fawn, of that chariot, in the mirror . . . What purity of line, it's amazing . . ." But there's nothing to be done about it, the current doesn't come through. He feels in all his gestures, in his words, in his intonations, something a bit stilted, a stiffness, an extravagance, it all lacks warmth, life . . . one is reminded of somewhat awkward, gross copies, made from memory, of a prescribed model, a perfect model with which he is familiar, and she too: she is comparing these dull copies with this ideal model, as she sits there on the sofa, very erect, very calm, just a little surprised, surely—but she doesn't want to show it—a little disappointed, frustrated . . . a picture of him is forming inside her, which nothing can ever erase, she's going to carry it away with her, keep it . . . this must be prevented, he turns towards her a face in which he does his best to express the admiration, the enchantment which are there, nevertheless, inside him, he feels them . . . "This amphora makes me think of those I saw in the museum in Arezzo, where there were some beautiful ones . . . Really, Maine, you're too generous with us, it's too nice of you . . ."

But it's not his fault, he's in no way responsible . . . There, he knows it, is what is keeping his feelings from flowing generously, freely, warmly, into his gestures, it's this lifeless mass there beside him, this heavy block . . . All his strength, all the waves he is transmitting diverge towards that, he must shake it, make it vibrate . . . "Don't you agree with me, Gisèle, that this amphora is as lovely as those we saw in the Arezzo museum? . . . Really, Maine is too generous with us . . . no, turn it a little this way . . . Look at that fawn, those horses . . ." But a few slight vibrations are the only evidence that a very weak current is passing through the lifeless mass . . . "Yes, you're right Alain, it's very lovely, it's enchanting . . ." There's nothing to be done, he knows it, however great an effort he may make, it only serves to increase, as always, this lifelessness, to add to this opposition . . . he must have the courage to stop short, to give up . . . he casts one more hesitant, nostalgic glance at the mantelpiece . . .

"Well, I'm glad you like it. I brought it back from my last trip to Italy. I was told that it came from Paestum, and it was guaranteed to date from the beginning of the fourth century . . . But of course, one never knows . . ." He nods assent, he protests: "Oh, that must surely be true . . . How could it be otherwise? You have only to look at this drawing . . . exactly the style of Medias, only more austere, less ornate . . ." She pulls herself up from the sofa, holds out her hand to him—a rather emphatic gesture, too, in which he feels something a bit ill at ease, a bit false . . . the aftereffects, probably, of the disappointment she has just experienced and which she has already overcome . . . "Come along, now, show me everything . . . You know I haven't seen anything yet, it looks like a magnificent place you have . . ." Chin up, now, she's leaving him one last hope, she's giving him a chance . . . he takes her hand, helps her up . . . "Yes, do, come with me. Excuse me if I go ahead of you, to show the way . . ." he walks just in front of her, turned towards her, the length of the long hall, he opens all the doors, that of the little linen room, those of the kitchen, the bathroom, wall-cupboards, everything here is hers, she's at home here, the queen is at home everywhere in the homes of all her vassals, over the château which she's visiting the royal colors float . . . She inspects with kindly curiosity, she inaugurates, she launches, unveils for others who will come after her, to admire, to marvel . . . The least thing arrests her glance, some tiny thing, that latticed cupboard for soiled linen under the dressing room window . . . "That's nice, they're very convenient, those gadgets . . ." Something slips inside him . . . a vague uneasiness, annoyance, like a very slight repulsion, he shrinks ever so slightly, he would like to turn aside, withdraw—it's his old defense reflex that comes into play in spite of himself, the one he feels . . . But where does he imagine he is? With whom? What is he thinking about? Against what is he trying to defend himself here? Against what platitudes? Against what narrow little material spirit? What pettiness? Here we are all lords and ladies, we can indulge ourselves like that, examining with an excited gleam in our eyes, with intense interest, almost envy, soiled linen presses with latticed ventilation, nothing we do here, amongst ourselves, can lower us, she can permit herself the luxury of deriving pleasure from "those gadgets," like the practical woman that she can be, and this is so admirable in her, so touching . . . weeding her own garden, planting her cabbages, keeping her accounts, quite so, liking to cook . . . Maine's juicy omelets, Maine's *carpe au bleu* . . . The little uneasiness has almost entirely disappeared, there remain only a few very faint traces, thin trails . . . with a little effort they'll soon be gone . . . He must back away a bit, he's too close to her, he must move off to a certain distance, so as to recover—he had lost it—a sense of reality, of true proportion . . . go stand with all those, and they're innumerable, whose hungry eyes avidly devour her picture when it appears on the television screen, on the covers of luxury magazines, in bookshop windows, project himself farther still, very far from here, from this rather vulgar woman, right beside him, pointing her large forefinger with its painted nail towards the cupboard, and see her as they see her, all those who, scattered in every corner of the earth, alone in their rooms, holding one of her books in their hands, their eyes raised towards her, gaze at her the way the faithful on their knees gaze at the Madonna, trembling and sparkling in the candlelight, crowned with precious stones, arrayed in satin and velvet, covered with gold pieces brought as offerings . . . He feels welling up in him the emotion, the surprise, the awe that they would feel if Germaine Lemaire in person were standing in the middle of their kitchens, pointing her finger towards their cupboards, stopping to admire the view from their bedroom windows . . . he has been too spoilt, he's been given too much, he's unworthy, he doesn't deserve it . . . he would like to retire into the background . . . she should look, rather . . . he's dancing attendance, he steps to one side, pulls the curtains farther apart . . . if she would be so gracious as to let her gaze . . . "That way, look, when you stand here, you can see, it's lovely, isn't it? The Seine, the barges, the reflections in the water . . ." She nods with an air of approval, of admiration, then turns, starts examining the room . . . "What beautiful proportions, and what a lovely light." He takes hold of her arm, all excited . . . "But you haven't seen anything yet, that's nothing . . . Come and see the dining room, my study" . . . Pride from some distant source, he's none too sure from where, surges up inside him, rolls its high waves . . . See my estates, my châteaux, these marks of my power, my titles of nobility, the valorous acts of my ancestors who were the first of my glorious line . . . admire my courage, my noble deeds . . . "This woodwork . . . ah, you like it? I thought it would be nice . . . It's quite ordinary wood, African okoumé. It all depends on how it is handled . . . That's a miniature my great-grandfather picked up in Persia . . . Here we've put a curtain for the time being. Later, we're going to put a sliding door . . . Ah, there, don't look at that . . . that was what drove my aunt to desperation. —By the way, what about your aunt? How is she getting along? She's not sorry? —My aunt? Certainly not, she's delighted . . . She's fixing up her new flat: she likes nothing so well. She looks twenty years younger. She wants the whole thing to be modern . . . the very latest style . . . She decided to get rid of what she calls her old rubbish . . . This chest of drawers, for instance, and this *bergère*, she left for us . . . The *bergère*'s nice, isn't it? —Yes, I had noticed it . . . It goes very well with the other one, that's a piece of luck, they match . . . And what about the leather easy chairs, are they forgotten? —Yes. Thank goodness, I think I won that round . . . And we've succeeded in getting rid of all the knick-knacks . . . Oh no, don't look at that door . . . —So, that's it, the famous one you told me about, you were so amusing . . . That's the one that caused your aunt such suffering? —Yes, she was sick over it, she called me in the middle of the night . . . —In the middle of the night? She laughs . . . Yes, yes, that's true, you told me about that . . ." He laughs too, he feels happy, very free, relaxed . . . "Yes, about the handle. The decorator—can you imagine it! had put a chromium-plated handle! But I must admit that chromium, or not chromium . . . Even with this one . . . I think one day we're going to have to . . ." She looks very attentively at the door . . . "No, really, I must say I like it . . . They're lovely, those old handles . . . Advancing a few steps, she takes the big heavy handle made of smooth solid brass, in her hand . . . Some people might find that a little

. . . farfetched here, but I must admit that I like that oval shape very much, the effect is very soft . . . it's a change from all these straight, rather cold lines . . . There are any number of doors like that in the South . . . You see them everywhere . . . in lovely houses . . . elsewhere, too, that's true, in those awful little bungalows they're building beside the road that follows the coast . . . But what difference does that make? It has to be seen here. And here, well, personally, I am not shocked by it, I think it's very agreeable, the effect is very nice." In one second, the most amazing, the most marvelous metamorphosis takes place. As though touched by a fairy wand, the door which, as soon as he had set eyes on it, had been surrounded by the thin papier-mâché walls, the hideous cement of suburban houses, like princesses whom an evil spell has changed into toads, reverts to its original aspect, when, resplendent with life, it had appeared framed in the walls of an old convent cloister . . . From the curved lines of its apex, of its polished oak medallions, there flows a shy, tender gentleness. It's a delightful surprise, it's the nicest of gifts, he performs a joyful pirouette, calls out: "Did you hear that, Gisèle, Maine thinks the oval door is very pretty. She thinks it looks very nice here." Delighted, emboldened, self-confident, he nods, pointing towards the little dark oak bench in the corner by the window: "And that, that corner under the window, do you like that?" She looks, she's considering it, and he feels anxious, the solid ground on which he was standing, starts to move . . . she hesitates . . . what does she see? what can she be thinking? . . . He waits. Finally, she makes up her mind: "Now there, really, I don't know. It seems to me that a good comfortable easy chair in front of that window, that view . . ." He stumbles, he's reeling, he hangs on . . . "Ah . . . Whereas we, that is, I . . . thought it was so pretty . . . it's an old church bench . . . —Yes, I see that . . . But I'm not so sure

. . ." Something is swaying, trembling over there, too, in the slender, silent figure that is busying itself about the tea table, something in it too has begun to totter, from one instant to the other, something may collapse . . . he perceives, coming from there, directed at him alone, in a mute language, their own language, an appeal, more than an appeal, an objurgation not to betray, not to cast under the heel of the outsider, in a moment of weakness, in a moment of despicable cowardliness, under the heel of the insolent, unmannerly intruder, their secret treasures which together, both of them, they have chosen reverently, fervently, contemplatively—warm, palpitating particles of life . . . peering through the window of an old farmhouse, taking each other by the hand . . . do come, come and look, Alain . . . sitting down side by side in little country churches, little mountain chapels . . . that bench . . . I wanted to carry it away with me . . . magical objects, bewitched trees . . . He calls her, he implores her . . . "Gisèle, listen . . . she must not desert him, she must join with him . . . this bench is very pretty, but perhaps here, in front of this window . . . it's true, perhaps a big armchair . . . what do you think? . . . it's perhaps an idea . . . —No, Alain . . . her voice is dry, cutting. His woeful cry arouses no pity . . . No, Alain, I don't think so . . . it is rejected gently but with firmness . . . Personally, I don't know why, I like it here very much, in front of this window, particularly . . ." He wavers, stammers . . . "Perhaps . . . well . . . we'll . . . well, we'll see . . . No, listen Gisèle . . . we'll have to see . . ." Her stern voice is calling them, calling him to order like a child: "Tea is ready . . . Come and have some tea . . ." They walk towards the table . . . "Oh, look, there, on the sideboard, what is that? She pauses . . . How very lovely it is, that Gothic virgin. —Yes, it's not bad, is it? I believe it belongs to the Loire school . . ." She nods approval with an air that expresses admiration, respect. With his hand he outlines in the air the head of the Virgin, the body of the Infant Jesus . . . "Yes, it's lovely, isn't it?" He would like to hide the other shoulder, that arm . . . however, no, it would be imprudent, there's nothing anyone can do, she will see, she has probably already seen, this is exactly what he had been dreading, he must forestall the danger, quick, take to shelter, protect himself, before it's too late . . . "I hesitated a long time, I went back several times. —Oh, was it very expensive? —Why, no, on the contrary, it was an extraordinary bargain . . . But I felt that there . . . she turns a blank gaze on the restored arm, and he beats a hasty retreat . . . Really, I can't say, that arm . . . it may be authentic . . . I thought, myself . . ." But she doesn't stir. She stares fixedly at the shoulder, the arm, she swallows them stolidly, her strong stomach digests them easily, her eyes maintain the calm, indifferent expression of a cow's eyes . . . Surprise, disappointment mingle in him with a sensation of relief . . . something changes place . . . there is a breach, a sudden cleavage . . . he feels that he is out of his element . . . the oval door is floating, uncertain, suspended in limbo . . . massive old convent door or that of a cheap bungalow . . . And the bench? . . . He would like to look away, to pretend that he has seen nothing, that he has not detected this embarrassing thing about her, like a ridiculous defect, a secret infirmity . . . "Come, let's go, the tea will be cold . . . But speaking of this statue, do you know whom I ran into? He slapped me on the shoulder just as I was wondering whether I was going to buy it or not. No other than Adrien Lebat, imagine. But he's not one whose advice I could ask, you know how he is . . . —That's true, for that sort of thing . . . How is he, anyway? What's he doing? —He seemed very well. Pleased, very self-assured, as usual. He asked me if I had news of you. He said that he would like to come to see you, that he kept intending to telephone you, but that he never has a minute . . . his book . . . his classes . . . examinations papers . . . In any case, he sent you his best regards . . . All of her features, her eyes, her gestures, have a look of happy vivacity as she takes her place at table, reaches for the teacup, sets the cup down in front of her and, pouting like a greedy child, chooses a cake. "So that was all he could think of, that he didn't have time? He's always rushed, it's been like that as long as I've known him. I know he's fond of me, but there's no way of getting him to leave home, to come out of his bear's hole, as he says. I tell him that it's just laziness, in reality . . . That makes him laugh . . . There we have it, Adrien Lebat is a real loafer. But he'll see, you make me think of it . . . I'm going to shake him up a bit . . . —Ho, ho . . . he notices in that little laugh of his something false, something malicious . . . and she looks at him, somewhat surprised . . . That makes me laugh, I don't know why . . . shake Adrien Lebat up a bit . . . I admire your courage . . . your optimism . . . he looks as though he would not so easily let himself be shaken up. There's something so ponderous about him, it would be like trying to move the *Arc de Triomphe*. No, better than that, *Mont Blanc*. With him, I always feel like looking up in the air, he looks so much as if he were throwing it somewhere very high up . . . considering you condescendingly . . ." She frowns: "You? —Well, 'you' . . . I mean everybody, all those like myself, all the pygmies at his feet . . . the poor ants scurrying about, understanding nothing . . . No, I don't know . . . Each time it's the same thing, I should like to come nearer to him, to communicate with him . . . it can't be done . . . He obstructs my view, I can't see a thing. —Well, well, how curious . . . With me, it's the contrary . . . he gives me the impression rather . . . it seems to me, that when you're with him, you feel . . . oh, I don't know, more intelligent . . . He's such a good listener . . . —Yes, he does listen, true enough, and very attentively. But with me . . . and yet I've tried many times . . . there's nothing to be done about it, nothing comes out. I certainly should not tell him stories about my aunt's doorhandles, it would never occur to me to talk to him the way I do to you. You know, what he lacks, really, is a little sense of humor, a little sense of the comic, the tragic—he hasn't so much as a trace—picked up just anywhere, in little things, taken at their very source, from life itself. Whereas he must have 'big' subjects. He soars on the heights. I can imagine his face if I were to talk to him about all that . . . leather easy chairs . . . In fact, despite appearances, he's rather like my father-in-law . . . 'aestheticism' . . . he stresses the consonants, they fairly hiss . . . Lebat, you see, has codes which he applies to everything . . . That's too convenient . . . he gets you both coming and going: bourgeois decay . . . class feelings . . . psychology . . . his latest fad . . . He's not alone, in fact . . . Ah, when he has said that . . . He's funny . . . shut up in a closed, congealed system. Not a breath of life can enter in . . . he takes no risks . . . he thinks he's well sheltered . . . And you know that he, himself, is the one that it leads to pure conventionality, to sterility . . . to inanity . . . Show him some perfectly simple thing . . . just anything, any object, a man, a work of art, his judgment will often be worse, less sound, than that of the corner grocer . . . he understands absolutely nothing . . . —Well, well, how partial you are . . . I'll defend him . . . That's not true. You'll be quite surprised: he wrote me a letter about my last book such as I think I have never received . . . full of subtlety, ideas, don't laugh, genuine, quite new ideas, his own, which made me think and taught me a lot. I'll show it to you . . . —Very well, perhaps, as regards somebody else's work, that's possible, I shan't insist . . . he may be quite intelligent . . . But as regards the actual raw material, the unelaborated material we start with, with which we work, from which we create . . ." She breaks into a little ripple of "silvery" laughter . . . "Ha, ha, ha, door-handles? Easy chairs? People's little manias? —Yes, just anything, you know that . . . It seems to me that if we really cling to them, they can lead to . . . —Really, you are funny . . . You can't pursue everything at one time . . . They're what constitute Lebat's force, those prejudices, those blinders . . . Each of us clears his bit of land as best he can . . . Your own, in fact, is not so far removed . . . —You're speaking of my thesis? Aaah, certainly, a thesis on painting . . . he perceives in his voice a dreary little sneer . . . that's something else, that's a serious matter . . . —Be that as it may . . . she looks about her . . . You know, I'm going to tell you—this raw material—things, people, when we apprehend them like that directly, when we stick to them so closely without any perspective, without applying any codes, well, all that . . . He has the sensation of having touched upon something very dangerous, in a moment of madness, of having set a mechanism going that nothing can stop, he's captured, caught . . . When all's said and done, all that's very amusing, but between ourselves, let's be quite frank . . . it's often, don't you think, pure waste . . . a certain leaning towards facility . . . Whereas he, Lebat . . ."

Everything about him is shrinking, growing smaller, becoming inconsistent, light—a doll's house, children's toys with which she has been amused to play a while to put herself on his level, and now she rejects it all, come, come, enough of this childishness . . . the sky is turning above his head, the stars are moving, he sees planets traveling from place to place, a sensation of dizziness, of anguish, a feeling of panic seizes him, everything is toppling, overturning, at once . . . she herself is moving away, she disappears on the other side . . . But he's not going to let her go, he can follow her, follow them out there, he's coming . . . only she must not reject him, she must not abandon him . . . he's with them, on their side . . . "Well, as it happens, all you've just said, I thought it a bit myself, when I last saw Lebat . . . He made me a little envious . . . I felt guilty . . . He gives an impression of such strength, such serenity . . . There's something about him, in his manner of soaring above everything, a sort of very rare . . . renunciation . . . He has achieved . . . I must confess to you that that's what I most envy others in life . . . an ascesis . . . He has within himself real unity, great purity, unalloyed . . . I thought all that, I too, the other day, while I was talking to him, I felt unworthy, I almost told him, like a child, that I should so much like to see him more often, become friends with him . . ."

But why doesn't she snub him, release herself, refuse to bend, to kneel with him before this stranger, why on earth doesn't she pull herself together, force him, too, to pull himself together . . . What has suddenly come over him? What's the matter with him? What is this excessive humility, this foolishness? Oh listen, let's not exaggerate, all the same. When you get going . . . Everything would fall into place again. They would feel at home once more, under the same motionless sky in which, as before, familiar stars would shine. But she bows her head respectfully: "Ah, that, yes . . . Yes. He's like that. I must confess that I admire him very much." He is seized with rage, a desire to tear her away from there forcefully, he would like to shake her, she should come to herself, she should wipe from her face, which has become all smooth and flat, that beatifically innocent, retarded smile . . . He thinks you're idiotic, he feels like shouting that at her, idiotic, do you hear, dull as ditch water, he told me you bored him stiff, that's why he never sees you . . . Only, he knows what is done . . . ah, letters like that one of his, nobody ever before in all your life . . . now really . . . isn't that touching . . . he is restraining these words that are rising up inside him, with all his might, other words, summoned from elsewhere, arrive hastily, repulse them, burst forth . . . "And yet, you know, that same day, that very time, he surprised me a bit . . . All at once, I had a certain doubt . . ." He feels himself blushing . . . but he can't stop now, the words are gliding, flowing, he can hold them in no longer . . . I had spoken to him of an article that had appeared about him . . . he had hardly listened, of course, he had an air of complete detachment, and I was like you . . . quite . . . quite . . . awestruck . . . Then, afterwards—we had already left each other—he ran to catch up with me, all out of breath: "Hey, there, Guimiez, about that article, tell me, who wrote it? what's the date?" She doesn't move. She plunges a hard gaze deep into his eyes: "Oh, that, really . . . Everything in him, everything about him is coming apart . . . You're very severe . . . I think we're all of us, really, a bit like that."

About the Author

The author of eleven novels, three works of criticism, a collection of plays, and an autobiography, Nathalie Sarraute (1900–1999) is well-known as one of the prime proponents of the New Novel, alongside Alain Robbe-Grillet, Robert Pinget, and Claude Simon. Among her books are *Do You Hear Them?*, *Martereau*, *Portrait of a Man Unknown*, *Between Life and Death*, and *Tropisms*.

Dalkey Archive Essentials

JOHN BARTH, *The Sot-Weed Factor*

ANNE CARSON, *Eros the Bittersweet*

JON FOSSE, *Trilogy*

ALASDAIR GRAY, *Poor Things*

AIDAN HIGGINS, *Langrishe, Go Down*

DAVID MARKSON, *Wittgenstein's Mistress*

FLANN O'BRIEN, *At Swim-Two-Birds*

ISHMAEL REED, *Yellow Back Radio Broke-Down*

NATHALIE SARRAUTE, *The Planetarium*

MARGUERITE YOUNG, *Miss MacIntosh, My Darling*